CW01430123

For more information, contact author Nina Jarrett. www.ninajarrett.com

LORD OF INTRIGUE

INCONVENIENT SCANDALS
BOOK FIVE

NINA JARRETT

ROGUE
PRESS

To the huntresses I have met along the way.

PROLOGUE

"Nothing alters a man's opinion of his ancestry quite so swiftly as being told he must wear it."

Impressions of England by an Unrepentant Foreigner

* * *

SEPTEMBER 1821, FLORENCE

Silence cloaked the room, heavy as velvet, after the pronouncement. The seconds dragged, each one stretching into what felt like minutes, as Marco remained lost in his thoughts. He supposed he should not be entirely surprised—given his parentage—but …

His gaze lifted. His mother, a handsome Italian dame with a mane of silver hair caught in a chignon, was staring blankly at the wall opposite her. Perhaps she was admiring the rich landscape framed in gold where her eyes rested. More likely, however, she was staring into the deep recesses of her mind.

1

Mamma had long since given up hope of reconciliation with the Scotts. Their unexpected visitor must have dredged up all manner of old sorrows: memories of her late husband, Peter—Marco's father—and his fruitless attempts to correspond with Marco's grandfather before Peter's untimely death from a fever more than two decades ago.

To Marco's left, his younger brother, Angelo, lounged with an air of incredulity, his legs sprawled out as he rubbed his jaw in dismay. He looked for all the world like someone trying to solve a complex mechanical puzzle befitting the engineering mind of da Vinci himself.

Finally, Marco returned his attention to the man from England.

Their visitor was something of a chameleon, this Englishman who represented important nobility. Marco found it difficult to place his age. He could be in his thirties or in his fifties. He had a certain vitality, despite his understated clothing and composed manner. His eyes, which could have been gray, blue, or green depending on the angle, spoke of great experience—a seasoned professional who had seen things. His clean-shaven jaw befitted the tidy and meticulous nature of his posture. Marco assessed that some might find him handsome, while others would forget they had ever met him at all.

Clearing his throat, Marco broke the oppressive hush in the elegant drawing room. "You are here to inform us that I am … the future Lord Blackwood?"

Mr. Long nodded, his lean face folding into an expression of measured sympathy, as if he could sense the storm churning within Marco's breast.

"That is correct. Your uncle, Lord Blackwood, has no sons to inherit the title. Your father was second in line until his untimely death. Therefore, you, Mr. Scott, are the heir. You will be the next Baron of Blackwood."

"But … I am a Florentine," Marco replied, his voice taut with disbelief.

Long's lips curved into a polite smile. "You may live in Florence, but half of you is English, Mr. Scott."

Marco raked a hand through his dark curls, agitated as he muttered, "*Maledizione.*"

"Do not curse, son," his mother chided, bringing him back to the present.

Marco released a humorless chuckle. "*Scusa, Mamma,* but truly—if there was ever a time to curse, is this not it?"

To his astonishment, his mother's lips twitched, and a moment later, she burst into laughter. The sound was startling, spilling into the room like sunlight breaking through clouds.

Angelo swung his head around, caught off guard by the abrupt shift in mood, before joining in as Marco and their mother doubled over in gales of incredulous laughter. They struggled to draw air from the force of it, tears of mirth dripping as they tried to comprehend how the tides had turned, washing them out to sea in a tempest of waves and stinging rain. The very floor beneath Marco's feet seemed to heave with the sheer shock of this unforeseen visit.

To his credit, Long refrained from censuring their lunacy, studying the gloved hands resting on his knees while he waited for the laughter to die down. Marco supposed he was accustomed to delivering unsettling news on behalf of his employers.

Mamma dabbed her eyes with a lace handkerchief before turning to their visitor. "*Scusa,* Mr. Long. We have waited over two decades for notice from Britain. I confess we had abandoned hope of … *riconciliazione?*"

The last was directed to Marco to assist with translation. "How do you say this … Reconciliation, Mr. Long? We had given up hope of reconciling with my father's family."

His mother bobbed her head in agreement. "My late husband wrote many letters, as did I, but none were ever answered."

"I understand the unexpectedness of this news." It was an adept response, acknowledging the bizarre nature of their conversation while not hinting at his opinion of Marco's grandfather—the late Lord Blackwood, who had not communicated with Peter or his family since their argument over Peter's intent to marry Marco's mother. She had mourned his father's death for years, before eventually remarrying a widowed friend of the Romano family.

Marco gave a nod of appreciation. "I thank you for traveling so far. You may inform the Baron of Blackwood that I have no desire to inherit his title. He can pass it on to someone else."

Long showed the first sign of tension, a slight swallow that caught Marco's attention.

Is there more to be revealed?

"As I stated, I represent Lord Saunton and His Grace, the Duke of Halmesbury. Your uncle, Lord Blackwood, is unaware of my visit to Florence."

"Then I suggest you inform him that the visit occurred, and I have denounced my interest in his barony."

Mamma shifted in her armchair, her long fingers smoothing the silk of her skirts. Marco's stomach sank; the measured gesture was a sure sign she had thoughts to share, and they would likely be aired the moment they were alone.

Meanwhile, Mr. Long adjusted his cravat—a pristine white linen tied in a simple, practical knot that suited his reserved demeanor. His hesitation drew Marco's attention.

"I must admit, Mr. Scott," Long began, his voice carefully composed, "despite my storied career, I have never delivered news quite like this. Your claim to the title … it brings with it a far more pressing concern. You see, the duke's father-in-law, Lord Filminster, was murdered—to conceal your existence."

The room froze as the words hung in the air.

Mamma gasped audibly, her hands clenching over her knees.

Marco's brows rushed together into a perplexed scowl as he cocked his head in question. "*Scusa* ... Perhaps my English is not as good as I believed—"

"You heard correctly," Mr. Long interrupted, shaking his head. His tone was low but steady. "Lord Josiah Ridley intended to notify the Home Office that you were the rightful heir. He was killed to prevent him from sending the letter."

Slowly, Marco turned to his mother.

She was leaning forward now, her expression anguished. "Josiah Ridley ... He is dead?" Her dark eyes glistened with sadness as she questioned their visitor, her voice tight with emotion.

"Who is Filminster, *Mamma?*"

She licked her lips, her poise intact even as her distress showed in the faint crease of her brow. To Marco, she was the very image of Florentine grace and sophistication, despite the turmoil that swirled around them. She turned to face him, her voice quiet but steady. "He was a friend of your father's. They attended Oxford together and corresponded often—until your father ... became ill. His letter of ... *cordoglio?*"

"Condolence," Marco supplied without hesitation.

His mother gave a small, grateful nod. "Yes, his letter of condolence was very kind."

Marco clenched his jaw, willing the conversation to end. This news was an unnecessary burden for his mother—a wound reopened after decades of healing. And as for him? He had no desire to dig into the English roots that had brought him nothing but pain and frustration in recent years.

Rising abruptly to his feet, his patience unraveled, Marco towered over their visitor, and his tone turned sharp. "What has any of ... *this* ... to do with us? These are British affairs for British people. You may inform your employers that we have been made aware."

Mr. Long did not flinch under Marco's pointed words. Instead, he remained seated, his calm demeanor unchanged as he responded, "The duke would very much appreciate your assistance in bringing the killer to justice. His Grace is prepared to pay for your travel arrangements. You should know that the duchess is distraught over her father's murder, and the duke—he has dedicated himself to helping others, particularly those with complicated origins like your own."

Marco's scowl deepened.

"Setting aside His Grace's wishes," Long continued, his tone softening, "would you not like to visit your ancestral home? To see the places where your father grew up, learn more about his life, and better understand the noble line you are descended from?"

Marco's gut twisted as Mr. Long deftly spoke to the buried desires of his youth. The man from England was clever, his arguments calculated to strike where Marco was most vulnerable. Those long-held dreams—the ones that had brought nothing but heartbreak—stirred within him, raw and unbidden. Years ago, he had tried to bridge the chasm to his English roots, and the bitter failure had left scars he had barely managed to conceal. Now, this conversation scraped at the fragile veneer of happiness he had painstakingly constructed, unleashing memories that left him winded with their intensity.

His mother must have noticed the shift in his mood. "Mr. Long," she interjected gently, her tone measured and polite, "my sons and I need time to discuss this. Perhaps you can return tomorrow, once we have had time to … *digerire?*"

"Digest," Marco responded.

"Yes, once we have had time to digest."

Marco exhaled deeply, relief flooding him even though he knew the reprieve was temporary.

When Mr. Long finally departed, Marco remained in the drawing room with his mother and Angelo. He had expected it—dreaded it, even—and sure enough, *Mamma* wasted no time broaching the topic he most wished to avoid.

She cleared her throat softly, switching to English—a family tradition, one she insisted on to honor the memory of Marco's late father. "It is because of her, is it not? The girl who … died?"

Marco swallowed hard and rose from his seat, crossing the room to stand by the window overlooking the courtyard. The scene beyond was tranquil: potted plants neatly arranged around a graceful fountain featuring Eros as a boy poised with an outstretched bow and arrow. Yet Marco's gaze was not on the present but on a distant memory, one that carried the weight of innocence lost.

It had been years ago when he first met the Dashwoods. Their visit to Florence had a dual purpose: to introduce their young son to the wonders of the city's art and architecture, and to seek a warmer climate with renowned therapies for their ailing daughter, Catherine Dashwood. A fragile English rose, Catherine had frozen Marco in place the moment he saw her. She was so delicate, so achingly beautiful, so unlike the spirited Italian girls who surrounded him. She seemed otherworldly, a rare and unexpected presence in his familiar world.

Englishmen often visited Florence during their Grand Tour, but unwed Englishwomen? They were a rarity, and Catherine's arrival had changed everything for Marco.

The Dashwoods had sought treatment at his family's business, the renowned *Antica Spezieria di San Lorenzo*. After exhausting every option in London, they turned to the pharmacy's traditional remedies, prescribed by Catherine's Florentine doctor. Marco's grandfather, learning that the Dashwood boy required a tutor, had volunteered Marco's services. It had been his first work outside the pharmacy, a thrilling new responsibility. Catherine, despite her frailty, had often accompanied their outings. Together, they visited the Uffizi Gallery and Pitti Palace, where Marco had introduced them to the masterpieces housed within those hallowed halls.

Marco had always been captivated by all things English, a fascination born of the father he never had the chance to know—who had died shortly after Marco's birth. But no curiosity about his heritage had ever matched his intrigue with Catherine Dashwood. With her flaxen hair, delicately sculpted features, and striking blue eyes, Catherine embodied what he imagined a British lady to be: graceful, demure, and heartbreakingly vulnerable. Yet beneath that fragility lay a quiet strength, a steadiness that soothed his exuberant Latin spirit and made him yearn to see the land of his father's birth.

It had not taken long for Marco to fall hopelessly in love. Young and naïve, he had been slow to recognize the truth— the shadow of death that clung to Catherine, draining her vitality with each passing day. In time, it became undeniable. Week by week, she faded before his eyes, her presence at the galleries growing infrequent until she could no longer join their outings at all.

Her parents, perhaps sensing how short her time was, allowed Marco to visit her at their villa. Those moments were both a privilege and an exquisite torment. Catherine had never complained of her condition, never revealed a hint of bitterness, meeting his attentions instead with quiet gratitude. Yet the changes in her were impossible to ignore: the way her slender frame grew gaunter, her luminous eyes seeming even larger as her features hollowed.

And then, one quiet night, death came for her—a dark veil descending to claim the fragile life that had so enchanted him. Marco received the news the next morning, the Dashwood household cloaked in mourning. Though he had known it was inevitable, the loss struck him like a thunderbolt, shattering his young heart into a thousand pieces—foresight had not softened the blow. Even now, the memory of Catherine's death squeezed the seat of his emotions beating within his left breast, the ache as sharp and fresh as it had been that first day.

"I have no interest in England."

His mother's expression softened when he looked at her, her tone brimming with sympathy. "I understand your … *sentimenti?*"

"Feelings," he corrected reflexively, the word slipping out before he had time to think.

"Yes, feelings." She nodded, her dark eyes growing distant. "I wish you had not endured such pain at so young an age."

"You were not much older when our father died," Marco countered gently. It was true. He had been a babe in her arms, and Angelo had been little more than a curve beneath their mother's heart.

Her lips pressed into a wistful line. "Your father loved his home. Leaving it broke his heart, but he chose me. We came back to Florence to build a life together." She paused, her gaze turning inward. "Sometimes I wonder … Should I have set him free? Would he still be alive if he had not returned to Tuscany?"

Marco spun on his heel, crossing the room with swift purpose. Dropping to a crouch beside her chair, he placed a hand over hers. "You cannot think like that, *Mamma*. If he had stayed in England, I would not be here. Nor Angelo. Nor Elena!"

At the mention of his younger sister—a spirited girl born of Bianca's second marriage—his mother's lips curved, but it was not the smile Marco expected. Instead, she quirked her head, raising her brows in quiet amusement.

Marco frowned, trying to decipher the meaning behind her expression. His emotions were raw, his thoughts scattered, and for the life of him, he could not understand what he had said to provoke such a look.

Angelo stirred from his languid sprawl, the light of realization sparking in his eyes as he sat up straight. "Ah, I see it now! Marco cannot regret the past because it has shaped who we are today. What has happened has happened—it cannot be undone, nor should it be!"

Marco gritted his teeth. *"Per l'amor di Dio!"*

"Marco!" His mother's brow puckered, her tone sharp with reproach.

He exhaled deeply, softening his tone. "My apologies, *Mamma*."

She regarded him for a moment, her expression softening once more. "I think this is important. You should see where your father was born and ... *scoprire?*"

"Discover," Marco supplied.

She nodded. "Yes, discover your roots."

Angelo leaned forward, his enthusiasm apparent. "I shall accompany you, brother! I wish to find my roots as well. Who knows? Perhaps London is in need of a Florentine pharmacy."

Angelo's fascination with herbal remedies and the family pharmacy was well-known. Yet, with so many uncles and cousins involved in the Romano business, his role had been limited to preparing medicines—a vital task, but one that offered little room for advancement. For months, Angelo had talked of leaving Florence to establish a new endeavor, a place where Tuscan medicine might flourish.

But he had not taken that leap. Florence was not easily left behind.

The crowded family business had prompted Marco to seek independence, turning to tutoring Englishmen on their Grand Tour. He had become a sought-after ... what did they call it? *Capo dell'orso?* Head of the bear. No—*bear leader*. The title amused him, but it also brought a quiet sense of pride. His work allowed him to live on his own terms, with rooms of his own and the ability to pay his way without relying on his grandfather's generosity.

Federico Romano rarely spoke of such things, but Marco could sense his quiet approval. His grandfather was proud that Marco had forged his own path as a trusted guide to the English.

Marco's hand slipped into his pocket, his fingers brushing the engraved surface of his father's gold pocket watch. The familiar weight was comforting, steadying him as he turned over the dilemma in his mind.

"I shall think about it," he finally said, though it was more a way of delaying the inevitable than a true decision.

He needed to take a damn walk.

Making a quick escape, Marco promised to return for dinner to continue the discussion. For now, the crisp winter air was a welcome reprieve. His boots struck a steady rhythm on the cobblestones as he strolled past elegant homes and entered one of Florence's bustling main roads.

As he walked, his gaze instinctively lifted to Brunelleschi's magnificent octagonal dome. The soaring structure of the great cathedral never failed to inspire reverence in him. The marble cladding gleamed in the afternoon light, its vibrant patterns a feast for the eyes. Marco paused, allowing himself a moment to savor the view, before resuming his pace toward a favorite *caffè*.

Marco claimed a table overlooking the bustling street and sipped his coffee as he waited for his friends to arrive, grateful for the prearranged meeting to provide distraction from the morning's revelations.

Sebastian and Lorenzo appeared together, locked in a heated argument, entirely oblivious to Marco's presence.

"We need to get the painting back. It is time to leave Florence, Sebastian! It is the only way forward," Lorenzo declared, his voice fraught with frustration.

"I shall not. We will find another way," Sebastian replied, his tone implacable.

"We have tried! *Porca miseria!*" Lorenzo exclaimed, throwing his hands in the air. His agitation was unmistakable as he paused to order his coffee at the counter. Turning back to Sebastian, he added sharply, "Are you a coward to hide from a woman this way?"

Sebastian's scowl deepened, and he straightened to his full, imposing height. Leaning over, he tapped Lorenzo's chest with a firm, warning finger. Though Lorenzo was tall and lean, Sebastian loomed over him, the tallest man of Marco's acquaintance.

The Englishman was a veritable giant, with a mane of bronze hair and a close-cropped beard that always put Marco in mind of a Norse warrior destined for Valhalla, hacking his way through one battle at a time.

Sebastian had arrived in Florence years earlier on his Grand Tour, ostensibly like the other young Englishmen. But unlike most, he had never left. A brother to an important nobleman back in England, he had chosen instead to remain in the city that had captivated him. Over time, he and Lorenzo had established a profitable partnership, trading art to wealthy visitors eager to bring a piece of

Florence home with them—a memento of the city's inexhaustible allure.

Marco could not fault their patrons; Florence had a way of seizing one's senses with a tenacious grip, so Marco understood the desire to recreate it in distant places, even if only in fragments.

Marco had been friends with both men for several years and always enjoyed their company. Lorenzo, passionate to the point of zealotry about art, often claimed his lineage to an apprentice of the great Leonardo da Vinci himself. His fervor could be exhausting, but fortunately, Sebastian's steady good humor typically tempered Lorenzo's intensity.

This, however, did not seem to be one of those occasions.

Lorenzo's sharp words had clearly struck a nerve, and realizing this, he displayed his palms in surrender, stepping back with a murmured apology. Sebastian relaxed almost instantly, his tense shoulders easing as his customary smile returned. Turning to the counter, he ordered his coffee, his tone now calm and measured.

Marco decided it was time to make his presence known. He raised an arm in greeting, and his two friends, spotting him at last, crossed the *caffè* to join him at his table.

"What is news, Marco?" Lorenzo asked, his dark eyes sparkling with curiosity. "Have you secured a new student?"

Marco exhaled, steadying himself. The moment of truth had arrived as he finally made his decision. "No. I am leaving for London instead."

The announcement was met with astonishment.

Sebastian's sharp gray eyes fixed on Marco, his shock evident in the way his expression stilled. Lorenzo, meanwhile, turned to Sebastian in triumph. "It is a sign."

Marco arched an eyebrow. Apparently, it was his turn to be perplexed. "A sign of what?"

"A sign that Sebastian and I must depart for England.

With you, of course. We shall enjoy the journey together!" Lorenzo declared, his tone self-congratulatory.

Sebastian frowned, draining his coffee in one swift motion before letting out a deep, beleaguered sigh. "I have no desire to leave."

"You must admit, it is a sign," Lorenzo pressed, undeterred. "We were arguing this very matter, and now our dear friend Marco announces he is departing for the great city of London. Fate itself is stepping in to point the way. It is time for you to return home, Sebastian. You are needed in England!"

Sebastian's gray eyes narrowed. "We have been debating this for months. Someone was bound to eventually plan a trip to Britain. It is not a sign."

Marco leaned back in his chair, observing the spirited exchange with equal parts astonishment and amusement. That he himself was leaving Florence to delve into his father's life still felt unreal. Yet, as his friends bickered, the notion of having their company on this journey grew steadily more appealing.

Angelo had already pledged to accompany him, waiting on Marco's final decision. And now, with the prospect of traveling alongside Lorenzo and Sebastian, the burden of his impending quest lightened. Perhaps this could become a grand adventure. It was not so different, he thought, from the groups of young Englishmen who arrived in Florence together, brimming with excitement to explore its artistic treasures.

"I am telling you," Lorenzo insisted, gesturing emphatically, "it is a sign. We must accompany our friend Marco!"

Sebastian shook his head, his voice firm. "I do not wish it."

Marco could sense that Sebastian was chafing under Lorenzo's relentless insistence. But there was something more—a deeper conflict that mirrored Marco's own feelings after Mr. Long's visit. Perhaps his mother was right: the past had to be faced. It had always struck Marco as curious that Sebastian had never returned to England, the land of his birth. Perhaps the time had come, just as it was time for Marco to explore his roots in England.

Perhaps … perhaps he should help persuade him?

"I would appreciate your company, my friend," Marco said, his voice warm but steady.

Sebastian met his gaze, the storm flickering in his gray eyes confirming what Marco had suspected all along. The Englishman had avoided returning home because, like Marco, he had ghosts that needed to be laid to rest. And perhaps, if they undertook this journey together, they might find a way to exorcise the past and return to Florence with lightened spirits.

Marco's words had struck a chord. He watched as Sebastian mulled them over, his broad shoulders stiff with unspoken tension. Lorenzo fidgeted, opening his mouth as if to interject, but Marco shook his head to silence him. The table itself seemed to hold its breath.

The Englishman's square jaw tightened; his eyes flickered, and Marco could see the moment when the decision crystallized. Suddenly, Sebastian brought a large fist down onto the table with a resonant *thump* that sent the cups clattering. His face split into a wide grin.

"Then we shall voyage to the green and pleasant land!"

Marco laughed, carried away by his friend's infectious shift in mood. Sebastian's use of William Blake's evocative words stirred a pang of bittersweet memory. Catherine Dashwood had adored reading such poetry, and Marco had taken to reciting it to her in the drawing room of her family's rented villa when it had become difficult for her to focus on the pages.

If they had ever spoken of his father's homeland, Marco thought Catherine might have approved of his decision to return to England. But they had never shared such a conversation. The thought dimmed his humor only slightly. The desire to visit merry England, that faraway land of his father's youth, was taking root in him again.

CHAPTER 1

*"The English are peculiarly gifted at making young women feel
both ornamental and in the way—often at the same time."*

Impressions of England by an Unrepentant Foreigner

* * *

NOVEMBER 29 1821, LONDON

olly's argument with Claudette Dubois began as most of their recent quarrels had. The lady's maid-turned-companion criticized Molly's appearance, drawing unflattering comparisons to her late mistress and lamenting her reduced station—now tending to a nobody with not even a title to her name.

Isla Scott, the dowager Baroness of Blackwood, had tragically overdosed the month before. Miss Dubois's duties had shifted to taking care of Molly, much to both their ire. But not as irritating as being informed just yesterday that the lady's maid had been elevated to paid companion so she might act as a chaperon for Molly.

"It is a necessity," Simon Scott, her cousin by marriage and de facto guardian, had stated. "We have four bachelors arriving from Italy, and only two of them are relations, and even they are not your blood relations. As you are an unmarried young lady, we must take steps to protect your reputation."

"*You* are not a blood relation, and I have lived here with you and your brothers for months since my mother ..." Molly's eyes had prickled slightly. The grief would hit her at unexpected times. Sometimes she could talk about her with nostalgic fondness, and other times ... she was overcome. "Since Mother was laid to rest," she finished thickly.

Simon had thrown her a sympathetic glance before replying. "You had my mother for propriety's sake. We should have immediately appointed Miss Dubois as your companion last month when I went away, but I was distracted by ... events."

"Lady Blackwood was hardly proper."

"Proper as far as society is concerned."

"Can we not find someone else? Miss Dubois is an aggravation beyond endurance."

"Not on such short notice. And not with two recent deaths in a single day—one of them a servant. It has frightened potential applicants away, but I assure you I am working on it. I do not wish to saddle you with the French poodle any longer than necessary, but we do not have a choice at the moment."

His logic was flawless, which was why Molly had resigned herself to Miss Dubois's resentful watch. Well ... for now, at least. Her musings were cut short by another irascible remark from the French retainer, whom in theory she was permitted to address as Claudette in private but ... She clenched her jaw, fighting the urge to push the other woman out of her personal space … *I do not wish to encourage familiarity.*

Not that this hindered Miss Dubois, who was pretty of face but foul of temperament. Not surprising, considering the wicked baroness had been fond of the termagant who had tended to her flawless appearance.

"Theez mourning gowns are *passé.* Your mother has been dead many months. It ees time to wear something with more … *coulier?*

"Color."

"*Oui*—color. You are a drab little … *souris?*"

"Mouse," Molly muttered with resignation, gritting her teeth. Attempting to put the maid—*blast!* Attempting to put the companion in her place would lead to a shameful quarreling which she was too weary to deal with.

"*Oui.* Lady Blackwood had to do ze mourning for her husband, but she was still … *élégante.* A great lady." Miss Dubois stopped to shake her head as she considered her new mistress with mild disgust. Molly fought the urge to slap her sulky face. The maid—*companion*—was dainty, with large doe eyes, high cheekbones, and a pointed chin, and liked to wear clothes a little more ornate than the usual fare of women in service. It was a pity her character did not match her exquisite exterior.

Molly glanced down at her lavender velvet gown and repressed a roll of her eyes. It was hardly rags. In fact, she was rather fond of it. But no doubt Miss Dubois found it too plain. The late Lady Blackwood had worn elaborate silk gowns, impractical in Molly's opinion. Isla Scott and the … poodle … seemed to have agreed on such garments. Perhaps it secured her position to encourage such indulgences; after all, such attire demanded constant fussing from a skilled lady's maid.

Unfortunately, Molly's patience unexpectedly snapped as she considered the hurtful words that Miss Dubois had been flinging at her since she had arisen from bed less than an hour earlier. "I will determine what is the appropriate length of time to mourn my mother, Miss Dubois!"

The maid drew herself up to her full height—it was not much—a familiar expression of haughty recrimination on her youthful face. "I was just tryin' to help," she responded reproachfully in her broken English.

Molly swiftly remonstrated herself. This was what happened every time she allowed the other woman to flare her temper. Claudette would act terribly offended, tugging on Molly's desire to be kind and respectful to her acquaintances, which left her feeling bleak and guilty despite all the insensitive things the lady's maid had said to provoke the reaction in the first place.

Not to mention, hearing Lady Blackwood held in such esteem after the baroness's evil deeds was a constant rough pebble in her slippers. But she supposed Miss Dubois was not familiar with those misdeeds—they had been kept private amongst the family.

"I understand you were trying to help ... but I am not ready to end my mourning period."

Claudette sniffed in wounded outrage. "I do not miss *ma mère* at all."

Molly bit back an inelegant snort. If Claudette's mother was at all like her daughter, it was little wonder the poodle did not miss her *in the least*. Molly would not miss Claudette *in the least* when Simon assisted her to find a new position in another household. Her own mother would have felt terrible regarding the situation that Molly had found herself in, especially after the criminal activities that had been brought to light in the wake of Lady Blackwood's overdose. Certainly, this had not proved to be the home of safety and security that the amusing Mrs. Carter had wished for her only child.

After doing her best to repair her companionship with Claudette, Molly escaped with a sigh of relief to meet Simon's wife in the garden. Simon had married his dearest friend, Madeline Bigsby, who lived next door. The nuptials had taken place just three nights earlier in the shared garden between the two grand London townhouses.

The new Lady Campbell was Molly's dear friend, and an unusual choice for the son of a baron to wed because Lady Madeline Scott was in trade, working with her mother at Bigsby's Stone Manufactory. After Simon had inherited a Scottish viscounty from his mother a few weeks earlier, he had finally been freed of suffocating expectations and pursued a love match with Madeline. Now he was no longer the heir to his older brother's barony, which Madeline had revealed was something Simon was privately pleased about.

Molly hurried down the gravel path, entering the garden that unified the two miniature estates which had been built nearly a century earlier by the Aldritch brothers. The two brothers had created the shared garden, and when they had sold the estates, they had ensured that the garden would remain intact with legal clauses included in the deeds. It was a beautiful space, bordered by silent gods staring down, with a huge urn of potted plants in the middle. Ordinarily they would be flowering in profusion, but not this late in the year.

Madeline was waiting for her on the bench below the urn, a cart laid out with tea by her side, a thick pelisse protecting her from the November chill, and a parasol crooked in her arm to shield her from the morning sun.

"Molly!"

"I am sorry I am late."

"Do not be silly. This is hardly a formal arrangement."

Molly sank onto the bench and sighed. "Miss Dubois

chose to lecture me about appropriate mourning periods. She has grown ever more obnoxious now that she is my *chaperon*." Molly emphasized the French pronunciation with sarcasm. "Any restraint she may have practiced has completely vanished since Simon promoted her to paid companion."

Madeline laughed, her amber eyes bright in the sunlight. "The yapping poodle? Yes, Simon has mentioned he feels terrible he has not yet found an adequate companion to take over. Rest assured, he is working on it."

"Amongst all the other arrangements he has to see to? I thought he was merely being polite when he stated that."

"Not at all. He is doing his best to see to all the details before he turns the management of the barony over to his nephew from Florence."

"The schooner bearing the Italians has arrived. Miss Dubois informed me that carriages have been sent to collect them from the London Docks."

Silence fell as they each contemplated the revelations of the past few weeks, Madeline finally responding in a worried tone, "They will be met with quite a muddle. I hope this Marco Scott is up to the challenge."

* * *

THE SQUAWKING of herring gulls was deafening when Marco peered with growing horror over to the docks of London from the swaying deck of the schooner that had been their home these past three weeks.

The gulls were perched on the ledges of the enormous brick warehouses lining the docks, the self-serving beggars swooping down to pick at scraps amongst the legs of the bustling crowd. Sailors from different ports of the world, weatherbeaten porters, and well-dressed merchants milled about while dockworkers with bared arms and filthy trousers hoisted crates back and forth using a system of pulleys. Huge sailing ships overshadowed their smaller schooner, which was intended only for passengers and light cargo. They rocked with the motion of the water while tall masts soared up, up, up into the skies above them with their sails neatly folded and thick riggings taut. Cold air wafted the odors of salt, soot, and rotting fish to assail his senses with an undertone of tobacco and spices.

Once his ears grew accustomed to the shrieking of the birds, Marco could make out the clanking of the pulleys hoisting goods, the bells and horns signaling the arrival of ships from far-off places, the shouts of crude men laboring to move the crated imports and exports, the gruff yelling of unknown languages, along with traders whistling as they hawked their provisions for the long voyages ahead.

It was nothing short of appalling to a gentleman of quality who had grown up in the gracious streets and piazzas of Florence.

"This seems neither green nor pleasant."

"The London Docks are the busiest in the world. Do not judge England by this, my friend!" Sebastian chuckled, patting Marco's shoulder in a gesture of encouragement before walking away to check on their luggage.

"I think it is all rather … what is *emozionante?* … exciting," Angelo remarked, his keen interest in the commercial activities ashore evident in his bright eyes.

Lorenzo paid no heed to any of them, quarreling with one of the sailors about the rough handling of his prized trunks, and Marco briefly wondered what was in them that had his friend so caustic.

After a lengthy disembarkation, the four men were finally settled in a fine carriage. The carpeted interior was rich, with leather squabs and plump stuffing. Marco relaxed back and watched the crowded streets as they slowly drew through traffic. After some time, the congestion on the roads let up and they passed by graceful manors interspersed with trees and gardens.

The carriage picked up speed, the wheels drumming against the road and occasionally jostling on the uneven surface while Marco's lids drifted shut. They had risen very early this morning to view their journey along the Thames, and the rocking motion of the vehicle had him soon dozing off.

A sharp, violent lurch had his eyes flying open only to see his large Nordic friend hurtling toward him before a broad and powerful shoulder collided with his ribs.

"Whoa! Whoa!" The coachman's panicked voice shouted from above, barely audible over the din of the horses' hooves as they struggled to halt, while a searing pain spread outward from the place of impact. Marco yelped in surprise as the entire carriage tipped precariously with a horrifying cracking sound—wood against earth—to deafen them. The four men tumbled about the interior with loud howls of protest as the chamber rolled, elbows and knees flailing about as they fought for purchase until finally coming to stop. They were piled in an ignominious heap, the carriage upended and Sebastian landing on top to crush them all down with his mighty build while Marco found himself flattened against the roof.

Is it still a roof if it is on the floor?

Marco panted, his heart pounding as he tried to catch his breath, but each pull of his lungs made the pain in his chest worse and he suspected he had cracked a rib.

Sebastian was the first to move, finding purchase to lift himself and heave his mighty shoulder against the door. It bulged but failed to open as the rest of the men slowly disengaged to squat against the walls.

"Is everyone all right?" Angelo peered around with worried eyes, ever the pharmacist interested in others' welfare.

Sebastian made no comment, fidgeting with the latch before attempting another powerful crash against the carriage door.

Lorenzo raised his head, his face gray with shock. "I appear to be unbroken."

Angelo turned to Marco, who had not answered because he was attempting to suppress the agony by pressing down on his rib.

"Marco?"

"I … may … cracked … rib?" he eventually wheezed in response.

Sebastian glanced back, his gaze determined as he heaved against the stuck door with another loud thud. From outside, the sound of the footmen could be heard in heated discussion with the coachman, then the door shuddered as if it were being yanked on from the outside.

The door finally opened and the servants began to help them out, an icy breeze blowing dust into the enclosed space so that Marco's eyes burned and he fought the urge to sneeze, knowing it would hurt like blazes to do so.

Soon Marco was lying on the side of the road, peering up into the blue, blue sky while Angelo explored his ribs with gentle fingers, palpitating the area to check for fractures. "I think it is badly bruised, possibly fractured, but not broken. But we must get it taped, in case. I have ointment and bandages, but this is …" Angelo looked about at the road and damaged coach. "I think we should attend to you at that inn. So we can clean you up."

Angelo's medicinal trunk was untied from the second coach before a footman was dispatched along with a coachman to continue the journey with the remaining luggage, empty the vehicle so it could return for them, and make arrangements for a wagon to collect the damaged carriage.

Sebastian and Angelo discussed the best way to lift Marco, opting to collect a sheet from the inn he had spotted across the road and use it to carry him into one of the public chambers.

Marco was barely listening, just focusing on catching his breath despite the pain. He was relieved to hear the rib was not overly damaged, that Angelo could not feel it moving from his examination, but he could tell it was definitely compromised. Soon he was carried by Sebastian and Lorenzo within the cradle of the suspended sheet, and Angelo had him laid out on a table in a private dining room off the main public rooms. A flickering fire warmed the room, and it was pleasant to be out of the chill.

Angelo was skilled at aiding people with minor injuries, as were most members of their family, which was something that would bring customers to their family's pharmacy. He assisted Marco to divest himself of the coat and waistcoat, lifting his shirt to bunch under his armpits. Angelo carefully applied a camphor-laced liniment, and the pain eased.

Marco sat up with help from Sebastian while Angelo bound his chest, then slowly struggled up from the table. "I need a *specchio* … a mirror?"

With more assistance from Angelo, he was reclothed and his cravat tied with a simple knot that would not aggravate, and Angelo issued a warning to keep his breathing shallow to reduce the aching.

"Are you well, my friend?" questioned Sebastian from across the room.

Lorenzo stood next to him with a distracted expression, glancing over to Marco as if he had just recalled the accident. Marco wondered if he should envy or pity the Italian's single-minded focus on whatever had brought him to England, even under such trying circumstances.

"England is only a little green and definitely not pleasant," growled Marco in resentment.

His friends broke into laughter, Marco managing a small smile at their good humor. Thankfully, no one was permanently damaged.

Angelo did not join in, his face twisted in worry.

"What is it, Angelo?"

"The coachman. He says that one of the wheels showed signs of tampering. As if someone wished to cause this accident. Is that possible?"

Marco frowned, sobering at the thought of why the duke and Lord Saunton had asked them to visit London. The duke's father-in-law had been murdered!

"I do not know, but we shall have to find out."

Sebastian, overhearing this, approached with a perplexed expression. "What is this? You think the accident was intentional?"

Marco stared up at his tall friend, trying to determine how much he wanted to tell the men who had accompanied him and his brother. They knew of the future inheritance, but he had not informed them of the murder investigation. It seemed unwise to speak of it openly, considering they were here at the duke's behest in the wake of the murder.

Recent news from London had informed them that the situation had been resolved. The letter had stated it was safe for Marco and Angelo to stay at the Blackwood estate, and the duke had promised to visit to explain what had come to light since Mr. Long had initially contacted them in Florence. Until he knew the details, Marco did not think it circumspect to openly discuss the sordid circumstances that had led Mr. Long to call on them until learning more about it himself.

"I can think of no reason. Perhaps the coachman seeks to conceal inferior maintenance?" Angelo raised an eyebrow in question, but remained quiet. "Perhaps this inn can feed us?"

The shift in conversation worked. Being such a large and energetic man, Sebastian needed a lot of food, so it was a matter of minutes until they were sitting in the busy dining room. Marco did his best to find a position on his bench that did not agitate his injury, while sipping on a British ale with a contorted face and mulling over his mixed feelings about the advantages of visiting his father's homeland. It had not been an auspicious introduction to England thus far.

* * *

MOLLY CARTER WAS in her room, reading quietly by the window and reflecting on how dull her life had become since her mother had died months earlier. She used to manage the Carter household in between calling on the neighbors with Mrs. Carter and sharing tea and biscuits with the vicar's wife once a week. Mother had been an amusing companion, sharp of wit but forgetful of her things, which had kept Molly busy. In their small country town, she had felt … useful.

Then she had come to live in the baron's household. It was all a bit of a muddle, her mother having named John Scott as the trustee of Molly's inheritance. Her mother had obviously meant the late baron, father to the current John Scott, but the solicitors had willfully misunderstood and turned her over to the son. Molly had gone along with it, not quite sure where to go as an unmarried young lady who was in mourning for her beloved parent, deciding she could determine her future once she had time to collect her thoughts. Which was how she had come to live in London at the baron's small Town estate.

The late baron had been married to her aunt. Despite a

lack of progeny from that marriage, the baron's second of three, Molly's mother had maintained a correspondence with her sister's widower, so Molly had learned from the reading of the will that she was to join the Scott household. She supposed her mother had considered it the very best connection she had, the Blackwood title being respected and endowed with great wealth.

Molly had not had much to do since her arrival. There had been the excitement of the coronation in July, of course. Followed by a few weeks of tense relations between the Scotts as tempers had inexplicably risen while Molly tried to stay out of the family upsets until eventually the underlying reasons had come to light. Simon Scott had been accused of murder. Lord Blackwood had collapsed, and the dowager Lady Blackwood had succumbed to a laudanum overdose.

So it was, for a short time, Molly had felt useful again, despite the gloomy circumstances, when she had been the only one entrusted with the baron's care. Fortunately, his health had gradually improved and the Scotts' tempest had worn itself out. Unfortunately, Molly's routine had receded back to that of boredom. And aggravation from her quarrels with Miss Dubois, which were not a welcome distraction. It was a blessing that Madeline had been visiting regularly due to her own convalescence the past month. But now that she had married Simon a few nights earlier, and Simon had moved his things to Madeline's family home next door, she did not come calling as much as she had been.

Molly supposed she should be grateful that she had, at least, integrated into the family after the disastrous October they had all shared. But it did not dispel the growing sense of disquiet about her future.

Reading in her room, cloistered in an armchair facing the back garden, had become a habit of late. Being in her bedchamber and sending her *shadow* out on errands had been a strategy to rid herself of Miss Dubois's company.

The sound of Miss Dubois's bedchamber door opening was an unwelcome disruption. Her chaperon had returned, presumably having had her fill of gossip in the kitchens. Appearing at Molly's door, she stared for several irritating moments before making an unexpected announcement with a smug expression.

"Ze guests from Italy, zey 'ave been in a dreadful accident! Ze carriage overturned!" Her companion clearly delighted in informing her of the salacious tidbit.

"What!"

"Ze trunks 'ave arrived, and zey 'ave sent a wagon to collect ze damaged carriage." Miss Dubois was reveling in the drama of an accident which could well have taken someone's life, but Molly knew her companion's retellings were often inaccurate at best. Nevertheless, she could not help the question that escaped her lips.

"Is everyone all right?"

The servant shrugged, as if this was an irrelevant detail to pay mind to, flittering away.

Springing to her feet in alarm, Molly rushed downstairs to find that the contingent from Italy was arriving, and Molly lamented her recent reclusive habits. Entering the family drawing room, she found both the baron and his and Simon's youngest brother, Nicholas, were there awaiting their visitors.

The current baron had been born from his father's first marriage, while Simon and Nicholas were products of the third marriage, so the difference in age was decades. The late baron must have been a virile man well into his fifties to sire sons with such vast age differences, and it was difficult to think of them as brothers.

She was gratified to note that John Scott had color in his

cheeks, and the pouchy flesh that had spoken to a man aging before his time had receded somewhat to give him a more toned appearance. He appeared healthier in the afternoon light, drifting in from the large arching windows. Certainly, years had been added on to his life after the revelations of last month, and without the late dowager baroness about to feed petty insecurities, John was turning out to be a generous and pleasant benefactor.

Nicholas was sprawled out, his injured leg propped up and a morose expression painted on his lean features, which could easily be mistaken for discontent, his mop of dark hair falling forward and his blue eyes vivid against his sallow complexion.

He had quit spirits around the same time that his oldest brother had collapsed, and it had been a bit of a painful recovery. Nicholas had neglected his health until he had become a rake-thin and haggard man in his mid-twenties, less than half the age of his oldest brother, but the two made quite a pair in their mutual convalescence, their fraternity perhaps more obvious than when she had first arrived. Molly suspected that the lack of spirits had made the younger man more aware of the condition of his injured leg, badly broken in his youth from a terrible fall, which he was now taking steps to rehabilitate. Despite the gloom of his sobriety, Molly was finding him easier to converse with than his inebriated version.

John greeted her with a grim smile. "Simon will bring our guests in to make introductions. There was an accident, so he is speaking with them and the coachmen in the mews, but their trunks have been brought in, so they should be here momentarily."

"Is everyone well?" Molly's voice was a little shrill, and she realized her nerves were still tattered from the prior month. The household was still dispelling the shroud of death and mayhem, and it had been most alarming to hear of another strange incident. A bizarre coincidence to have one of their carriages overturn so soon after the macabre occurrences in October that had led to two deaths under this very roof.

"I believe so. Simon is overseeing the situation, and he did not mention any significant injuries."

Molly took up a seat on the settee next to Nicholas, and suppressed a huff of annoyance when Claudette Dubois hurried into the room to take a seat near the door to chaperon her "charge," and cause Molly to feel like a girl in short skirts instead of an adult woman of five and twenty.

It was not long before Simon arrived, escorting the men from Italy. They included, to her surprise, a huge Norseman. Molly immediately suspected his identity because of his resemblance to a certain acquaintance they had made last month.

Following him into the room was a tall, lean Italian dressed in the manner of an artist, who she assumed must be one of the friends. Then a shorter and younger man with medium brown hair, bright brown eyes, and an air of keen interest entered to peer about the room. But it was the last man to enter the room who affected Molly's equilibrium in unexpected ways as a frisson of excitement roared through her veins.

He was as tall as his artist companion, perhaps six feet, but a gentleman with wavy hair as black as soot. With broad shoulders, and a lean build, he had a sculpted jaw of steel which was shadowed with stubble as if he were due for a shave after his long journey. Soulful black eyes set within a strong, olive-toned face, and framed by thick lashes, spoke to a troubled past. A man who had experienced things.

There was only one person whom he could be. Molly acknowledged within the deep recesses of her heart that, much to her chagrin, she was inconveniently captivated by the one who was the baron's new heir—Marco Scott—the man who would take Simon's place in their little household.

She bit her lip in dismay. His proximity was going to play merry hell on her sensibilities over the coming days because Marco Scott was temptation clad in fine Italian wool. Even in that moment, her fingers itched to reach out and explore the muscular shape of him. She hurriedly curled them in her lap to quiet their agitation and focused on regulating her breathing, which had fallen apart like a castle built of sand being lashed by a great downpour, while her heart pounded loudly in her ears.

"Zooks!" she murmured, causing Nicholas to shoot her a quizzical glance as he struggled to his feet for introductions.

CHAPTER 2

"An English household is a maze of titles, teacups, and unspoken
grievances—navigate with care."

Impressions of England by an Unrepentant Foreigner

* * *

*M*arco's ribs throbbed with a persistent ache
that dulled his senses, but the Blackwood
townhouse had astounded him. It had been bigger than he
had anticipated, more of a grand villa and formal gardens
befitting Rome itself. Standing next to a twin estate, the
manors had elegant colonnades, crowned with impressive
porticos, and from the rooftop stone gods silently stood
watch over the two households while chimneys bellowed
cheerful smoke into the chilled air.

He and Angelo had peered at each other in amazement
after their carriage had come to a halt, and they had slowly
realized they had arrived. Disembarking, they stood staring
upward at the edifice.

"Not what I expected," commented Angelo in a low voice.

"And what were you expecting, young Scott?" Sebastian had come to stand behind them, surprisingly light on his feet considering his size.

"It is as if we are back in Italy," replied Marco in his brother's stead, fully aware why Angelo was nonplussed. "It is very elegant. Especially considering the route from the docks."

"And I told you not to judge England by its docks. It is both green and pleasant, yes?" their Norseman friend asked in a humorous tone.

"*Sì.*" Angelo's expression displayed his awe.

Entering the house, they were met by Simon Scott, who seemed most concerned over their accident. Marco realized this was the man who had lost the right to the Blackwood inheritance because of him, but his uncle, who was only a handful of years older than himself, exhibited no resentment about his change in circumstances. He ushered their party to the mews to discuss what had happened, where they had inspected the damaged carriage.

They failed to conclude whether the accident had resulted from sabotage, but Simon, whom the servants referred to as his lordship, continued to inspect the damage with keen interest. He appeared worried when he finally rose from his haunches and declared they should go inside to meet the Scott family, along with Lord Blackwood.

As they walked the path through the garden back to the house, Marco asked the question hovering on the tip of his tongue.

"Mr. Scott, perhaps my understanding of English titles is not as good as I thought. As the brother of a baron, why do the servants address you as a titled gentleman?"

Simon Scott hesitated, causing all five men to come to a halt mid-stride. His lean face bore signs of strain as he stroked his close-cropped dark beard, and his blue eyes were shadowed. Marco sensed that there was much to learn about the troubles that had plagued the Scott household in recent months.

"I inherited the title from my mother when she recently … died. Which makes me a Scottish viscount. Lord Campbell at your service." He dropped a curt bow, opening his mouth as if to say more, then glanced at Sebastian and Lorenzo as if to remind himself they were in mixed company. Which Marco could not fault. He and his own brother had not made their friends privy to anything related to the murder or the attempt to prevent information about Marco's existence from reaching the officials of England. "We … have much to discuss … But … we should make introductions and allow you to refresh yourselves. Meanwhile, please address me as Simon. It will avoid confusion with so many Scotts in residence."

Marco gave a nod of assent, not quite grasping all of it but hoping it would become clearer once they could speak more freely. The last letter from the duke had been confusing, writing of events that made Marco's head reel. He suspected this was because much of the sensitive information had not been included in the correspondence that would have shed light on its contents.

They continued along the path, entering the townhouse from the back, and Simon led them into a drawing room down the hall. Marco guessed it was where the family gathered, similar to the one in his mother's home.

Plump armchairs and settees in a soft dove gray were grouped informally, while ornate cornices and an intricate chandelier stole the focus of the room. The walls were covered in watered silk of the same gray, while large oil portraits of ancestors glared at them with the serious demeanors of English nobility, haughty in heavy gilt frames.

A fire glowed cheerfully in the large fireplace, and leaded glass windows soared to the ceiling across the room, with elegant drapes to frame the view of the garden they had just crossed. It was early winter, so much of the garden was resplendent in hues of rich browns and deep reds, while some of the foliage maintained their evergreen colors.

The room was both inviting and foreboding at the same time.

Simon made introductions, beginning with the baron. Lord Blackwood, the oldest brother of Marco's father, rose to his feet with a little trouble. He seemed aged beyond his years, but he had a warm smile, insisting on shaking hands with all of them in a gesture of welcome. His grip was firm and his color pink, which Marco supposed was good because the baron had recently suffered ill health, according to the duke's letter. Would his father have resembled the baron if he had lived?

"You have the look of your father, young man. Something about the shape of your eyes and the line of your jaw." The baron looked bemused, as if staring into the past.

Marco gave a brief bow in acknowledgment. "My mother has told me this, too, Lord Blackwood."

Next they were introduced to an attractive young woman with glossy brown hair, lively hazel eyes, and the warm tones of someone descended from Mediterranean roots. Her gown hinted she might be in half mourning, but it was flattering.

"Miss Molly Carter, may I introduce Mr. Marco Scott?"

"*Buongiorno*, Miss Carter." Marco took up her gloved fingers and dropped a bow in the Italian manner, which was less formal than the stiff Englishmen.

"Miss Carter is our cousin," Simon explained.

The young woman inhaled sharply, quickly interjecting, "By marriage! … Not … by blood."

Her color heightened along with her pitch, and after

initially cataloging her as a relation not to pay attention to as a woman, Marco took another look at the young lady. He noted his increase in interest as he took in the rich brown curtain of hair caught in a coif. Her velvet gown of lavender was the perfect foil for her honeyed skin tone and pretty hazel eyes—flecks of brown, gray, and green sparkling like jewels set in an oval face with a determined little chin to punctuate.

Miss Carter was tall for a woman, just a few inches shorter than himself, and she had a capable air about her despite her obvious bashfulness at meeting him. To his dismay, Marco found himself enjoying her implied esteem, and somewhere deep in his soul an echo of agreement sounded as he became aware of her in turn.

It would not do. Marco had no plans to remain in Britain, and it was inconvenient that he would be living under the same roof as an attractive female during his stay. Not to mention that the fragility of Englishwomen was a source of painful reflection. But Miss Carter's lashes fluttered in abashment and Marco's lips curled in response; the urge to appease her embarrassment overruled his caution.

"Perhaps you can explain the … *complessità?*"

"Complexities," Sebastian responded from behind him with amusement, and Marco suppressed a wince that his friend had noted his approval of Miss Carter. Marco realized he still clasped her fingers, and reluctantly released them, mirroring Miss Carter's bashfulness as he finished his reply. He returned his hand to put pressure over his injury in an attempt to distract his English friend.

"Perhaps you can explain the complexities of our relations when we have a free moment?" He did his best to quell any indication of flirtatious interest, but he knew the astute Sebastian would mock him when the opportunity arose.

A glimmer of a smile crossed her features, and Miss

Carter's blush spread out, to his masculine satisfaction. Marco moved on quickly before their exchange drew untoward attention from his new family, noting that both Simon and the baron appeared bemused by other worries and had not noted the spark between him and their mutual cousin … *by marriage*.

* * *

BUTTERFLIES WERE fluttering and swooping in her stomach, her heart beating a little too quick in her chest, and her palms were damp within the confines of her gloves. Marco Scott had a deep accented voice which thrilled her to her toes and made her yearn for things she did not usually think about. Courtship. Weddings. Babies with shocks of dark hair and big, black eyes.

She did not think of herself as a typical female, so it was quite a revelation to discover that her brain could melt and her pulse quicken at the sight of a striking gentleman.

As the introductions continued, she observed that Nicholas was grim, shifting on his feet as if his leg might be hurting him. She winced in sympathy. Ever since he had quit spirits, the young man had suffered both from the effects of the drink and the unresolved pain from his injury, which he was taking steps to address with the help of their new friend, Lady Trafford.

It was not the best time for him to be meeting so many new guests; the introductions were keeping him on his feet for some time, and she wondered if she should step closer to his side to assist. Perhaps she could fold her arm through his and allow him to shift some of his weight onto her?

By the time the younger Scott, Angelo, was being introduced to Nicholas, she predicted from his pallor and the narrowing of his blue eyes that he was about to turn terse.

Angelo and Nicholas were about the same age, despite being from two generations. Angelo was a cheerful, brown-eyed young man of about five feet ten inches, with hair closer in shade to herself than his older Latin brother, but she supposed they had English blood in their veins to cause the disparity in appearance. It was strange to think that Nicholas was Angelo's uncle when no one could be faulted for mistaking them for cousins.

Molly began to move over, worried that Nicholas needed her assistance, when Angelo grabbed his hand to enthusiastically pump in a friendly handshake. Handshakes were usually conducted between close friends, few Englishmen engaged in such practice with strangers, but she could see how Angelo might be confused by how the baron had greeted them thus in a gesture of familial friendship.

Nicholas, however, was in a declining mood and thorny because of his recovery state. Staring down at their grasp in abhorrence, he yanked his hand away with an abrupt movement that nearly pulled their shorter guest off balance. Everyone paused, their attention shifting to the two men. Nicholas had a fierce glower on his face as he turned his gaze up to meet Angelo's look of surprise.

"That is not how it is done!"

"*Scusa?*" Angelo responded in confusion, his boyish face perplexed.

"You should not touch me! Gentlemen bow in greeting! Did you not see how your brother did it?"

Molly did not know what to do. Angelo was reddening at the unexpected onslaught, while she knew Nicholas was being a curmudgeon because of the physical pain that must be intruding on his mood. She had not witnessed him being so intolerant before, but she knew that years of hard liquor was working its way out of his system, and that he had been complaining for days about the stiffness of his injured leg.

Angelo, to his credit, straightened to his full height to defend himself. "I thought English were meant to be polite!"

Simon cleared his throat. "I apologize for my brother, Angelo. We are a house in mourning, and tensions are running a little high."

Nicholas growled in the back of his throat, limping away to drop his thin form onto the sofa. And awkward silence descended until Simon smiled politely and continued the introductions, evidently concluding he would skip Nicholas altogether in the interest of peace and diplomacy.

Returning to her seat, Molly watched as tea and biscuits were brought in along with candied nuts. Their guests appeared mollified as they quietly sipped on their hot beverages while the baron asked them about their journey across the Mediterranean, and marveled at the excellent time they had made from the port near Rome.

"Are you all right?" Molly whispered in a low voice.

Nicholas gave a curt nod. "Not an auspicious beginning with new family," he muttered back while the discussion at large turned to sailing ships.

"Is it your leg?"

He bobbed his head, stretching out a hand to knead above his knee. "I was a terrible heel."

Molly twisted her lips. "I am afraid you rather were."

"Not my brightest moment. When Marco Scott inherits from John, he will recall that I am a dreadfully rude reprobate and cut me off."

"Perhaps you should get some rest and then make an attempt at peace with the young man."

Nicholas soughed, heaving with the force of the exhalation. "Does he have to be so … enthusiastic?"

Molly glanced over to where Angelo was regaling the baron with the sights they had seen on their journey, poetic over the blueness of the ocean, the puffy white clouds, and the herring gulls that had greeted them in an exhilarated chorus upon their arrival. He was animated as he spoke, and she experienced a quiver of worry for Nicholas and his new relations. In his current state of rehabilitation, he could not be more disparate to the clear-eyed young man from Italy. Their ages might be comparable, but their temperaments were decades apart. Even when Nicholas had still possessed his humor, it had been of the dark, sardonic sort.

"Perhaps it will do you good to spend time with someone who embraces life so wholeheartedly. The pall of death in this household has been a misery, and you are working hard to change the course of your life."

Nicholas turned away in defeated disgust, and Molly reached out to pat his hand in commiseration before being distracted by the fascinating Marco Scott who was speaking about his injury from the accident earlier. Her heart fluttered, and she quickly forgot Nicholas's troubles as she soaked in the sound of his accented voice. She was well aware that Marco had noted her state of mild infatuation when they were introduced; her private habit of being direct had inadvertently intruded to reveal her attraction.

Cousins by marriage, not by blood?

Could she have been more obvious about what she was thinking?

Subtle, Molly Carter! As subtle as a hammer to the head!

Such a sophisticated man was likely entertained by such bungling antics from a country gentlewoman who was nearing spinsterhood. She thought maybe she had seen an answering flash of interest in those soulful eyes, but perhaps that was merely wishful thinking. Or perhaps Marco Scott was a glib flirt.

Nevertheless, she wished to remain when the rest of their guests arrived so that she might be in the same room as him for a while longer. It was a novel experience being so intrigued, and she wished to know more about him. Did his character match his handsome exterior? The way to find out was to spend time in his company.

Molly shifted her gaze to the French poodle at the door, keeping watch over her. If she asked Simon for permission to attend the private gathering to brief their new relations on the secrets of the Scotts, he was going to point out that she could not be alone with so many men. And he would never allow the gossiping Miss Dubois to overhear the discussion of such private affairs.

Blast! Being a single woman was such a complicated affair!

On the other hand … Molly nibbled on her lower lip as she considered her options. Just weeks earlier, she had prevailed on cousin Simon to allow Madeline to come to dinner despite the lack of propriety. And now the two were married. Not precisely connected facts, but she had discovered something then. Simon did not like to turn down her requests, even with poor arguments for her case. He had little experience with female relations and was disinclined to disappoint her. And it helped that he liked her. If she could form a solution to the chaperoning which put Claudette Dubois's inquisitive ears outside of hearing distance, might he allow her to remain in the room when the gentlemen met?

* * *

Marco was recounting the bizarre accident from that morning, describing what it had been like to be thrown about in the carriage. He had glanced at Miss Carter across the room, but after realizing she was now staring back at him, he had made a point to not look in her direction.

Fortunately, right around the time the compulsion might have overridden his good sense, the butler had entered to announce the guests they had been waiting for. An older man of medium height with the rigid posture of a military man and a round, friendly face, the butler made his announcement with a slight Scottish brogue.

"What is it, MacNaby?" queried the baron.

"His Grace, the Duke of Halmesbury, and Lord Saunton, the Earl of Saunton."

Two men entered, one a Nordic god from the halls of Valhalla and, for a moment, Marco thought it was Sebastian. Several inches over six feet, broad shoulders, slim hips, and blond hair with gray eyes, but it was the quiet air of English authority along with the fastidious state of his attire that revealed it not to be his longtime friend. Nevertheless, Marco turned his head to confirm that Sebastian was yet sprawled in a wingback chair near the fireplace, his long legs crossed before him.

They rose to greet the guests but, as the Viking's gaze swept the room, he froze to settle it on Sebastian with a tensing of his facial muscles. Marco's friend had not risen, but was staring back at the newcomer with a challenging expression that Marco had not observed on previous occasions.

"Sebastian?"

"Duke."

"What are you doing here?" The duke's tone was angry and confused.

"Never say you missed me, brother?"

The duke's jaw set in firm lines, and he barked out a response. "We are family, you … you … arse!"

As soon as the words left his lips, His Grace froze and turned a deep shade of red before he turned to find the young woman in their company. Licking his lips, he dropped a quick bow, clearly mortified at his loss of composure. "My apologies, Miss Carter."

The shorter of the two newcomers, presumably the earl who was a handsome man with sable hair and emerald eyes, swung his head back and forth between the two, then strode forward to lean down and clap Sebastian on the shoulder. "It is good to see you, cousin! When did you return?"

"Lorenzo and I accompanied Mr. Scott and his brother. We arrived this morning." Sebastian rose to his feet, reluctance etched in the lines of his colossal form. Marco had always thought that his English friend could have been a subject for the great sculptors of the Renaissance with his impressive form. In the current mood, he could represent Hades himself.

"Did you think you might inform us? Were you aware that we were coming to call this afternoon?" The duke's tone was stern, and Marco grimaced. If the Scott family drama was not enough, apparently they were now to bear witness to the melodrama of the Markham family unfolding as if they were an audience at a theatre. How had he not recalled that Sebastian's important nobleman of a brother was a duke?

Sebastian gave a small roll of his shoulders as if attempting to squash some potent emotion. "I was unaware you had a connection to Lord Blackwood, and I would have paid a call when I had the chance."

The duke frowned. "Of course I know Lord Blackwood. The peerage consists of a finite number."

"I suppose I should have thought of that. Certainly, I did not expect to encounter you so soon upon my arrival."

The older brother gave a frustrated shake of his head, his fuming evident. "I have not heard from you in a year! I have a wife and an heir who have never met you, and another child on the way. How—" The duke cut himself off, his eyes flickering to the others in the room as if he had just recalled where he was. "We need to speak in private."

"Then I shall pay a call to Markham House so we can … catch up … And I shall meet the duchess and your son."

Marco turned his head to Angelo, catching his eye to raise his brows in question. Angelo shrugged in nonplussed response. How had they not known that Sebastian was estranged from his family? He supposed they might have guessed by the fact that he had never left Florence, nor mentioned anyone from England.

However, it did bode well that keeping Sebastian and Lorenzo in the dark about the Scotts' difficult circumstances would be an easy matter if the two partners were to be distracted by their own troubles.

Since the additional guests had arrived, it was time to learn what precisely had happened these past months, including the mysterious death of Lady Blackwood, Simon and Nicholas's mother. But first, they would have to politely disengage from their companions, who did not need to be included in this particular discussion.

CHAPTER 3

❦

"In English society, threats are rarely announced—they are simply seated across from you."

Impressions of England by an Unrepentant Foreigner

* * *

Claudette Dubois glowered through the study window, her delicate features set in anger as she shifted from foot to foot on the terrace outside with her ire most evident as she tugged a shawl close to combat the November cold.

Molly turned away, concealing a smug smile at the minor victory over her repugnant companion. Her negotiation with Simon had granted her entry to the private meeting, with the stipulation that Miss Dubois must be able to observe her at all times—through the window.

He had cautioned the occupants of the room to keep their voices low so that the chaperon would not overhear their conversation. The Scotts, Molly, the Italian Scotts, and the duke and earl had opted to move their chairs closer to the baron's desk, and had turned their backs to make it harder for their voices to travel. It was a strange arrangement, but no stranger than the events of the past weeks, so only the Italian men appeared to be mildly confused by such lengths to accommodate Molly.

It had been surprisingly easy to convince Simon, but John had supported her request. She supposed it might have to do with her having nursed the baron when no one else could be trusted to do so. John had informed her numerous times that he was impressed by her gumption.

Simon stood behind the baron, his face grim. "I suppose I must reveal the dark plots that have shadowed our home, especially in light of the accident this morning. We had hoped to welcome you and your brother under happier circumstances, but the possibility of sabotage requires vigilance over the coming days."

"Sabotage?" Molly covered her mouth in shock. Was she the only one who had been unaware that a carriage accident might not have been an accident at all?

Marco, who was sitting close to her due to her machinations with the seating arrangements, glanced in her direction. "The coachman believes the wheel was tampered with, but we could not find conclusive … *prova?*" His nose wrinkled, and he peered around for a translator.

"Evidence," Molly replied without hesitation.

Those soulful eyes returned to her, warm appreciation in their black depths. "You speak Italian?"

"My mother was passionate about opera. She conversed with me throughout my youth."

"You are still … youthful." His sculpted lips curled into a devastating smile that ignited heat in her lower belly, excitement fizzing through her veins.

Molly blushed at the compliment. She was considered

close to being on the shelf by society's standards, but Marco evidently did not agree. It was still otherworldly that he appeared to notice her as a woman when he must have his pick of beautiful Florentine women, and she could not help the hand that rose to check her hair. Marco's eyes followed the gesture, and she quickly lowered it.

Zooks, Molly, what if he is just a flirt?

Even so, she was flattered to receive any of his attention as someone unaccustomed to being in the presence of a male who attracted her so.

"As I was saying," Simon interjected, "I had hoped to not reveal quite so much about private affairs, but in light of … Well, I will have to explain the circumstances of my mother's death or none of this will make sense. Lives have been lost, and both the baron and my wife were nearly killed, so this is not the time to be coy. It would be appropriate for each of us to take steps to maintain our safety, so John and I have decided to reveal all that has happened."

Molly leaned forward, nibbling on her lip and realizing she would finally learn the entire truth rather than the tidbits she had garnered.

"My mother was not a sane woman. Since her marriage to the late baron in her youth, she had sought to drive a wedge between her husband and your father. She wished for me to become the future baron and took measures to ensure this would happen. Your father—my older brother, Peter—was considered an opponent because he had left England with a wife and could bear an heir." Simon gestured to Marco and Angelo. "So she devised a plan to intercept mail from Florence. She recruited servants to her bidding, so this must be how she went about it. And she knew well that the two of you existed."

"My parents attempted several times to reconcile with our grandfather," Marco replied.

Simon nodded. "It was not a brilliant plan because the truth was bound to come out at some point, but I cannot attest to her intelligence, only to her commitment to her cause."

The duke shifted in his seat. "My father-in-law, the Baron of Filminster, visited London for the first time in decades and had the misfortune to sit beside Lord Blackwood at the coronation."

John huffed a dry chuckle. "It was unfortunate for Lord Filminster, but as it turns out, rather fortunate for me."

His Grace nodded. "Lord Filminster questioned Lord Blackwood about his succession in a rather inflammatory manner, which resulted in the baron informing his family of the encounter. This is how the dowager Lady Blackwood learned of it, and that night she visited Filminster's home to negotiate with him."

Simon snorted in disgust. "She hoped to seduce him into keeping the secret, but that did not work."

The duke laughed humorlessly. "My father-in-law was not a pleasant man, but he considered Peter a friend and he had principles of a sort, so we surmise that he told her he had written a letter to the Home Secretary to inform him of Marco's birth. Lady Blackwood took exception and clobbered him from behind."

"Which was when the investigation into his murder led them to me," continued Simon. "Which, as my brother has stated, was rather fortunate for us because it came to light that he was being poisoned by my mother to hurry my inheritance, and due to a timely intervention, he is still with us."

Molly perched forward, the unfolding story fitting in some of the missing pieces. "And what of Madeline?" Looking about, she realized not everyone present knew who she was. "Simon's wife as of three days ago."

Simon cleared his throat, seemingly overcome at recalling

the day John's poisoning had come to light after he had collapsed. "My mother tricked her into drinking tea laced with arsenic and accused her of trying to trap me into marriage. Lady Blackwood did not consider Madeline the right sort of bride, not being of the peerage. She must have known she would soon be found out, and it was a last desperate act to bring about the future she had envisioned. I was to be baron and to wed a proper high society wife who would elevate her bloodlines even further."

Molly sat upright, perceiving she was about to learn the ugly truth of that day, rather than the edited version.

"Which was when my mother took an overdose of laudanum. Despite the coroner's finding that it was an accident—and I implore confidentiality with this information—Lady Blackwood committed suicide."

It was as Molly had suspected.

* * *

Marco slumped back in his seat with shock while his brother sprang to his feet with a horrified expression. The tension in Simon he had sensed upon their arrival now made sense, and he was at a loss for words.

"*Mi dispiace tanto* … I am so sorry."

The words hung suspended in the air, and the room went quiet. Miss Carter shifted her gaze to the window, and he realized she was ensuring that the paid companion had not overheard anything. He followed her look to see that the dainty little creature who served in the role was still in her position outside the window, but showed no signs of having heard the appalling announcement.

Angelo slowly lowered himself back into his chair, blinking with thoughts that must have been spinning as fast as his own. He could not imagine the horror of such an event. It was terrible enough that his father had died when he was so young, before Angelo had even been born, but how much worse would it have been to lose a loved one to suicide?

Yet … considering she had committed murder … where would she be placed within the circles of hell? *Phlegethon*, the boiling river of blood, was reserved for those who committed violence. But suicides became part of the Wood of the Suicides, being transformed into gnarled trees in a barren forest. It was quite the philosophical puzzle to consider which was worse—the violence committed against others or the violence against oneself.

"I am so sorry," he repeated to Simon, then turned to his other uncle, the belligerent young man who had lost his temper at Angelo. Nicholas Scott was glum, fixated on his boots. "My …" Marco sought for the word. "… condolences."

Angelo turned, noticing to whom Marco was speaking. "I am sorry, too."

Nicholas jerked his head away, rejecting their sympathies, but his discomfort was obvious.

Eventually, once Marco had time to grasp the tale of the Scotts' woes, he frowned in confusion. "Why are you concerned about the accident if the baroness is dead?"

Simon swallowed. "Because she had an accomplice, possibly two. One of the footmen had assisted her, but he jumped to his death when he heard about her death."

"And the other?" This question came from his left, in a thready voice with perfect English enunciation. Miss Carter was a woman of fortitude to keep her wits about her. He could barely comprehend such events, yet she had lived through them.

"I was with my mother when she said her final words. I pointed out that despite her Machiavellian methods, the heir had been found and I would not inherit. She … Her last words … She implied that she had taken steps to prevent that."

Miss Carter leaned forward into Marco's peripheral vision, her pretty face worried. "You mean that she might have had someone else enthralled into assisting her?" Her hazel eyes flickered to the window, her expression bemused as she stared at her companion outside, who was clasping herself in a tight embrace in an effort to retain her body heat.

The baron cleared his throat, taking some time before speaking. "We had hoped it was over, but the incident with the carriage suggests we must take precautions. In the event that Isla—Lady Blackwood—had another accomplice to ensure that Marco, or Angelo who is next in line, cannot inherit."

"You are suggesting that someone tried to kill us this morning?"

"Yes, and another attempt might be made. It is why we apprised you of the facts. We nearly lost Madeline because of our lack of caution, and we will not allow any further misadventure. It could be an accident, or it could be …"

The duke exhaled heavily, then declared what they were all thinking. "Attempted murder." He shook his head. "I could have lost my brother without even knowing he had returned home. It seems fantastical that someone would risk killing four people, along with the coachman and footmen, just to target two in the vehicle. Surely it must have been an accident?"

Simon shook his head. "We must assume the worst. It is the safest course. Which is why … I am taking my bride to Scotland in the morning. We shall visit my new estates to ensure she is out of harm's way. My mother was quite obsessed with severing my connection with Madeline, and after nearly losing her, I will not risk it. I am afraid I cannot assist in sorting this out. We were to share dinner here this evening, but she cannot set foot in this house if there is even a possibility of harm befalling her."

Struggling to his feet, the baron patted his brother on the back. "Agreed. Considering Isla's obsession with bloodlines, Simon must see to Madeline's safety, and we shall put our heads together to resolve this matter."

Marco rose to his feet, walking back to the other side of the room with a gesture for Angelo to join him.

"What the hell have we stepped into here?" he muttered in a low voice.

Angelo rubbed his face, his expression solemn as he sought an answer. "It could be just an accident. After such events … perhaps they are seeing shadows where there are none. What reason would an accomplice have to continue this madwoman's quest after she is gone? I understand their … *attentzione?*"

Marco struggled to think of the English word, his thoughts swirling in his head. They had known that something odd had happened, and that the dowager baroness was dead, but this was a hornet's nest. "Caution!"

Angelo nodded. "I understand their caution, but perhaps it is nothing."

"Will this delay my return to Florence?"

His brother shook his head in cheery rebuke, his usual good spirits restored in an instant. "We just arrived. Give England a chance. I wish to see more of it. Discover if a pharmacy is needed here. How are your ribs?"

Marco chuckled, his mood lightened as he rubbed his aching chest. "They are much better. You are determined to bring Florentine medicine to the world."

Shrugging, his brother grinned. "It is the best, and I could find my own place in this world doing something that is meaningful."

Reaching an agreement, they returned to their seats.

Lord Saunton offered a commiserating smile. "It is a lot to take in. We apologize for greeting you with such grim tidings."

"I do not know what all of this means. We thought we would settle matters with the baron about how to handle the title now that Lord Filminster's murder had been solved, but I suppose we must address this first. How do we even proceed?"

Simon leaned over the desk, pushing a pile of notebooks forward. "These are my mother's journals. I read them once to uncover the truth of what happened, but I was not looking for an accomplice. Perhaps there is a clue in there somewhere, but if I am leaving, who is to read them? It shall need to be someone who knows about the situations she is referencing and our family tree. However, they are … unpleasant."

"I shall do it," said Miss Carter in a bright tone, though her face showed some reticence to the notion, and Marco found himself impressed at her resilient offer to read the ravings of a homicidal lunatic despite her misgivings.

"I appreciate that, Molly, I do. But this is not appropriate reading for an unmarried woman."

The baron coughed into a handkerchief. "I think it is important that you take Madeline away after all she went through. Her poisoning was more violent than my own, and she plays no role in this, so I shall read the journals."

"No!" The taciturn one, Nicholas, rose from his seat to limp forward. Reaching the desk, he picked up the journals to tuck them under his arm. "Simon has done enough, and you are recovering your health. This is my task to complete because she was my mother and … I have done nothing to assist. This will be my contribution."

Simon contemplated his younger brother for several seconds, doubt written on his features until he finally agreed. "Perhaps that is the right thing. There are three years' worth of entries missing. The period when Mother married our father. I searched for them, and it seems that they should exist. Considering what is in these journals, I shudder to think why she might have thought those were the ones to get rid of."

Nicholas bobbed his head. "She could have misplaced them, I suppose."

"That is doubtful. She kept these locked in her writing desk, and considering what her journaling reveals, it is unlikely she would have allowed them to go missing. Perhaps she destroyed them."

As he listened to the exchange, Marco's concern was that Simon did not seem to consider that the accomplice might be in the study with them. The baron had been poisoned, so it was not him. Perhaps the attractive Miss Carter might possess some unknown motive to forward the murderous quest, although she seemed rather pragmatic, so he did not think so. And, if they were considering those with a close relationship to the dead baroness, would the ill-tempered Nicholas not directly benefit from his and Angelo's deaths?

He shuddered lightly at the direction of his thoughts. Angelo was right. The creeping gloom that his English family had been living with was contagious, causing even him to see monsters in the shadows. Talk of heinous poisons did nothing to lift that shroud of dread.

But the carriage incident could have merely been an accident.

* * *

SIMON SAT at the desk John had vacated. Although the baron's stamina was improving, he still required frequent periods of rest, but Molly was pleased that his complexion was more healthy with each passing day. The gray pallor, from when Lady Blackwood had been slowly poisoning his tea, was disappearing, and he had more vigor.

Their visitors had left, and Angelo and Nicholas had retired to their rooms to leave Molly, Marco, and Simon to discuss some details before his departure. Molly saddened that Madeline would be leaving; their daily teas together in the shared garden between the Scott and Bigsby homes had been the only brightness in her otherwise dull days.

"I have written down some details of affairs that need attention. The baron must sign anything official, but I have been managing the estates in his stead for some time now. Which means there are some estate matters that may arise in my absence for you to see to."

Marco had resettled in a wingback chair facing the desk, his fingers drumming the padded arm to mark his tension. "You understand I intend to return to Florence. I cannot … how do you say this … take up the mantle when I will not remain here to manage the Blackwood estates."

Molly's stomach dipped in disappointment at hearing his intentions to return to Italy, but she supposed it was better to be forewarned rather than get her hopes up about any sort of potential match. Unfortunately, it did nothing to curb her fascination with the handsome gentleman. Was this how the men Isla Scott had seduced had felt about her?

Ugh! I hope not.

Simon stroked his bearded chin, leaning back in his chair to contemplate the new heir. "I am afraid you are the future Lord Blackwood with hundreds of servants and tenants, not to mention thousands of subjects, relying on you. Whether you reside in Florence or in England, there is no avoiding the responsibilities of the title. You can learn something of it now, or when the baron departs this world. I recommend sooner rather than later would be in your best interests."

Marco frowned. "I am a man who makes his own choices."

"And your choices must include what to do with issues that affect the estates and the people who rely on you. I understand this was unexpected." Simon paused as if in reflection, his expression softening to one of sympathy, before resuming. "My advice is to learn something of the duties of the title while I am away, and calculate how to incorporate them in your future path. I myself have several titles I have inherited from my mother, but I wish to pursue a future in stone manufactory, so I have hired a good man of business to see to the estate work who will report to me. There are rewards to be had from this, I assure you. And the baron is in residence to discuss these matters."

Marco raked through his lush waves. Molly wished she could whip off a glove to finger through the silky strands of black and discover if they were as soft as they appeared. She wondered what his scent might be, but she could not discern it from this afar.

"*Cazzo!*" He winced, his eyes flickering to Molly, who smiled back in innocence as if she had misunderstood his curse.

"What of Miss Carter? Why is she included in this discussion when everyone has left?"

"The baron is the trustee of Miss Carter's estate. With him incapacitated, I have acted on his behalf, but there are some details related to her trust that will need to be seen to urgently because it has been more than six months since Miss Carter joined our household after her mother … left us … so I wished to discuss this with the two of you before I leave."

Molly's mouth fell open, aghast at the news. She had not realized that Marco would be essentially acting as her guardian in Simon's stead. It seemed somehow wrong to be contemplating what his firm lips would feel like pressed to her own, when he was to act as ... as ... as her de facto parent!

From the corner of her eye, she could see that Marco's brow had furrowed, and she wondered if he was having a similar thought. The frisson of mutual awareness during their introduction seemed almost shameful in light of this announcement.

"Someone is going to have to explain to me my relationship to Miss Carter," Marco finally responded. Molly thrilled slightly at the underlying note of rejection. It suggested that perhaps a familial tie was undesirable to him, but that could be wishful thinking on her part. Perhaps he was just irritated at the additional responsibilities.

Simon gave a nod of his head. "It sounds like excellent dinner conversation, but for now we shall consider the details of the trust that need to be attended to. The baron will need to sign off, but you must prepare the documents that are required with our solicitors."

Dear cousin Simon was focused on removing his bride from danger posthaste, or Molly suspected he would have noticed something was amiss between her and her—*ick*—substitute trustee, who even now was glancing at her with discomfort. But, despite everything, Molly was excited to think they would be in residence together, and perhaps her trust would provide a reason to spend some time alone together.

Then she remembered her chaperon, turning to the window to find Miss Dubois shooting daggers from her large brown eyes as she shivered in the cool air, which would have grown frostier as the meeting had progressed. Molly was going to pay for making the vicious French poodle stand out in the cold, but overall, she thought it had been worth it to attend the meeting with the men.

CHAPTER 4

"A determined lady with a chaperon is still a determined lady—just one with a shadow."

Impressions of England by an Unrepentant Foreigner

* * *

NOVEMBER 30 1821

"*N*o more colors of mourneeng. Zis ees *mieux*. Not very good, but *mieux*."

Molly curled her lips in repressed aggravation. She was not prone to sarcasm, but Miss Dubois brought out some of her base instincts, to be sure. "I am thrilled that you slightly approve of my attire." She was not. She did not care a whit what the poodle thought.

"Lady Blackwood would advize to wear silk wiz zo many … *admissible?*"

"Eligible."

"Zat ees it! Eligible gentlemen, but zis ees … *mieux?*" Claudette Dubois wrinkled her delicate nose as she sought the English word, and Molly restrained the impulse to provide it because she was hardly going to assist her chaperon to condescend. "Better! Zis ees better!"

Molly huffed under her breath, but she was pleased at her reflection. Preparing to retire to bed the evening before, she had decided to turn the page and begin a new chapter. As much as she missed her mother, it had been months since her passing, and it was time for her to set her sights on the future.

It has nothing to do with a certain Italian gentleman.

Or maybe it did, but if his presence acted as motive to leave her mourning behind so she might think about what she wanted from this life, then so be it. She had spent the last few years nursing her ailing mother in the country, enjoying her company, but her youth had slipped by until some would consider her on the shelf—too old to wed—but there were yet gentlemen who might consider her age acceptable.

Truthfully, she did not even know if finding a match was her aim—she did not know what her aim was because until now her only aim had been to get through the day without grieving until she could consider her options. The recent drama of the Scotts had been a gloomy but effective distraction. It was just such a relief to feel any interest in anything after months of feeling removed—distant—from the world at large. The grief of losing her closest companion, a wonderful and amusing parent, had a way of making time stand still. The rest of the world continued to move forward while one was caught outside of it, merely an observer standing in the cold with one's face pressed against the window. Yesterday, time had begun to move once more, as if she had suddenly found an entrance back into the world of the living.

Molly suppressed a grin at the memory of Miss Dubois's

ire at being literally in such a position the afternoon before. She was not a vindictive person, but after contending with the poodle's condescension and criticisms since the death of Lady Blackwood, it had been retribution for all the rebukes she had swallowed in the interest of peace. The poodle's constant admiration of the murderous Lady Blackwood, whom she apparently adored with single-minded obsession, was grating, but Molly could not blame her for it. Miss Dubois was a shallow woman who revered appearances, and she was not aware of the foul misdeeds committed by her former employer.

Or is she?

Molly glanced at the servant who was fussing over her gown, straightening and shaking bits of it out as if Molly would not walk away and the minute rearrangements not be undone within seconds. She nearly groaned aloud when she recalled that Simon had departed London, so any hopes of a new companion were delayed.

How fanatical about the dead dowager baroness is she? Would she know how to sabotage a carriage wheel?

Miss Dubois seemed too delicate to do anything approaching that kind of manual labor.

Molly returned her attention to the mirror. Her military-inspired spencer, the sort that had become fashionable during the Napoleonic Wars as homage to their soldiers, was green with sleeves of gold and attractively tied with black loops and ornate buttons running down the front. The matching gold bodice was hidden from view, but her skirts matched the spencer, and the ensemble brought out the gold and green flecks in her hazel irises while complementing her complexion. She hoped it might draw eyes—a very particular, soulful pair that had appeared in her dreams throughout the night.

She was excited to descend for breakfast, and she had the

seeds of a plan to distract her chaperon. But even the presence of her dogged shadow could not hinder her interest in seeking out the handsome Marco Scott.

Once they were in the hall approaching the breakfast room, Molly decided it was time to enact part of her strategy. "Miss Dubois! I just realized I have come down without my gloves!"

The poodle paused, peering down the corridor and then back to Molly's naked hands, clearly at a loss as to what to do.

"Do you mind? I plan to go to the gardens after breakfast, and it is ever so cold."

Miss Dubois was torn, both of them aware that there were now six unmarried men in residence, and only four could claim any familial relationship with Molly, which meant she was on duty as chaperon. But her sensibilities as a lady's maid made the tug of clothing duty overwhelming.

"*Oui*, I shall fetch zem for you and return right away."

"The green ones. To match my gown."

Molly smirked as the maid walked away. Miss Dubois thought she would only be gone a few minutes, but Molly had buried one of the gloves in the wrong drawer during the night, so she was hoping it would take ten or more minutes. Time she could spend searching out Marco. It was ruthless, but she would not allow the annoying companion to thwart her effort to learn more about the intriguing gentleman.

Molly hurried to the breakfast room, hoping to find Marco there, but a conversation in Italian had her coming to a halt. It sounded a little heated, and she was unsure about making her entry as she eavesdropped with a mild flare of guilt. But she had a goal for her day, and she would not be prevented from achieving it.

"You must call on the lady today, dear friend."

"I cannot, Lorenzo! I have promised the duke I would visit Markham House today. He is quite put out that I did not inform him of my arrival."

"But, Sebastian, we must secure the painting. It is essential to our cause."

"I am well aware, but it must wait for another day."

"Pig misery! You always have excuses! What is it about this woman that makes you such a craven?"

Molly recognized the curse. Her mother had loved music and opera, but she had also possessed a wicked sense of humor along with a copy of *The Classical Dictionary of the Vulgar Tongue*, so Molly had enjoyed a ... well-rounded education. The thought instigated a sharp pang of longing for her irreverent parent. It had been just the two of them since her father had died a decade earlier, and it was still an adjustment to recall that Mama had been buried months earlier. She shook it off because she was weary of being gloomy. Two deaths and two almost-deaths within this household in the past few weeks had done nothing to lighten her mood, so she was going to pursue her newfound interest even if it could not lead to anything. There was no reason to not savor Marco's presence while she could. Other than befriending Madeline, his riveting appearance was the only happiness she had enjoyed this year.

"Mind yourself!"

The last was growled in a menacing tone, and nothing was said for several seconds until, finally ...

"My apologies."

Molly took this as her signal, silently backtracking a few

feet before stomping her slippers hard on the wooden floorboards to announce her approach before she entered the breakfast room. As she suspected, the only guests it contained were the Norse brother to the Duke of Halmesbury and his artist friend, both of whom were completing their meals with earnest intent while two footmen stood at attention by the sideboard where the breakfast platters were laid out. The servants' presence explained why the men had been speaking in Italian—for privacy, she supposed.

"Good morning, Lord Sebastian. Mr. di Bianchi!" she exclaimed with good cheer, despite her disappointment that Marco was nowhere to be seen. Soon she was settled in her seat to eat her eggs and ham, when Miss Dubois rushed in with a nervous expression and Molly's gloves clasped in her hand.

Molly ate in silence with Miss Dubois, the two men leaving soon after she had seated herself, and wondered what to do next. Thankfully, she had organized more than one delay for her intrepid chaperon, but perhaps she should ensure she located the elusive Italian before she played her next card. It had been a novice mistake to send for the gloves too early, and the gambit was now wasted.

Eating her meal in haste, with a grumbling Miss Dubois complaining she had not finished drinking her tea, Molly pulled on her gloves and began searching the rooms before finding Marco in the library. Nicholas was seated in a wingback chair near a window with his injured leg propped up on an ottoman and a stack of expensive journals on an end table. He was reading with an expression of distaste from one of the thick leather-covered tomes which were tooled in ornate gold patterns along the spines and borders, an intricate thistle embossed onto the front covers. Isla Scott's journals might well have been custom-made, from their luxurious presentation.

Ignoring him, Molly focused on Marco who was seated near a library table reading what appeared to be account books, far simpler and more businesslike than Nicholas's stack. He was dressed in buckskins that hugged his lean, muscular legs to perfection. His black coat and snowy white linen emphasized his sooty hair, olive skin, and soulful eyes with elegant impact, while his black riding boots gleamed in the morning light. She had heard of the craftsmanship of Florentine tailors, and Marco's elegant form was evidence of their skill.

"Good morning, Marco," she chirped in a voice that was more breathy than she had intended. Miss Dubois shot her a look, but she ignored it. During her meeting with him and Simon the day before, she had solicited an agreement to use their given names. She had reasoned, with Simon looking on, that they were of a similar age and shared a familial relationship.

It was a shameless ploy, because she had earlier made a case that they were not related by blood. Was she playing both sides? Indubitably. Had Marco appeared perplexed because he still did not know how they were related, other than he was her trustee? Unquestionably. Had Molly wanted to hear her name said in his deep, accented voice? Without a doubt.

"*Buongiorno*, Molly." He rose to drop a small bow, and Molly blinked in shivering delight to hear her name spoken with his accented lilt, while doing her best not to blush like a chit in short skirts as she had yesterday on multiple occasions. Some experience with courtship would have come in handy right about now. For a woman of her years, she had a surprising lack of knowledge about flirtation.

Behind her, the butler entered with a tea tray. MacNaby walked it over to where Nicholas was sitting, placing it on a free table nearby and politely gaining his attention. The household was a little short-staffed, what with the longtime footman, Roderick, falling to his death upon news of the baroness's suicide the month before. She grimaced at the memory, quickly turning back to pose her question to Marco.

"I was hoping to show you the gardens this morning. They are most impressive, even at this time of the year."

Marco hesitated before giving a nod. "That sounds delightful." He turned to pick up his gloves from the table.

Molly thrilled, almost rising on her toes with glee. She had not seen him since the afternoon before. Everyone had settled on retiring early to their rooms, and dinner had been brought on trays to their respective bedchambers.

Molly had shared supper with the baron in his private drawing room, something of a habit since his collapse the prior month, except this time Miss Dubois had been there, too. With Lady Blackwood deceased, Simon away in Scotland for several weeks touring his inherited estates, and Nicholas in the perpetual grump of recovery from his days of hard drinking and carousing, it had been a pleasant evening ritual for her and John as they grew to know each other better by sharing stories about her aunt—who had been his first stepmother—and her own mother.

Last night, however, it had frustrated her to her core that there had not been a communal supper so she might partake in Marco's company, so she had devised a plan to spend some time with him this morning. Simon and Madeline had spent the evening preparing to leave this morning, while their guests from Italy had been disinclined to socialize after their long journey and the carriage accident.

She smiled, gesturing toward a terrace door. As they reached it together, Molly turned with a contrived gasp to stare at Miss Dubois in consternation. "Oh my, I have quite forgotten my bonnet!"

The poodle scowled before obviously recollecting admonishments from the late baroness about the damage that emotions did to one's youthful appearance. Molly could pluck the thought from her companion's head as she quickly relaxed her face into placid lines. "You must wait 'ere!"

Marco raised his sweeping black brows at the impertinent tone, but refrained from comment as Miss Dubois spun on her heel to hurry away. Molly watched her depart the library on the heels of MacNaby's exit with smug satisfaction. Every single bonnet had been removed during the night to a closet beneath the stairs where cloaks were stored. Not the cloaks worn currently, but the ones in deep storage, which were infrequently needed. It would take some time for her pestilent chaperon to find even one. Just to be sure, Molly had even removed the bonnets of the deceased baroness, too. Even if Miss Dubois gave up and returned, it should buy a good half an hour if Molly was wily about her tour of the gardens. The servant would expect her to make straight for the shared garden, the jewel of the twin estates, so Molly intended to take a different route and prolong her time alone with the man who captured her interest.

Glancing over at Nicholas, she confirmed he was still absorbed in his reading before turning back to give a wide smile to the gentleman waiting by the terrace doors.

"Shall we?"

He assented, politely opening the door and stepping aside to allow her to exit, and Molly was encouraged by his cooperation.

Outside, he offered her an arm, and with tingling anticipation, she took hold of it. He was strong, his upper arm muscular, and Molly had to remind herself to breathe lest she swoon from heady delight. He smelled of shaving soap, leather, and starch, his masculine scent a physical sensation that arrowed down to settle as a pulsing awareness in her lower belly. The urge to press closer had to be firmly denied as they walked to the stairs to descend to the garden where she discovered that the weather had warmed up overnight.

Instead of leading him through the back garden toward the walled sanctuary that was the jewel, though she wished she could take him there, she guided him to the left and around the corner of the manor. It was the least interesting part of the garden, mostly just a line of hedges along the property line with a narrow lawn, and Molly searched the attics of her mind to find a compelling justification for the route she had chosen.

Peering up, she considered the ivy creeping up the side of the building, but the singular thought that came to mind was to point out that the footman, Roderick, had plummeted to his death from the baroness's private sitting room on the third floor. Not a subject that would add to the romantic ambience of their walk, so she kept walking while she sought for something else to show him.

Coming to a stop below a sentinel which guarded the parapet, she pointed up. "Here is Mars. Although he usually depicts power and strength, I believe he was placed here to symbolize a love of the classical by the men who commissioned the building."

Molly wanted to kick herself. It was the first thing she could think of to say, their tour of the garden being conducted in silence for the first several minutes. But had she really lectured an actual bear leader from Florence on Roman symbolism? A man who tutored the sons of noblemen on this very subject? Molly was afraid her weak excuse to spend time with him was as transparent as a sheet of glass, but she had never had much practice with subterfuge.

Blushing, she turned to find Marco regarding her with amusement in his dark eyes. "I hate to correct you, but I believe that is Romulus. I believe Mars is standing watch at the front of the house."

"Is it? How can you tell?"

Marco pointed up at the head. "The military attire misled you, but he is wearing a laurel wreath and holding a scepter. These are symbols of leadership to emphasize his role as the first king of Rome."

"Oh." Her tone was disappointed. He must think her the worst ninny. After impressing him with her knowledge of his Continental language, she had regretfully followed it up with a gauche lack of classical knowledge. "I suppose I do not understand ancient Rome as well as I thought."

He turned back to look in her face, lifting a gloved forefinger to tuck a stray lock of hair behind her ear in a gesture so intimate she nearly lost the capacity to breathe. "It is not to be helped. You have not taken your Grand Tour or attended university. Many of the young Englishmen arrive in Florence with a faulty understanding, which is why they pay me to educate them."

His kind words eased her embarrassment as his hand fell away, and they stood gazing at each other for several seconds, until Marco eventually queried in a husky voice, "Molly, how are we related?"

She was enthralled by the windows to his soul, which spoke of the emotional events of his past, while his question slowly filtered into her brain. "We are not. I mean ... we are ... but ..." Inhaling deeply, she gathered her wits. "My aunt was married to your grandfather. His second wife. They did not bear any children together. We are second cousins by marriage."

Marco nodded. "That is ... good." Then he raised his head back to stare up at Romulus, tensing beneath her fingers where she was holding his arm.

Next, he embraced her tightly and threw them both to the

ground. She landed on the grass with a low rustle of clothing and a thud disproportionately loud, considering all their layers of fabric to mute their fall.

Despite her bemusement at being pressed beneath his body, she turned her head to find a large stone urn had shattered in the very place they had been standing a second before. She swung her gaze up to confirm that it was one of the twin urns that flanked the Roman god, who even now peered down at them with seeming concern, then looked back to Marco in shock.

* * *

THE STRIATIONS of Molly's eyes had utterly fascinated Marco, shining like opals in the pale winter light, when he heard a scraping sound from above. Swinging his head up, he thought he saw a flicker of motion, as if someone might be positioned behind the depiction of Romulus, when he noticed that one of the urns—the one right above them— appeared to be toppling over.

Flinging himself at Molly, he tackled her to the ground, almost in sync with the resounding thud behind him that confirmed he had acted just in time.

His first instinct was to jump up and run inside to find the roof, but he realized he did not know the way and if someone had pushed the large urn off the roof deliberately, they would have more than enough time to get away. If there was an assailant, the fact that they were familiar with the house would make it easy to run off while he lumbered around trying to find the right staircase.

He turned his attention back to Molly to check on her, becoming aware of her rounded breasts pressed against his chest, and his groin notched so neatly between her skirted thighs. Attraction sizzled, and his loins responded to her proximity with firing heat. Raising himself on his forearms, only to be riveted by blazing eyes which shone with a mixture of alarm and desire, he was captivated by the infinite constellations in those opalescent irises.

He shifted, attempting to untangle their limbs, and discovering that she smelt like cinnamon to further thicken his blood. A tide of heady passion made it difficult to think, while his mouth watered at the possibility of tasting that sweet spice on his tongue. Molly panted in agitation, squirming beneath him to set off a new riot of sensation, and their gazes were locked until hers flickered away to focus on his mouth. Everything around them receded as his head descended ever so slowly, the shouting of his conscience no match for the inevitability of the moment as his lips found hers in search of an ecstatic binding of their souls and bodies.

He had had a paramour or two over the years, but they had an arrangement of expediency to see to their mutual needs. He had avoided any hint of anything more meaningful because it reminded him of Catherine, which inevitably reminded him of the father he had barely known. It was not that he had done anything so crass as to swear off romantic love because his mother had been widowed so young, followed by losing Catherine before they had even had a proper beginning. It was more an instinctual aversion to pursuing deeper emotions.

This heightened awareness of the pragmatic gentle-woman who dealt with the harshness of life with fortitude and composure was something new—something he was not prepared for—but her lips were so soft against his, and before he could stop himself, he swept his tongue over the seam of her lips, growling in approval when they parted to allow him entry.

She tasted of cinnamon as he had hoped she would, and

he distantly wondered if it was blended into her tea, but hunger took over and thoughts were washed away. The very ground wavered beneath them as if he were back at sea, his ardor mounting as he explored her mouth with infinite interest before gliding away to taste her creamy skin and nuzzle against her neck. Molly was all woman, kissing him back, while soft curves fitted against him as if they were made for each other, and he found himself nudging against the warm embrace of her thighs in search of—

Marco lifted his head, gasping for air, and rolled off her to massage at his ribs. "My apologies."

Molly said nothing, recovering her breath as they both lay on their backs and gazed up at the pale sky. Finally, she rolled over and began to rise. "No apology required, but Miss Dubois might happen upon us at any moment."

Standing up, they inspected the smashed urn while they brushed grass off their clothing. Marco noted with relief that no grass stains were visible on the fetching green and gold ensemble she was wearing.

"Two potentially fatal accidents in two days? You are either terribly misfortunate to experience such a string of bad luck or …"

"The devil beckons."

Molly sighed. "Do you think someone could have deliberately pushed it?"

He raked through his hair. There was so much to think about at once. Another close call with death? And he should address the ravenous kiss with her, but he understood she was attempting to compose herself before they were joined by the chaperon.

"It is a distinct possibility," he replied.

They would need to speak about what had happened, but it would have to wait. Marco was angry with himself. Molly was an innocent, and their little flirtation had got out of hand. He did not intend to stay in England, so why was he dallying with a well-bred woman who deserved his respect?

Nevertheless, it was a struggle to regret their passionate embrace. He could still feel the womanly form of her against him, and his loins were protesting the abrupt loss of contact. The urge to sweep back in her arms and tumble her to the grass was a distinct pressure to further conflict his tumultuous thoughts.

CHAPTER 5

"Trust not the smiles of kin, for even roses grow thorns when ambition blooms."

Impressions of England by an Unrepentant Foreigner

* * *

*M*arco returned inside without Molly, who said she might have an appointment for tea before heading farther into the gardens at the back of the house. Entering the library from the terrace doors, he immediately noted that Nicholas and his journals were absent. The only sign he had been there at all was the askew ottoman and the tray of tea, which appeared untouched.

Firming his jaw, he mused that the most likely suspect was the uncle who had been second in line to inherit the barony, but was now fourth in line with the revelation of his and Angelo's existence. The younger man had both personal motive and a close connection to the original murderess, Lady Blackwood. Was Nicholas's limp enough to prevent him from scaling about the roof? It was certain Marco needed to keep an eye on him.

A movement in the corner of the room drew his eye to find that Lorenzo was browsing through the stacks with a bored expression.

"Lorenzo? What are you up to?"

His friend flinched in surprise, apparently having been absorbed by his thoughts. "Marco! I am keeping myself busy. Sebastian has gone off to visit his family, and left me to amuse myself."

Marco caught the tone of remonstration. The other man was rather intense—one with a crusade—and his single-minded attitude toward his pursuits sometimes prevented him from understanding the demands that others faced from their own lives.

"To be fair, Sebastian has been gone from England for six years and his family must be eager to speak with him."

"It is not the purpose of this journey."

Marco snorted with reproach. "Ah, but your obsessions with your own family are legendary, my friend. You understand that Sebastian must see to his obligations?"

Lorenzo responded with a wry laugh. "You are not wrong. Nevertheless, I am impatient to see to our affairs here in London."

The two men had not revealed the purpose of accompanying him and Angelo to England, but it was sure to have something to do with Lorenzo's ancestor. The one he had talked about these past years that Marco had known him. Matteo di Bianchi, who, according to Lorenzo, had been one of the greatest painters of da Vinci's time. Unfortunately, there was little evidence of this, but considering his friend's vast knowledge of art, and his profitable trade in such, Marco accepted there must be something to his grand claims.

"Have you seen Angelo?"

Lorenzo nodded, turning back to consider the books. "He returned from a walk. You can find him eating breakfast."

Marco thanked him, hurrying to the breakfast room to find his brother so he could discuss what had happened out in the garden. The brush with death, not the kiss with the surprisingly sensual Molly.

Entering the breakfast room, he found Angelo finishing his meal with two footmen on duty. His brother looked up with a wide grin. "Marco, you must accompany me on a walk later. This neighborhood is magnificent."

"We shall see. May I speak to you? In private?"

Angelo raised his eyebrows in question, but forked up the remaining eggs on his plate and chewed in haste. Marco took the opportunity to speak with Duncan, the head footman who had greeted them on the docks the day before. He asked how to get to the roof, and Duncan withheld any questions about his strange request, informed him the route was complicated, and offered to escort them there. Marco agreed, then turned to find Angelo rising to accompany them.

* * *

MOLLY ENTERED the walled garden alone, finding Madeline seated on their bench, waiting for her with a cart of tea. Her ploy to rid herself of Miss Dubois had proved quite effective, and she relished these stolen moments with her friend. Marco had mentioned something about visiting the roof after their harrowing brush with death, but she needed time to clear her thoughts—particularly after the searing tumble in the grass that had shaken her to the core. Neither of them was ready to address … the kiss.

"I did not think I would see you before you left!"

Madeline lifted her head from the book she was reading

to smile. "I insisted I enjoy tea with you before we depart. Simon is quite impatient to leave, but considering we did not even share supper together last evening, I want to bid you a proper farewell."

Molly found herself unexpectedly nostalgic as she dropped on the bench with a glum pout. "I shall miss you! An entire household of boys and nary a woman in sight to speak to."

Madeline's lips quirked into a mischievous grin. "What of your Miss Dubois?"

She groaned, clenching her fists at the skies in mock anger. "Curses! She does not count. She is an entirely different species. Far more of a vain, shallow vessel such as Lady Blackwood than an actual human woman."

"I see you have given up your mourning attire. Did the poodle wear you down?"

Molly tensed, uncertain if she wanted to reveal her infatuation with Lord Blackwood's new heir until she had time to sort through her thoughts on what had just happened. It seemed awfully frivolous to admit she had wished to look her best because of Marco. "I ... decided it was time."

"I think you are quite becoming. Those colors suit."

She looked down at her gown, noting it was a little creased after their passionate tumble on the lawn. "Thank you."

"With four new bachelors in your home—have any of them caught your eye?"

Molly blushed, studying her kid gloves while feeling the heat racing up her neck and her ears burning with the intensity. "Not especially."

Her friend's laugh tinkled in the morning air as she shut her book to set it aside. "Perhaps you can write to me when you are ready to speak on it."

"Do you think … if I were to meet a gentleman … How would I go about prompting a courtship?"

"Hmm … I suppose it would not be so different from establishing a friendship. You could talk about common interests, and learn about each other. As the affinity grows, if there is any attraction, things should progress along their natural course."

Molly leaned forward, her interest captured by the topic despite her inclination to keep her thoughts private. "And if they do not? You waited so long for Simon to come up to scratch? Is there nothing I could do to … hurry it along?"

The question made her feel guilty when she saw the flash of regret in Madeline's eyes. "We did spend far too long apart. If I were to do anything differently … Well, I would have cared less about society's restrictions on my behavior and spent more time making things happen. It was difficult to reconcile the rules of etiquette with my more aggressive business instincts, but when I released those arbitrary inhibitions, Simon and I finally forged a path together."

"But forging your own path was fraught with peril."

"The poisoning?"

"You could have died."

"Not a traditional risk within a courtship, but without risk, life has no meaning. There is no possibility of achieving one's goals. You shall have to weigh it up. What would your mother say if she were here?"

"To say what fits, not what is fitting."

"There you go. Trust your instincts and speak from the heart."

Molly giggled nervously. "That is far easier to contemplate than it is to actually do."

"I suppose if the opportunity arises, you will take matters into your own hands. I know that both Simon and John are most impressed with your fortitude at nursing the baron when you were needed. My husband is quite regretful to leave you in the lurch with Miss Dubois. He had hoped to leave you with more humored company."

Shaking her head, Molly reached to clasp her friend's hand. "Do not concern yourself with my problems. Securing your safety must come first. Even now—" Molly wanted to inform Madeline of what had happened, but to do that would reveal the object of her feminine interest, and she was not quite ready. Recollecting that Marco had just survived what was possibly a second murder attempt, she realized Madeline must leave for Scotland despite her desire to complete their conversation. "Thank you for taking the time to share tea with me, but it is time to depart. It is not safe to delay when Lady Blackwood loathed you with such seething venom. If there is an accomplice hanging about—I could not bear it if you were harmed again."

Madeline turned her palm over to squeeze Molly's and released it to rise. "Good luck with your gentleman. Write to me if you wish."

Molly watched the viscountess leave, and thought about her yapping companion. Miss Dubois had been aware that Marco would be in the garden. And leaving to collect the bonnet would have provided an opportunity for her to go to the roof. Could the French poodle be a disciple of Lady Blackwood's reign of terror? Might she execute her ladyship's desires from beyond the grave out of misguided loyalty?

She shivered at the thought, hopping to her feet to prepare a cup of tea while she had some solitude to enjoy it without the perpetual nipping of her chaperon. Returning to her seat to savor the rich aroma wafting from her cup, Molly wondered what her mother would say about handsome Italians with firm, sculpted lips. Would she approve of Molly's sly machinations to get Marco alone, or warn her of seductive kisses and the ruin to be found in pursuing such yearnings?

* * *

Duncan led them up a servants' staircase. Ascending behind the tall footman, Marco noted when they reached the third floor where his chambers were. He had been placed in the deceased baroness's rooms, which were well-appointed for a gentleman. He wondered if they had removed the signs of the female occupant, because the colors and furniture were quite appropriate for him.

The footman continued on, heading up to the attic level where he led them down a long corridor. One side appeared to be the servants' quarters, while the other would be storage rooms. Duncan led them to the end of the hall, where he opened a window that overlooked the roof. Pointing out, he indicated the walkways and ladders to safely traverse the top of the building. Leaning out, Marco discovered stone-faced gods watching the neighborhood from pedestals interspersing the short skirt of the parapets that ran along the roofline. The roof itself was cluttered with chimneys puffing smoke up into the chilled sky, decorative turrets, and the domes of cupolas that allowed light into the lower floor.

Marco inspected the window for any signs that might indicate if someone had deliberately pushed the urn, but it was well used, so there was no method of assessing if someone had accessed it within the past hour. Angelo waited without comment, although he had to be perplexed by this strange quest.

Thanking the servant, the two brothers gingerly climbed out the window and proceeded to make their way to the side of the building where Romulus loomed. Reaching the towering statue, Marco inspected the now empty pedestal near the base of the god's feet where the urn had stood. Then he walked carefully over to its twin to inspect the difference.

Not being fond of heights, he made sure not to glance over the parapet at the drop of three floors, in addition to the basement level, which was making him queasy to think about.

Angelo leaned over to peer down, his perplexment evaporating as he apparently concluded what they were about.

"Were you down there when it fell?"

Marco nodded. "It was a narrow escape."

"Was it deliberate?"

Returning to the empty pedestal, Marco took his time answering. "The urns are fixed in place by their weight, unlike the statue, which is both cemented and doweled to the roof. If I were to choose a weapon, it is the obvious choice. And here near the edge—this appears to be chipping as if someone pushed it over."

Angelo leaned down to examine closely. "There is a small gouge here where it was positioned that suggests that a lever was used. A pry bar, perhaps? It is fresh."

Marco combed his fingers through his locks with a hiss. "So you agree. Someone is trying to kill me?"

"It seems too great a ... *coincidenza?*"

"Coincidence."

"*Sì!* Two near deaths in two days. It is too much."

"We should go home."

"I wish to stay. I think this little island holds potential."

"You understand that if someone is trying to kill me so that Simon can inherit—they will try to kill you, too."

Angelo shrugged. "We need to find this man and stop him. There is no choice in this because we cannot leave a potential murderer on the loose."

"Is that your good sense speaking, or your desire to open a pharmacy?"

His brother smiled, his youthful face lighting up with the optimism he was known for. "One does not … *precludere?*"

"Preclude."

"One does not preclude the other. We are on an adventure, and our prize is cornering a dangerous criminal. We cannot leave our new family exposed to risk. Uncle John is ill and Molly is under our protection, with Simon leaving. He might have left already." They had settled on addressing the much older baron as uncle, but due to their proximity of age with Simon and Nicholas, their two younger uncles had insisted on first names.

Marco frowned, thinking of Molly. Indeed, he could hardly desert her to such criminal intent. There could be no leaving England until this culprit was unearthed and prevented from doing further harm.

Reluctantly, he realized that their uncle Simon had trusted them to keep this household safe. Having heard the details of what the baroness had done, he understood Simon's priority being to remove Lady Campbell from the area. The falling urn only proved that Simon was not overreacting. His bride might well become a target due to her perceived inferior bloodlines. Not inferior in Marco's eyes, but in the eyes of someone loyal to the baroness. Having been introduced to her the day before, he could attest that Lady Campbell was an enchanting and intelligent woman who was superior to the more arrogant sons of the nobility he had encountered in Florence. But the dead baroness had not viewed it that way.

Angelo interrupted his thoughts with an unexpected question. "Do you know why Sebastian and Lorenzo accompanied us?"

"No. Do you?"

His brother shook his head. "They are behaving quite

strange. I interrupted yet another argument about the woman and the painting."

"I do not know, but I think this woman must have something to do with why Sebastian has never returned home. Back in Florence, I saw something in his eyes. Our tall friend is haunted by the past. Perhaps he is nursing a broken heart."

"He is always in such a good humor. It is difficult to think of him pining after a woman."

"You forget when he first came to Florence. Back then, he was chasing skirts like a demon. He made me worry about his very soul, not to mention the risk to his health. Thankfully, he relented his pursuits after a few months."

"It must be quite a woman to capture his heart."

"Our friend possesses a very large heart. Just like the rest of him."

Angelo chuckled before sobering again. "What do we do next? How are we to investigate … this?"

He waved at the bare pedestal, returning Marco's attention to the devil dogging his heels since his arrival on English shores.

"I do not know. I suppose we are waiting for Nicholas to read those journals. In the meantime, we must maintain our vigilance. Assume that whoever is trying to kill me will try to kill you, too."

"They have failed twice and they will continue to fail. Fortune favors us, brother."

"But sharp reflexes are essential. *Mamma* will curse me to the deepest depths of Dante's hell if I allow anything to happen to you."

CHAPTER 6

"It is in solitude that a man meets his conscience, and in temptation that he proves whether he has one."

Impressions of England by an Unrepentant Foreigner

* * *

*M*arco was restless, pacing the small drawing room attached to his bedchamber. It was an elegant room, appointed in green and blue with landscapes of Scottish lochs and soaring mountains. He dropped into the ivory chaise lounge, leaning back into the green and blue tartan cushions, and admitted sleep would not arrive soon. Perhaps he should read through the copious notes Simon had left him about managing the barony's holdings. His uncle must have invested great time and thought into the notes written in a simple, leather-bound notebook which was resting on the writing table under the window.

Marco dismissed this notion, too agitated to focus his thoughts and do that task any justice. After promising Simon he would consider the work with a view to the future, it did not seem the right time to tackle it.

Agree to stay in England? This is madness!

Remaining in this strange country was an impossibility. He had known this journey would be difficult, raising uncomfortable troubles from the past, but the addition of the creeping menace in the shadows had done nothing to make this island realm hospitable.

There were so many thoughts swirling around in his head, and it was difficult to pick which one to focus on. It was difficult to assimilate that there was a killer stalking him. Not merely someone who wished him ill, but someone who was taking an active interest in bringing about his death. What prompted a person to pursue such ghastly goals?

Another persistent problem, making sleep impossible despite the lateness of the hour, was the memory of Molly's soft curves pressed against him, soft thighs bracketing his hips, and the taste of cinnamon lingering on his tongue to produce yearnings he was not familiar with. The desire to seek her out was ever-present, but he had reined in that desire with an iron fist. She was a young lady, and if he had no intention of remaining in England beyond sorting out what to do about impending duties to the title, he had no place spending time with her or encouraging the growing affinity between them.

He was tempted—she was tempting—but it was not the conduct of a gentleman of honor.

Reaching the peak of impatience, Marco jumped to his feet and stalked out to find something to do. The halls were wreathed in flickering shadows, dim sconces on the walls the only light to assist him in finding his way. The house was silent, save for the occasional creak of its timbers settling in the late hours to punctuate the night as he reached the main staircase and descended. Upon reaching the ground level, he strode purposefully toward the library, flinging the door open with a flash of frustration—only to be met by the soft glow of an oil lamp and a yelp of surprise.

"Molly?"

She was seated in a wingback chair by the fireplace, dressed in a belted night robe which begged for his fingers to undo the knot and discover the details of her night rail. Was it thin like a shift? Would her dusky nipples be visible through the thin layer of cotton?

Maledizione! Control yourself!

"I ... yes ... it is me. I am reading."

"And why are you not reading in your bedchamber?" He winced, realizing that the mention of a lady's bedchamber was not the sort of discussion polite society engaged in. There was a lamentable lack of propriety between him and the young woman, when seduction must be avoided at all costs.

"Miss Dubois ... my drawing room has been turned into her bedchamber because ... because of all the unwed gentlemen in residence."

"What of it?"

"She growls and yaps in her sleep like a—it is difficult to ignore."

"You cannot be here!" he snapped in reply. He was not angry at her, but rather himself for the persistent wish to untie the belt that was all that lay between him and the sight of her feminine form. What would she look like without the compress of stays and multiple layers of clothing? It was galling that he continued to be so fascinated after the stern lecture he had administered to himself only minutes earlier.

She swallowed hard, putting her book down on an end table and rising to her feet. His gaze fell to her naked feet, so dainty on the rug where she now stood, and he groaned low in his throat in protest. Through the thick robe he could see her full, unbound breasts plumping the velvet fabric, while from the region of the belt, her hips flared to make him itch with longing to explore her hourglass form. A plait of rich brown hair was draped over her shoulder, diverting his thoughts to releasing that silky curtain to cascade over the pillow of his yet unvisited bed.

He knew well that at some point he needed to address their passionate kiss under the pale winter sky, but this seemed the worst of times. The awareness that they were alone, past midnight, and unlikely to be interrupted, was causing his attraction for her to ratchet up to unmanageable heights. He had already lost his head once. He could not afford to do so again.

Before he lost his self-control, Marco turned to cross the room, so he stood far from temptation. When he turned, he found to his dismay that Molly had followed him as silent as a ghost.

"Are you angry with me? It is because … of what happened … earlier?"

"No, I am not angry with you. I am angry with myself for taking advantage."

"Oh." Her expression was that of disappointment, and he scowled.

It was likely that the kiss they had shared was the first she had received. Although passionate in her response, her inexperience had been obvious, and Marco realized he had just spoiled that moment for her.

Reaching out, he cupped her chin to lift her gaze back to his. Her eyes were magnificent in the reflected light. "I am sorry, *mia bella*. The … kiss was delightful, but it is inappropriate for me to take advantage of you so."

"I enjoyed it very much," she confessed in a husky voice that sent shocking sensation rushing through his veins.

"As did I. But I plan to return to Italy and you deserve a respectful courtship, which I cannot give you."

"Why not? We like each other and ... I could go to Italy."

Marco shut his eyes, drawing in her cinnamon scent and seeking an answer that would not hurt her any further.

"You do not wish this, Molly. I am just a bear leader—a tutor—and you are a well-connected young lady. You must seek a man who can give you what you deserve."

"But ... I want you."

"And I am greatly honored, but this is wrong. I am not the man for you. I do not desire this title or these obligations, but this is your home. Our flirtation must end, and I apologize for my part in it."

Molly pulled away, her face dejected as she backed off from him. "The title cannot be discarded, I am afraid. Simon said you have a choice to learn about it now, or be forced to learn about it later, but learn about it you will have to do."

"I do not know what I wish to do about it, and it would not be fair to give you any expectations when I am not in a position to make any promises. The danger that lurks in this home has me distracted, not to mention my dishonorable behavior in the garden." He winced, realizing he had done it again. Spoiling her first kiss with regrets and apologies. But what was he to do? He sincerely wished there was a simple resolution to the strange conundrum he was buried in. A title he did not care to have. Menace still lurking in this house of suicide when he had thought the matter settled with the death of Lady Blackwood. A tempting and courageous beauty who fired his blood in unexpected ways. Had he inadvertently committed some cardinal sin to find himself entering the first circle of hell?

"You are a captivating young woman, but you must forget what has happened between us. It cannot happen again." With that, he withdrew from the room with what dignity he could muster after wronging her so. He could have handled it with more finesse, but it was the best he could do while his thoughts were in turmoil and he had no straightforward path mapped out for how to reconcile his obligations to this Blackwood title. He had resisted coming to England, and his instinct to stay away was proving correct.

* * *

MADELINE'S ADVICE had been terrible! Encouraging her to speak from her heart? All she had done was ruin the enjoyable flirtation between them by rushing to talk of commitment. They had only met the day before—what had she been thinking? That a single glorious kiss—the first she had ever received—was going to make a sophisticated gentleman of Florence fall head over heels with a gently bred, almost-spinster from the English countryside?

There was no doubt she was an idiot of magnificent proportions!

Stuff, stuff, stuff, stuff!

She wished to howl her frustration at the heavens, but that would hardly help. Instead, she kicked a doorframe with her slippered foot so she could vent her frustration without drawing any curious ears from servants who might be on duty. Then muttered a curse at the resulting pain. Pain which proved she truly was an idiot!

If she were honest, Madeline's advice had been to spend time with her gentleman and allow things to take their course. But they had both been surprised when he had entered the library, so the discussion had been anything but natural.

She had promised herself not to get her hopes up about a match, knowing from their meeting with Simon that Marco had no intention of remaining in England, so she should have enjoyed their flirtation as a welcome respite from her mourning and boredom. Instead, she had spoken to her friend this morning about contriving a courtship. What had she thought? That she would provide the enticement the gentleman needed to decide his place was here as the future heir to the Blackwood title? Apparently, she had exaggerated notions of her personal charms. It was mortifying to discover she was more like her irritating chaperon than she would care to admit.

Walking back over to the chair where she had been reading, Molly flopped down to stare at the ceiling. Their kiss had been sublime. She could still feel the hardness of his body pinning her to the ground, and the smell of his shaving soap lingered in the air. Following him across the room had been a bid to solicit a second kiss.

Like a clinging wallflower.

She had lost all semblance of common sense to pursue him so. A woman was meant to be alluring. To allow the man to chase her. Her only justification was that she could feel the magnetic pull between them, and she wished to prod it along, but her efforts were clumsy at best.

"But I am not willing to give up," she whispered into the night. Despite his reservations, Marco made her feel beautiful, and his interest in her was obvious. And some of her efforts had worked out, after all. She had contrived to get them alone and been rewarded with a passionate kiss. And their botched interaction here in the library had caught them both off guard. Perhaps patience was in order. Marco had declared he was struggling with the unanticipated demands, and being stalked by a killer had to be unsettling. She had had time to assimilate all the violent events in this house, while he had just arrived to be greeted by not one, but two potentially lethal incidents, and he had been in England less than two days!

Her optimism trickled back. There was still a possibility that Marco could remain in England, and all signs were that he did find her appealing. Perhaps the kiss had set them off balance, and she merely needed to return to her plan to learn more about him. Allow a friendship to grow.

Soothed, she rose to her feet, taking up her oil lamp and her book to return to her chambers.

She grimaced. Her and Miss Dubois's chambers now. Her chaperon had had her own room in the servants' quarters, but since her promotion a few days earlier, she had moved in to Molly's drawing room.

Which made Molly feel like a child with a nursemaid. A nasty, niggling nursemaid who compared her unfavorably to a violent murderess at every opportunity.

To be fair, Miss Dubois does not know the baroness was a killer. At least, I do not think she knows that.

Molly reached her rooms, turning the handle to Miss Dubois's room as quietly as she could to swing the door open where she found the French poodle sitting up in her bed. Her companion pushed the curling hair from her face, rubbing bleary eyes. "Where 'ave you been?"

"I could not sleep, so I went to fetch a book." One advantage she had ferreted out from this unwanted partnership was that Claudette Dubois was a heavy sleeper. It was unusual for her to awaken in the middle of the night.

"You must ah-waken me to … *accompagne?*"

"Accompany."

The poodle nodded. "*Oui,* I must accompany you. Lady Blackwood was a weedow, so zis sort of zing was not necessary." Miss Dubois waved at her new bedroom with disdain, making her feelings about the arrangement clear.

"Ah, but as a widow, she did not require a companion. Are you not pleased with your promotion to paid companion?"

Miss Dubois's distaste was palpable at the question. "But a lady'z maid to a baronezz!"

"That is true," Molly replied in a sympathetic tone which she did not feel in the least. *Poor* Miss Dubois! The horrors of her descent from serving an elegant viper like Lady Blackwood, to being promoted to serve unfashionable Molly from the country. The sheer tragedy of it all!

Molly decided she had had enough. Smiling pleasantly, she bade her chaperon to return to sleep with an assurance she would remain in her bedchamber. Fortunately, she had the book to keep her company or she would toss all night thinking about that devastating kiss she had shared with Marco this morning. If only she could ignore the noise emitted by her sleeping watchdog in the next room.

CHAPTER 7

"In the quiet drawing rooms of England, it is not always strangers who plot your end, but those who sit beside you, sharing your tea."

Impressions of England by an Unrepentant Foreigner

* * *

DECEMBER 1 1821

*A*ll things considered, when Molly awoke, it was the memory of their kiss that was foremost in her mind, and Marco's admonishment to keep away had receded in importance. Patience was in order, but the possibility of something developing between them was not out of the question.

She had no stratagems to spend any time with him, but she would think of something. They needed to talk more, learn about each other, if she was to develop her rapport with him. She could hardly expect to earn his undying esteem, and him to choose to remain here in England, if he had no inkling who she was as a person. They had barely conversed, but the searing kiss proved he was aware of her as a woman.

Miss Dubois had just finished fixing her hair, although Molly was musing that she had done these tasks herself in the past, and would happily do so again if she could rid herself of her annoying companion. A knock on the door interrupted the increasing chafing of ignoring the critical prattle she was subjected to each morning, and Miss Dubois crossed to open it. Duncan, the head footman, was revealed, dropping a polite bow.

"The baron requests your presence in the study, Miss Carter."

She nodded, collecting her shawl as a defense against the morning chill and stopping to pull on her gloves. Then, with Miss Dubois at her heels, she made her way to the lower level.

When she entered the study, she found Nicholas had taken up a seat, his injured leg propped up and the stack of Lady Blackwood's journals beside him. The baron was seated at the walnut desk, his wispy gray hair a halo around his head, but she was pleased to note the pink in his cheeks. John was recovering since his slow poisoning had been uncovered by Lady Trafford, a skilled healer, who had begun visiting on a regular basis to see to his health. Even Nicholas, despite his grumpiness, was filling out. No longer rake-thin, the young man was developing muscle.

"Molly! You look lovely this morning."

She smiled, a hand coming up to check her hair. Relenting on her mourning period had lifted her spirits more than she had anticipated, and she was enjoying rediscovering her wardrobe from before her mother's death.

"How are you this morning, John?"

The baron grinned. "Better than yesterday."

She chuckled in response. It had become a running jest since his collapse, when Molly had been the only one trusted to take care of him. Back then, they had not known who had been behind the attempt to kill him off slowly with micro doses of arsenic. As Molly had joined the household a few months earlier, she was the only person in the house who had not been a suspect other than the baron himself. Those had been strenuous days, but they had developed a friendship from their time spent together.

John turned his attention to Miss Dubois. "I am afraid this is a private discussion, Miss Dubois. Would you mind observing from outside as you did before?"

The Frenchwoman sagged slightly, curtsying with a plaintive, "*Oui*, milord," and departing the study through the terrace doors to take up her post.

Crossing the room, Molly took up a seat in one of the armchairs. "What are we about?"

John tilted his head toward Nicholas. "My brother has completed the reading of the journals."

Nicholas grimaced, his lean face painted in disgust. "It was as unpleasant as Simon warned. My mother was not a well woman. Reading the details of her madness was horrible but edifying, and I have gained a great understanding of evil."

Molly winced, recalling that Simon had said they were not suitable reading for an unmarried woman. Which would imply that poor Nicholas, and Simon, had had to sift through the discussion of carnal relations within the venomous writings.

Volunteering her services two days earlier had been done with severe reservations, but she possessed a sense of duty to the family who had endured so much. If she could have spared them, she would, but Simon had deemed it inappropriate. She supposed that as Isla's offspring, they felt an obligation to shield others, not to mention to uphold as much privacy and dignity as they could under the circumstances.

John interjected. "We are waiting for Marco and Angelo to join us, so we might discuss the possibility of an accomplice."

This information was more unsettling than she had anticipated. She desired Marco's company, but she had yet to decide how to act when she next saw him. After months with no tangible plan for the future, she had glimpsed a possible path, and she wanted … she wanted … she wanted to explore the potential.

* * *

MARCO AND ANGELO were just completing their breakfast when the footman who had assisted them the day before to find the roof entered to inform them that the baron had requested they join him in the study. They headed down the hall, entering through the door one at a time. Marco came to an abrupt halt behind his brother, realizing Molly was there.

Guilt over his outburst last evening, as well as kissing an innocent woman, had kept him up all night, so he was still feeling on edge. When he had fallen asleep, he had suffered a variety of disturbing and inappropriate dreams. Being crushed under a falling Romulus, as well as being flung by an overturned carriage. Not to mention the other sort—lush breasts cupped within his palms while the scent of cinnamon wafted through the air, causing his mouth to water with a ravenous hunger for creamy skin and delectable curves.

He knew he needed to make up for his poor behavior, but he was not ready to see her yet.

Angelo paused, noticing his hesitation in entering, and followed his gaze to where Molly was sitting. Looking back at Marco, his younger brother raised his brows in query, but Marco did not respond. Comprehension lit up Angelo's face, and with great deliberation he walked in to take the seat farthest from Molly.

Marco gritted his teeth in irritation at his brother's manipulation, before continuing into the room to drop into the remaining armchair closest to the object of his lustful phantasies with a curt greeting.

Uncle John straightened at his desk. "I wish to remind everyone present to keep your voices low. Miss Dubois is observing from outside." He bobbed his head in the direction of the windows, and Marco saw that the companion was leaning against the stone balustrade as she watched their gathering with a resentful expression.

Molly's chaperon did not appear to be an endearing creature, despite her physical attractions, and Molly's transparent efforts to rid her from their company the day before would confirm his suspicions. He shuddered to think what it would be like as an adult, just a few years younger than himself, to have a thorny nursemaid following him about as if he were a tiny tot in short pants. Which made his guilt arise again for his clumsy bemoaning of proprieties the night before. His nerves were on edge, and he had not employed any charm to reject her interest in him as a man. How capricious his disposition had grown since setting foot on these Albion shores!

"My brother has completed studying Lady Blackwood's journals, and we wish to discuss the implications." The baron's low voice reminded Marco that he was not here to mull over his inadequate dealings with the woman sitting a couple of feet away. "Given the possibility that his mother has left us a disciple to mete out further death, I wished for us to meet as a family so we can formulate a plan if there is reason to suspect we are in danger."

Angelo perked up. "My brother has confirmation that he is being targeted."

Uncle John frowned, turning his gaze to Marco. "What is this?"

At the edge of his vision, he could see Molly shifting uncomfortably as he tried to think what to say. "I … was walking in the garden when I came to a stop beneath the statue of Romulus." He gestured to the side of the building. "A urn came tumbling from the skies directly at my head, but I was able to leap away. When Angelo and I visited the roof, we found that it might have been levered over the edge with a pry bar."

Nicholas groaned, dragging a hand through his mop of dark brown hair, which was in need of a cut. "That is unfortunate news. I suppose that confirms we do have cause for concern."

The baron shook his head in dismay. "Indeed. If there is an accomplice seeking your death, it means that I might become a target, too. Isla—Lady Blackwood—was attempting to clear the way by hurrying my death. Is there anyone else who might be considered expendable?"

"Not me. Simon would inherit with or without my presence." Nicholas sounded sour in his response.

Molly cleared her throat before chiming in with the same notion he had yesterday on the roof. "Angelo. He would stand in the way of Simon inheriting, if that is what this is about. Which seems likely because that was Lady Blackwood's obsession. She would have wanted rid of you, Marco, and Angelo to clear the way for Simon to be the baron."

Marco was impressed—she had calculated the list without hesitation, proving again that she was no wilting flower of high society, but a resilient woman with a strong mind. His mother would like this Molly Carter if they ever met.

Nicholas contributed his thoughts in the same sour tone as before. "And I can confirm from reading these ... toxic ramblings ... that my mother was obsessed with Simon rising to the rank of baron while I ... I was a mere tool to ensure his perpetual guilt. She seemed pleased in the aftermath of my accident that Simon blamed himself, using it to her advantage to persuade him into doing his duty. You, Marco, and Angelo *are* the three people who stand in the way of any plot she may have enacted before she died."

John sighed heavily, slumping back in his swivel chair to think. "And what do the journals reveal? Do we have a list of potential suspects?"

"I do not have a definitive answer. One name that came up was Dr. White."

Molly glanced around the room before adding to what Nicholas had said. "Dr. White is the family physician. He supplied Lady Blackwood with laudanum, which was how she ... took her life. He disappeared the day we discovered John was being poisoned. We thought it was probably to avoid trouble for failing to notice the signs of arsenic poisoning, but perhaps it was because he had willfully ignored the symptoms to assist the baroness."

Angelo cocked his head to consider this information with a studious expression before finally responding. "How would Dr. White access the carriage or the roof of this house? To do so, he would need a servant to allow him entry."

"Which means we should still be looking for someone within this household," agreed Marco.

"If I may suggest someone else?" Molly was nervous, licking her lips as if reluctant to proffer a suspect. The urge to lean over and clasp her delicate fingers in encouragement was unexpected, and Marco made a point of relaxing into the plump padding of his chair before he worsened the tense situation he had created with her.

"Who?" queried the baron, his interest obvious.

Molly's eyes flickered toward the figure beyond the window. "Miss Dubois. Her affinity for Lady Blackwood borders on fanaticism. She mentions her dozens of times a day, and she is quite put out to be my companion instead of servicing a '*beauteeful baronezz*'."

Marco almost laughed out loud; Molly's impression of her fawning companion was comical, despite their macabre discussion.

"Interesting. What would her motive be?" Uncle John mused.

"According to these"—Nicholas waved at the stack of journals—"Lady Blackwood paid a footman in the Ridley household to gather information after she killed Lord Filminster. Perhaps she has made arrangements to pay Miss Dubois for completing her crusade." Nicholas pulled a face. "I had to read all about it. There is not much about Miss Dubois in the journals, but I can confirm that my mother had a liking for the maid, so she might have had a strong enough relationship to corrupt Miss Dubois into perpetuating her crimes."

The baron nodded. "Then we should observe Miss Dubois. Perhaps someone should search her room for any evidence? Molly could keep her occupied."

The baron's outrageous suggestion, so easily offered, had Marco and his brother exchange looks of surprise. This household had been under attack, which explained the equanimity with which its residents conspired to investigate even as Molly hissed in rejection, clearly alarmed at the thought.

"And what if she is innocent? That would be a terrible invasion of privacy for a man to go through her things. No—I should do it if we are to be so sly."

It was a thoughtful gesture, Marco thought, considering he suspected Molly did not like her companion in the least.

Her proposal of Miss Dubois as a potential murderess confirmed her dislike of the servant, but she still took pains to treat the woman with what respect she could afford.

"If you remain in your room to read, Miss Dubois could be called away. Perhaps I could interview her over her change in roles and deliver some directions about how I want Molly to be serviced? I should be able to drag that out for an hour if I choose to blather on like old men are wont to do."

Molly nodded at the baron's suggestion. "That would work."

"So we have Dr. White and Miss Dubois on the list, but cannot see how White could do it without help from inside the house. Any other suspects, Nicholas?"

He shook his head, and the devil seized Marco. It was difficult to shake the thought that Nicholas himself had a motive to assist his mother, and it was high time someone proposed the possibility.

"What of Nicholas himself? How can we know he does not wish to clear a path to inheriting? Should someone else read the journals when he has much to gain if we are all killed?" Angelo's face fell with alarm, and Marco realized he had overstepped. Perhaps raising the subject was circumspect, but he was afraid his lack of sleep, along with the pressure of knowing someone wanted to kill him, had caused him to be sharper than was good judgment. Even Molly had reached out a hand to pacify Nicholas, who had straightened to glare at Marco in anger.

"I did not help my mother to kill a peer of the realm to cover up your existence, and I did not poison my own brother!" He jerked a hand toward John, bristling with outrage as he responded in an angry but low voice which reminded everyone present of Miss Dubois, all eyes shifting to the window to ensure the companion could not overhear their conversation before Nicholas returned his heated gaze to Marco. "I certainly did not assist her to overdose my own father. Nor did I assist her to poison Simon's bride!"

Marco raised his hands in appeasement. "I apologize for how I stated my question, but as someone who is unfamiliar … You have a close relationship with her, and you would benefit if we all died. How can we know you are not a suspect?"

Nicholas rose from his chair, awkward because of the limp, as he straightened to his full height. "Because she was a homicidal lunatic who had no time for her damaged son! Anyone here can confirm that we did not, in fact, share a close relationship. My mother was a vain woman who liked her shallow and *pretty* pursuits." Gesturing down at his leg, Nicholas continued. "With an injury like this, do you think she considered me worthy of her attentions? But feel free to read her journals if you wish to know what she thought of her … spare … son."

The hurt that emanated from the younger man could not be feigned, and Marco slowly comprehended the challenge it must have been for Nicholas to read his mother's private musings. To discover firsthand what she thought of each of her family, including Nicholas himself, while reading about the crimes she had committed and her warped reasons for doing so.

"My deepest apologies, my friend. I had not considered how uncomfortable it must be, and I meant no disrespect."

Molly reached out a hand as they stared at each other, the tension palpable, to clasp Nicholas's. "Please, Nicholas, calm yourself and take a seat."

Heaving a shuddering sigh, the other man settled back into his seat, his face wreathed in pain. Molly turned to Marco. "Your question is understandable under the circumstances, but as someone who witnessed the baroness interact with Nicholas, I can confirm that her disdain for him was marked. I cannot recollect a single instance when Lady Blackwood directed any conversation in his direction. And Simon would not have left the journals with Nicholas if he had even one thought that Nicholas could be involved. We may have been naïve about the evils a person is capable of before recent events unfolded, but I can assure you we now possess a much-heightened awareness."

Reluctantly, Marco's esteem for the young woman grew. She had inserted herself to bring peace with sincerity and eloquence, and he could not help admiring how she faced the pressures of life as well as any man he knew. Molly was not only comely, she was a force to be reckoned with. Her future husband would be a fortunate man to have such a strong partner by his side. And, just for an instant, he pictured that husband to be him.

"I second Molly's observations. After his accident, Lady Blackwood had little time for her younger son," the baron interjected. "I could not and would not consider my brother as a suspect. It is much more likely someone has been paid to pursue her goals than that Nicholas would assist in such demonic activities."

Angelo cleared his throat, offering his thoughts in a bright tone intended to improve the prevailing mood. "I think it is best if we can all remember that we are family. We may have just met, but the bonds of blood can make us strong if we work together."

Despite the troubles they were currently facing, Angelo's optimistic declaration made Marco's lips quirk into a slight smile. His brother was a good friend to many, and Marco was glad Angelo had joined him on this bizarre trip to England. "Agreed. Again, my apologies. I did not understand the situation, but now I do."

"What should I be searching for? Do we have any ideas?"

Molly's attempt to shift the subject was obvious, but welcome.

Nicholas gestured to the journals. "One of these. Each volume has about three years' worth of entries, and we have a period of three years which is not covered here. My mother pulled these out as her confession to clear Simon's name in the aftermath of her suicide, so if she tasked an accomplice to complete her work, it is possible she gave the missing volume to that person."

Marco studied the journals with their distinct rich leather, gold tooling, and embossed thistles on the front. "Did you search the house for it?"

Nicholas looked to John for an answer.

"Simon did have a search done, but I cannot speak to how thorough it was. At the time, we were not aware that there was still danger roaming these halls."

"Angelo and I will conduct another search. It is something … *tangibile?*"

"Tangible," replied Molly immediately, and they exchanged smiles. Marco was relieved to see that she did not hold a grudge for his clumsy rejection last evening, proving she was far more sensible than he under the current circumstances.

"*Sì*, it is something tangible for us to do to help."

CHAPTER 8

"In the great houses of England, secrets do not hide in the shadows
—they are folded into linens, tucked into books, and whispered
behind locked doors."

Impressions of England by an Unrepentant Foreigner

* * *

"*H*ow do we search for the missing journal?"
Angelo asked when they entered the library,
which they tended to gravitate toward, having some of their
things stacked on a table.

Marco sighed heavily. "I suppose … we … Honestly … I
do not know."

His brother nodded. "We could begin on this floor. Search
all the public rooms, starting here in the library. Then we
will tackle one floor at a time."

"What of private rooms? Or servants' quarters? Or the
butler's pantry, or kitchen cupboards? How do we explain

what we are doing to the staff in the kitchen?" Marco was genuinely interested in hearing what his bright and optimistic brother would come up with.

Bemused, Angelo paced up and down in deep thought, until he spun on his heel to face Marco. "I do not know. If we begin with this floor, we will rule it out. Along the way, as we gain some experience in searching, we will calculate the next step, and then the next, until eventually … we will finish the search."

Marco groaned. It sounded like a tiresome task that might take the better part of the week in a house of this size filled with decades of accrued furnishings, books, *objets d'art*, and a thousand other nameless things. "We should get started."

Heading to the end of the room, they each tackled a different stack, dropping down on their haunches to peer at the lowest shelves. Marco ran a fingertip over the spines of the books to help him focus as he sought a book the same size and binding as those Nicholas had in his possession. Perhaps Molly's search would fare well, and she would unmask Miss Dubois as Lady Blackwood's accomplice. One could hope, after all.

After ten or more minutes, his thoughts were turning decidedly maudlin with such a repetitive task as he began a new set of shelving. Embarking on this journey had set him on a path of danger, and he felt a twinge of nostalgia for the simplicity of life in Florence.

Angelo interrupted the pangs of homesickness with an unwanted question. "You hold Molly in some esteem?"

The sudden shift of subject pushed him out of kilter, not being prepared to discuss what had happened. "Molly is … courageous. Of course I hold her in my esteem."

His brother snorted a half-laugh. "It is plain that you find her"—Angelo paused, searching for the English word— "comely."

"What would you know of that?"

"I saw how you were looking at her when we entered the baron's study. It has been a long time since I have seen that expression."

Marco stopped, turning to scowl at his brother in irritation. "What expression?"

Angelo paused, cocking his head as if he was working something out. "A mixture of yearning and regret. It is how you looked when you were tutoring Mr. Dashwood and his sister. Before she …" He did not complete the sentence, grimacing his own regret for mentioning it.

"Before she died." There was no point in skirting around the truth. Even now, the sense of loss echoed in the region of his heart, but perhaps the distance from Florence was helping because it was not as sharp as it had been.

"Molly might heal your heart?" Angelo asked, his face hopeful.

Marco turned away to continue his search. "That is ridiculous. We must see to my duties here and then return to our home in Florence."

Despite his rejection, the desire to spend more time with the young lady was compelling. She had … what was the Scottish word Sebastian had explained to him during their long voyage … gumption. Molly had gumption, along with an alluring form. The sensation of her breasts pressed against his chest returned to haunt him, as did the scent of cinnamon that had been present in the spiced tea they had drunk during the meeting in the study. He resolutely pushed them aside to continue the tedious task of checking the shelves.

A change of subject was in order, Marco decided,

recalling their conversation on the roof just yesterday. "Have you learned anything about what brings Sebastian and Lorenzo to London with us?"

Angelo chuckled. "You are changing the subject."

"What of it?"

His brother relented as he continued his perusal of his shelf. "I overheard them discussing that the lady whom Lorenzo wishes Sebastian to visit is still in London, despite the lateness of the Season, and has not left for the country."

"Lady? As in a noblewoman?"

"I believe so. Sebastian said he will call on her when he is ready, but his reasoning sounded like an attempt to delay. His reluctance is frustrating to our Italian friend."

Marco burst out laughing. "Delay Lorenzo? Does he not know better?"

Angelo grinned, continuing his task with great earnestness. "They have an unusual partnership, but it works somehow. Sebastian is good-humored, while Lorenzo is compulsive. Between the two of them, they sell a lot of art. I suspect our friends are far wealthier than we know because neither of them spends much coin, but I heard from a customer that they sold a sizable collection to a comte for several thousand pounds just before we left Florence."

Marco whistled through his teeth. "That much? Perhaps I am in the wrong line of work."

"Heir to a baron? I think you can rival them for income, brother. It is I who needs to establish a pharmacy to make something of myself."

Marco clenched his jaw, irritated by the reminder of his confusing circumstances. Angelo had made his thoughts clear on the subject. He believed Marco should accept his new role as part of a grand new adventure, while Marco yearned for the simplicity of tutoring. If only their roles were reversed—his brother would happily step into the role of a future baron as an exciting new chapter in life, but Marco was struggling to find such acceptance. Thus far, he had encountered an enticing and feminine reason to even consider it, but that was hardly a sufficient motive to alter the course of his existence, surely?

* * *

MOLLY ENTERED Miss Dubois's bedchamber with the burden of guilt weighing her down. She felt terrible about searching the servant's room, but the baron had summoned Miss Dubois to his private sitting room, where he spent most of his days, to allow Molly to begin, so this was her chance to do the lamentable deed.

I will feel more terrible if Marco is killed.

That was a poignant thought, the distress so sharp it cut like a knife into her belly. Squaring her shoulders, she closed the door to contemplate the room.

She would begin with the bed. Crossing over, Molly dropped down to peer underneath but found nothing but a pair of soft leather slippers. Sitting back on her haunches, she lifted the mattress carefully, so she did not disturb the bedding, and ran a hand underneath, feeling for anything hidden out of sight. Encountering a purse tucked deep, she pulled it out to untie it and empty its contents onto the bed. Several rings and necklaces of gold and silver spilled out onto the quilted coverlet.

Picking one up, she inspected it closely to see if it was Pinchbeck jewelry, but it appeared genuine rather than a cheap alloy. The color was a true gold, rather than the brighter brassy imitation stuff, but it was not conclusive because Molly was not an expert in such, and she had heard some Pinchbeck pieces were so well rendered as to fool even an experienced eye.

Molly put them back in the purse and returned the purse to its place under the mattress. But it was an unusual find— they appeared to be too expensive for an unmarried servant on fixed wages. Claudette Dubois had a larger collection than Molly herself, though Molly wore little jewelry because her own tastes were simple. Could they have been gifted by the dead baroness?

Or, worse, payment for future services?

She found nothing else in the bed, so moved on to search the bedside table and then the chest of drawers. Again, she was startled by several fine stays and shifts that rivaled her own in quality. However, there was no journal amongst Miss Dubois's belongings. Molly continued to the trunk at the end of the bed, wrought in a hardwood with brass fittings. Sitting back on her heels, she wondered at how Claudette could afford such nice things. It lent credence to Molly's supposition that her companion might indeed be one of the servants embroiled in Lady Blackwood's schemes. If the baroness was her benefactress, these lavish items would make sense.

Checking her timepiece, Molly realized her time was running out. She finished searching through the trunk, which was mostly seasonal clothing folded away, before studying the room for any signs of her search. Satisfied, she exited the bedchamber. She should return to her own chamber to read, but being separated from her chaperon had created an opportunity to seek out Marco to repair some of their rapport after the disagreement in the library the prior evening.

* * *

SIMON'S LOVE for the barony and its people was evident as Marco read his uncle's notebook. It had been passed to him with such little ceremony on the day of Marco's arrival. *"I have written up my notes to help familiarize you with the baron's estates and tenants. Read it while I am gone, and please write to me about any questions you have."*

Simon's words had been a glorious understatement, as Marco had quickly discovered when the baron had invited him to make use of the study earlier.

Simon had detailed each estate, along with specific mention of the long-term tenants of each. His attention and knowledge were far more extensive than Marco had realized because his uncle had informed him that the family spent most of their time in London. He had thought them to be absent landlords with little regard for the people under their influence. But the notebook revealed Simon had paid an annual visit to each of the estates these past years, since his father's time, when he had taken over the management of the Blackwood holdings in the late baron's stead.

Tenant farmer Mr. Frank Jameson oversees a 400-acre plot—one of the larger farms on the estate. He is married to Wendy, the eldest daughter of a neighboring farmer, and they have one adult son, Caleb, and two younger children, Sandra and Mark. Mr. Jameson employs several laborers to assist with the cultivation of his extensive farm, and I have tasked the steward with overseeing the improvement of the drainage ditches along the west perimeter. These efforts are intended to boost Mr. Jameson's crop yields and, consequently, his income. The enhancements should increase the fertility of the soil and prevent waterlogging, but I have yet to receive word on the progress. The work is to be completed by winter, and I expect a full report shortly.

It was not an isolated entry. Another that caught his

attention was for a lessor tenant but with the same attention to detail.

> *Tenant farmer Mr. John Wright manages a 90-acre plot on the eastern side of the Elmstead estate. He and his wife, Mary, work diligently, and they have two young daughters, Emily and Ann. To help improve his yield, I have instructed the steward to supply Mr. Wright with additional seed for the next planting season and to repair the broken fencing that has allowed livestock to stray into his fields. These efforts should bolster his crop production and reduce unnecessary losses. Ensure the steward follows up regularly, as it is essential that all tenants, regardless of size, have the means to thrive for the good of all involved.*

As Marco read through the notes, the complex issues of land management were drawing him in as he realized that the estates were composed of living people who worked the lands. Each tenant represented a family with children, and in some cases, laborers, who in turn supported wives and children of their own. The baron's holdings comprised communities of people who relied on the Blackwood title for good governance and leadership.

Despite his lack of experience in such affairs, Marco found himself enthralled by the writings that evoked such context for the humans influenced from this desk with the stroke of a quill upon paper.

It was a far cry from tutoring spoilt and moneyed young men of the aristocracy who had just completed their time at university and were now frolicking in Italy while they completed their classical education. Some were serious about their education into the wonders of the art and culture that Florence had to offer, but others were far removed from the reality of men who toiled, and this notebook made Marco regret that his uncle Simon had never had the opportunity to take his own Grand Tour. He would have been an excellent student, sensitive to the humanity depicted by the old Masters. They would have enjoyed their time together had he done so.

It was daunting to learn that there was far more to this stewardship of the barony than he had thought, and he understood the concerns Simon had expressed about the attendant responsibilities. His uncle was worried about the people affected by the change in inheritance. Realizing this did nothing to reduce the stresses of the past few days. In addition to protecting himself from attempts against his life, he must now worry about the people affected by what was happening here in the Scott household?

"*Maledizione*," he muttered, something of a habit of late. Shutting the notebook, he decided that was enough for the moment. Perhaps he should return to the search, while Angelo currently worked his way through the shelves behind the baron's desk. "I thought these upper classes were idle."

Angelo glanced over his shoulder, balanced on a small stepladder so he could reach the upper shelves. "The notes imply otherwise?"

"I suppose you will be gratified to hear that our uncle is a responsible and benevolent manager. He knows these estates intimately."

"That is good, no? It means our family is contributing to the well-being of society."

"Sometimes, brother, your positivity is appalling."

Angelo chuckled. "You would rather I was pessimistic? I think *Mamma* would caution you that you should be wary of what you wish for."

Marco grinned. "If you are going to bring *Mamma* into it, I suppose I would not have you any other way."

Just then, the study door opened, and a head popped around the corner. Marco's eyes were riveted, taking in

Molly's iridescent eyes with a sudden craving for the taste of cinnamon and cream.

"Oh, hullo!"

His brother stepped down from his ladder, smiling broadly as he crossed the room. "Molly, you finished your search?"

"I did. I thought I might inform … you … of what I found."

Angelo nodded. "We are most interested. Why not speak with my brother while I continue my search in the next room? No time to lose if we are to reveal a scoundrel." With that, he turned to wink at Marco before disappearing into the hall beyond to leave Molly alone with him.

She entered and shut the door behind her, even as Marco groaned inaudibly at Angelo's obvious maneuvering. His little brother wished to encourage his flirtation with Molly. Walking around the baron's desk, he came to a stop a few feet from where she was now hovering and wringing her hands together in an agitated manner.

"I must apologize for last night, Molly. I was … unkind."

"No, I understand that you have much to contend with. Two murder attempts in as many days? You must be tense."

"Nevertheless, you were standing by my side when that urn crashed down. I should have been more sensitive."

Molly frowned, as if his sympathy was upsetting her, but he did not know how to apologize under such circumstances. It was quite outside the realm of his familiarity, this strange attraction between them.

"Miss Dubois had a selection of gold and silver jewelry that seemed costly for a woman of her circumstances," declared Molly, apparently deciding that a shift in conversation was in order.

"You think … perhaps a payment?"

"It could be, but beyond that, it is hardly conclusive. Miss

Dubois had not a single book in her possession, though she had some fashion periodicals along with some circulars, suggesting she is hunting for a new position."

His brows shot up. "Does that surprise you? That she is seeking a post?"

Molly shook her head, a lock of hair falling loose, and he clenched his fist lest he reach out to touch her again. It was not the done thing. They should not be alone as they were, and he needed to keep his hands to himself. "Not at all. Simon tasked the baron's man of business to find a new companion for me for when he returns from Scotland, but no luck yet ... Miss Dubois and I do not get along very well."

"Then we are still in the dark about this muddle."

She nodded, nibbling on her lip which he recalled carried the hint of cinnamon on its plump flesh. Marco folded his arms lest he lunge in to feast on her soft mouth for the second time but could not wholly help himself. He reached out to tuck the wayward tendril behind her ear, eliciting an audible gasp that pleased him as a man. She was affected by him.

"I suppose ... I believe we should find respite from the pressures in this home. The baron and I have not been anywhere much since Lady Blackwood's death, and I grow weary of this pall of gloom. A sojourn to the country might provide us with insight if we can clear our heads for a short while. Visiting Elmstead would be a wonderful way to spend the day."

"Elmstead? That is the baron's property in Hertfordshire?"

Molly arched a rich brown eyebrow in surprise. "It is. A small but valuable estate due to its proximity to London. If it is acceptable to you, I shall propose to the baron that we visit in the morning. That will give the servants time to prepare."

"That would be delightful. Angelo and I will continue our

search, but I would enjoy seeing something of this green and pleasant land I have heard so much about, but yet to encounter for myself."

She laughed, cocking her head to peer at him with a sympathetic expression. "Your welcome to merry England has not been as favorable as one might have hoped."

Marco gave a short bow. "To second chances."

CHAPTER 9

*"The most dangerous woman is not she who is armed with daggers,
but she who is armed with purpose."*

Impressions of England by an Unrepentant Foreigner

* * *

DECEMBER 2 1821

Two carriages were carefully inspected before setting off in the early morning, soon leaving London behind to traverse the country roads. Green hedgerows and trees bedecked with the last leaves of the season lined the roads as they drove, so that barely anything could be seen from the windows, but the baron settled back into the luxurious squabs with a happy sigh.

"I think you were right, Molly. A day to Hertfordshire is just what the doctor ordered."

Molly smiled, enjoying the fact that Marco was sitting

across from her on the other bench, his fingers laced over his flat midriff as he watched the passing scenery. He wore a thick woolen coat as a defense against the cold but appeared quite comfortable despite the seasonal weather.

"It is both green and pleasant," he commented, leaning forward in interest as the thick bushes obscuring the view finally broke to reveal the rolling hills of Hertfordshire. The woods in the distance were were mostly bare but some rich reds, browns, and oranges remained while the yews were striking in their deep green to frame the gold of rolling fields and create a kaleidoscope for the senses—a view so beautiful it fairly took one's breath away.

The butler, MacNaby, and a small contingent of servants had departed the afternoon before to open the manor for the baron's party of guests, and Molly was looking forward to showing Marco the grounds of the bounteous estate. They had elected to forgo breakfast and eat when they reached Elmstead.

A low growl of a hungry stomach broke the silence, and Molly glanced sideways to find her chaperon glaring out the window. Miss Dubois was quite put out to have to wait for her breakfast, her mouth firmed in sour lines and her shawl hugged close against the chill. Molly suspected that her companion was not much interested in the countryside, not unlike her former mistress who had preferred to remain in Town year-round.

"It ees a long drive for somezing we could do at 'ome, *non?*" she complained. As a lady's maid, she would have eaten when she first arose in the kitchen with the other servants, but as companion, she had to wait to eat with Molly. Yet another point of contention between the two of them.

"Ah, but then we would not enjoy the fresh air."

Molly turned back to find Marco suppressing an amused smile at her admonishment, and she winked in acknowledgment. Miss Dubois was not an enjoyable fellow passenger, but Molly had squashed each of the servant's laments with a cheery rejoinder which, thankfully, meant she would fall back into a bristling silence for a good twenty minutes or more. The truth was the other woman was not well suited to the role of paid companion, being far better at the work of a lady's maid.

Eyeing Marco with the excuse of their proximity, Molly could not stop the stray thought that entered her head.

If I were to wed, I would no longer require a companion.

She nearly groaned out loud. It was one thing to covet time with the handsome Italian, and another to leap to the thought of marriage. She knew he liked her, but she did not want to get her hopes up, that he liked her enough to marry! Unfortunately, her infatuation was growing in leaps and bounds, and she did not know how to curtail the phantasies of an unmarried woman wishing for more than her solitary existence.

What the blazes happened to patience, Molly Carter?

Molly settled back to listen to the rhythmic sound of the carriage wheels on the hard-packed earth of the roadways, interspersed by the rustle of a breeze disturbing fallen leaves, and turned her attention to the view. The baron, who was sitting next to Marco, dozed off for a little while, but Molly determined that to be a good thing as she did not wish John to overexert himself.

Eventually they passed the outskirts of a village, a grouping of charming stone cottages with thatched roofs to break the monotony of the landscape, and Molly realized Elmstead was close. She gathered her shawl closer and fumbled around for her basket. The view gave way to manicured hedges and stone walls to mark the boundary of the baron's estate, and within minutes the carriage slowed, turning into a private lane.

An archway of towering elms lined the drive, opening up to reveal a small Palladian manor house, the symmetry a perfect juxtaposition to the formal front gardens, and the baron shifted in his seat, awakening with a bleary appearance as he rubbed his face.

"I present to you Elmstead, Marco. One of your future holdings, dear boy. It is hopeful that there will be no brushes with death today."

Molly glanced at Miss Dubois in alarm at the indiscreet comment, but the servant was not listening, peering out the window in interest. "Do you sink ze breakfast ees ready?"

The carriages drew to a halt in front of the towering portico, and MacNaby came forward as the footman opened the door. Molly and Miss Dubois alighted, standing on the drive while they waited for the baron and Marco. When the baron appeared, MacNaby called out in a hearty greeting, "Ah, your lordship! The tide's in your favor today. You've arrived just in time for a fine breakfast from Cook."

Molly blinked, a strange feeling of recognition causing her to pause. "Were you in the Navy, Mr. MacNaby?"

The butler bowed in acknowledgment. "Aye, Miss Carter. In my distant youth I served on HMS *Bellerophon*, but I left when I finished my contract, which was how I came to join Lord Campbell's household in Edinburgh."

She smiled broadly in response. "My father was a captain in the Navy. He used to speak of the tide's favor frequently. It was startling but pleasing to hear it after so long."

"Captain Carter? I served on his ship briefly nearly forty years ago, before *Bellephoron* was launched. HMS *Thunderbolt* which sailed out of Plymouth?"

"Yes, I believe that was one of his commands. How odd that we never made the connection!"

"It was a lifetime ago. I do not usually speak of that time,

Miss Carter, but I can confirm Captain Carter was well respected by his crew."

"Thank you, Mr. MacNaby. That is good to hear." She smiled, a little sad to think of her dear departed papa, but it had been endearing to recall such a touching memory. Something she had not thought about in years, since his death more than ten years earlier.

Nicholas, Angelo, Lord Sebastian, and Mr. di Bianchi disembarked from the other carriage to join them, Nicholas grousing that he needed to eat. To her delight, Marco walked up and offered her his arm, and en masse, they made their way inside to find the breakfast room.

* * *

THE WEATHER WAS cool but mild, and the farms surrounding the delightful Elmstead reminded Marco of Tuscany, and he thought what it might be like to be master of these lands.

Simon's notes remained in his mind, and looking to the east, he realized he was gazing at the tenant farm of Mr. Wright and his wife, Mary. He wondered what it meant for them that they had two young daughters. Would they attempt to have another child? Did Mr. Wright worry about the future of his farm if they did not have a son to toil the fields in the decades ahead, or would his daughters one day marry so their husbands would take his place when he was too old to labor in the fields?

This title was a concern for the multitude of people involved, and the weight of the unknown bore down on him. Marco loved his current career as bear leader to the wealthy sons of the aristocracy because he spent his days immersed in art and architecture. Florence was the greatest city in the world, and he had planned to walk its elegant streets until he drew his last breath.

But now, Simon's notebook had opened a new world. One where a dutiful lord could improve the lives of many through good governance, and it was intriguing to consider such a role. If executed with responsibility, he now understood it to be a rewarding endeavor that would be a life well spent. As the future Lord Blackwood, he could ensure the wealth, health, and happiness of hundreds of servants and tenants, and thousands of constituents within his domain.

This visit to Elmstead had him at the crossroads, contemplating two different futures. In this regard, his uncle Simon had succeeded in providing insight into the role he was being asked to step into.

Turning back from the window, Marco stared up at the large oil paintings of the picture gallery. Generations of Scotts stared back at him, and Marco realized that his own father had once visited this house. It provided a strange connection to the past to contemplate his father as a boy, running through the halls, perhaps being chastised for boisterous behavior by stern tutors.

"It is very different from the London home," he commented.

Sebastian was staring up at a pastoral landscape with great interest. "This is a Turner. The signature is hard to read, but this is his style. What do you think, Lorenzo?"

Lorenzo came to stand by his side, considering the calm river that ran under a stone bridge and was framed by trees. He twisted his face in haughty disgust as he gestured with great disdain.

"Bah, Turner, the Englishman who indulges in landscapes and dares to upheave the perfection of form, light, and composition laid down by the great masters of the Rebirth. What is all this swirling, tempestuous brushwork? These wispy, almost formless depictions of nature—it is sheer mayhem when compared to the exactness of Leonardo, the harmony of Raphael, or the majesty of Michelangelo. This amateur's use of light may fascinate, but where is the clarity, the precision, the ideal proportions that elevate art to the divine? His heavens are dramatic, yes, but do they evoke the sublime grace of a Botticelli horizon or the architectural symmetry of a Palladian landscape? I think not."

Angelo and Sebastian burst into gales of disbelieving laughter, Nicholas scowling with seething irritation, while Molly and the baron blinked in confusion at the scathing criticism of one of the great painters of England. Marco swept his hand over his mouth in alarmed perplexment, searching for a suitable rebuke to such eloquent arrogance.

Sebastian calmed himself to speak first. "As you can hear, Lord Blackwood, Mr. di Bianchi struggles to form his opinions. It is our hope that bringing him along on our travels will further his education so that he might contribute some of his thoughts to the world."

Uncle John shook his head, chuckling at the facetious explanation of their guest's rude assessment. "I believe that Mr. di Bianchi suffers from a surplus of opinions."

Marco finally found his tongue in the face of such an unexpected onslaught. "I apologize for our priggish friend, Lord Blackwood. He grew up in a barnyard and has yet to learn how to conduct himself indoors." As they were not all family present, he elected the formal address for his uncle.

At this, even Lorenzo chuckled, his expression wry as he realized his vehement dissection of Turner's talents. "I apologize if I insulted your art, Lord Blackwood. My friends will tell you that I am enthusiastic about my cultural history, and I forgot myself."

To his credit, the baron shrugged, his amusement evident. "It was certainly entertaining. Perhaps when we return to London, you can censure my collection there. It will wile away an otherwise boring afternoon to hear such distinct opinions from someone as knowledgeable about Renaissance art as you."

Molly giggled at this. "A Grand Tour in the privacy of our galleries. I think it is a superb notion, Lord Blackwood."

After that they visited the garden, the noon sun having sufficiently warmed the day to stroll about, and Molly and Miss Dubois accompanied Marco into a maze at the end of the garden. It was composed of evergreen yew hedges, but the oaks, elms, and chestnuts had divested their leaves upon the ground. The brown and russet leaves rustled and crunched beneath their feet as they entered the opening of the puzzle of foliage, but within a few feet, Miss Dubois stopped in her tracks with a stricken expression.

"I do not like zis. Ze sides are too close, and I feel crushed."

Molly frowned, having told Marco that she wished to show him the fountain at the center of the maze. "They are not that close. No closer than the walls of the servants' corridors in the attic at home."

"But zere are bugs and creeping, crawling zings. Ze baronezz never made me do such zings." The chaperon shuddered in repulsion.

Molly's irritation was evident when she responded, her tone brooking no argument, and Marco was impressed by her steel. "I am going to visit the center. You can accompany me or you can wait here."

Miss Dubois looked into the maze and swung her head back to the exit. "I ... eh ... I shall wait 'ere. Do not be long!"

Even with the bonnet shielding her face, Marco did not miss the glow of triumph that crossed Molly's features as the servant hurried out to stand outside the maze in agitation. His lips quirked, having some inkling what drove Molly to seek these brief flashes of freedom. The life of an unwed Englishwoman was restrictive, but she constantly fought those bonds as someone with something of a wild spirit despite her polite demeanor.

"Shall we?"

She took his arm, and he flexed in reaction as he caught the scent of cinnamon again. Despite his wishes to maintain his distance while he sorted through his rampant confusion over his future, a future until these past weeks he had considered settled, it was ever tempting to steal a moment with her when the opportunity arose.

Despite Molly's arm being curled around his, he soon found himself being pulled along with the aggressive young miss. She had requested the baron write down the directions to the middle, and now consulted her page frequently.

"Why are you in such a hurry?" Marco finally asked, after she had yanked him around yet another corner.

Molly blushed. "The faster we reach the middle, the longer we can spend there."

"Ah, you are worrying about Miss Dubois?"

"I am."

This raised a suspicion in the back of his mind, and Marco frowned as they hurried through the tightly clipped yews. "Did you know Miss Dubois would refuse to enter?"

Molly hesitated, licking her lips. "I do not know what you mean. How would I know such a thing?"

"It strikes me that you have made a great study of your shadow."

She glanced at him briefly but continued their ramble with the single-minded attention that reminded him of his friend Lorenzo. "And what of it? What would you do if Miss Dubois dogged your heels like a foul-tempered French poodle, yapping and snarling even when there is no one to fight?"

With that, she swung them around a corner, and the center was revealed. Marco stopped, a little stunned by such a riveting installation in such an unexpected place. A small country estate? What riches the Blackwood title must control!

It was a magnificent fountain, drained for the winter, but magnificent nevertheless even to a Florentine accustomed to beauty. Diana, the goddess of the hunt, was blowing a horn as if to summon the wild spirits of the woods to follow her on her chase. She wore a short, flowing tunic which revealed long sculpted legs strapped in sandals, as she stared into the distance where her prey must be racing away with dread, or perhaps excitement, a majestic stag running by her side.

Staring up at the eerie face carved of stone, Marco was struck by the likeness. He looked down at Molly, who stood in awe, as if transfixed. He returned his gaze to Diana.

Their similarity was uncanny, and a shiver ran down his spine as Marco realized that, perhaps, he was the prey and there might be no shaking Molly from her quest to join with him. There was something about the young lady. Something unrelenting about her force of will.

His dismay was offset by the rush of heat from thinking about Molly's slender legs bared to him … clinging to his hips … which he fought back while his thoughts reeled. He was ill-prepared to commit to a life here, so far from everything he knew. There was no denying she was pure temptation, even now the subtle fragrance of cinnamon made his mouth water, but would merry England, and the huntress at his side, release him if he chose to return home as a bachelor? Or had he entered the otherworld from which escape was not possible?

Yet … what would it be like to have a woman of such strength at his side? Success would be inevitable with such a determined and enticing partner.

Marco was afraid that visiting Elmstead had made his thoughts even more confused. Was he now contemplating accepting this fresh path that fate itself had thrust at him? None of this was what he had planned for himself. Within just weeks, his life had changed so drastically, not to mention there was still a killer stalking him back in London. How was he to make monumental decisions about his future when he did not know if he would survive the week?

And what of the risks of giving away his heart a second time? Watching Catherine fade away had decimated him. He did not know if he could survive allowing himself to love again, when death could steal his other half. Was it not safer to maintain his independence and return to Florence as an unmarried gentleman to live his life as he had the past few years? It had taken a long time to carve out some peace after such a terrible loss.

Clearing his throat, he decided to stand his ground before things got out of hand. "Molly, you understand I do not know if I shall remain in England?"

Her eyes found his, confusion in their depths, and he realized that while the past few seconds had been rather ground-shaking to him, she had no notion of what he had been thinking.

"I know."

"Then you understand we cannot come to any agreement? You and I?"

She looked down, her disappointment plain despite her attempt to hide it. She finally answered in a thick voice, "I know."

"There is much for me to consider. About this title. About Florence. I cannot say what the future holds. We must resolve this danger first, and then, perhaps, I can find some … *chiarezza?*" He stopped, irritated that his English had failed him at such a pivotal moment.

"Clarity," she replied, her shoulders sagging slightly in defeat.

"*Sì*. I need to find clarity, and we must not imagine things are something more than they are. I do not say this to hurt you, but I cannot make any promises and it is best we do not pursue anything while I sort this out."

She sucked in a deep breath, staring at the empty basin of the fountain. "I know."

Laying out the hard truths should have brought him some comfort, but it did nothing to ease the sense that he was standing at a fork in the road, wholly uncertain which route he should pursue to find his happiness. The sense that the most important decision of his life was before him, but he did not know which path would lead to the heaven of a fulfilled life versus which path would lead to the hell of regrets.

He reached into his pocket to stroke the etched surface of the timepiece he had received from his father and wondered if Peter Scott had faced a similar decision when he had argued with the late baron about his intended marriage to Marco's mother. What would his father say if he were here now? Which path would he counsel Marco to take after all the struggles he had faced until his life had prematurely ended? Would he have encouraged him to take Papa's place in England, or dissuaded him from giving up what he had built for himself in Italy?

Perhaps it was time to escort this party home so Angelo and he could resume the search for the journal and end this plot to kill him so he might be freed to consider his choices.

CHAPTER 10

"He who dreams of fire must wake swiftly—or risk finding himself consumed."

Impressions of England by an Unrepentant Foreigner

* * *

The drive home was mostly silent. The baron had fallen asleep. Marco watched the view with a pensive expression, and Miss Dubois appeared mollified as a result of having her breakfast, so she was leafing through one of her fashion periodicals.

Molly stared out the window, but she was thinking about the conversation in the maze. She was pushing Marco too hard. But knowing that, and knowing how to ease the pressure while still spending time in his company—this required a level of finesse she had not developed. She had never esteemed a gentleman so intensely.

It was a conundrum, she decided, the twisting of her fingers the only sign of distress she permitted. If she did not spend time with him, there was no possibility of attracting him into a courtship. However, for the second time, he had declared he could not pursue a match with her. The entire situation was mortifying, but the thought of living with regrets was just as uncomfortable.

If she did not at least try … even if he would never court her … was she willing to give up the opportunity for at least one more fiery kiss before she bid him farewell?

Molly's chances of marriage receded with each passing year. Because of her mother's long illness, she had never properly come out, then came the period of mourning. Just as that was ending, the baroness had died. Which, in effect, had mostly ended Molly's chances of being introduced in society. She now lived in a household devoid of a female sponsor, and with a convalescing baron who was regaining his health. He could not attend any events with Molly any sooner than the Season next year.

Marco's arrival and the events of the past few days had brought to light that her marriageable years had passed by without notice. Would she remain the step-cousin to a baron forever? Was there no larger role for her to fulfill? Was this her fate? To disappear into irrelevance, her entire life lived in the perimeters of society while her friends and cousins carved out their part in this world until, eventually, John passed on to the next life and Marco became the head of the family? Would she be forced to watch as the man she wanted, the man she would be beholden to, married some other woman while she slipped further into the shadows?

Perhaps she should have raised such an essential subject with Madeline when she had had the opportunity.

Perhaps she should ask Madeline about securing a position at the stone manufactory. At least then, if she worked, she could create a life of her own. A life which could gain some meaning.

Molly's turmoil spread until she was afraid she might be experiencing a full crisis of the soul as she struggled to fix upon the purpose of her existence. She had always considered herself a pragmatic person who could be relied on, but what if she never had anyone who relied on her? Was she to spend the rest of her days as a companion to an aging baron?

Simon or John could probably help her to make some sort of practical match, she supposed, but what if she did not want that? Would that not mean she had changed her position from keeping an aging baron company to that of keeping a nameless husband company?

I have no choice. I must try.

Somehow this made her feel better, and her spiraling thoughts gathered back together into a resolution. The connection between her and Marco was powerful. He would not be dissuading her interest in him unless he agreed that a match was a distinct possibility. She had been attempting to practice patience during their outing, but somehow, their visit to the fountain had caused him to reject her for the second time. It had been so wholly unexpected. She had thought that the outing was going rather well. That they had been enjoying each other's company without coercion. There was no indication of what she had done to provoke him so, but she could not give up, so she would change her strategy.

Such a course might lead to regret, but not as great as the regret she would experience if she simply gave up. The attraction between them was unprecedented. How could she ignore it?

Arriving back in London, Molly headed upstairs with Miss Dubois to prepare for dinner. Her thoughts remained occupied as she washed and changed into evening wear, turning over different ideas in her mind. None felt right, so she wound up conversing with Nicholas and John throughout the dinner in order to avoid Marco, who laughed with his brother and companions at the other end of the table, until she could devise a plan to proceed.

Eventually, as she laid her head on her pillow, Molly realized perhaps Marco was right. They needed to find the culprit behind the attempts on his life as the priority.

From the next room, she could hear the nocturnal sounds of the sleeping Miss Dubois. Recalling the jewelry she had found, Molly wondered if Claudette had sufficient malice to attempt to kill a man. Twice.

And who else in the household might have been corrupted by the baroness? Perhaps she should speak with John and Nicholas about servants who might have spent time in Isla Scott's company. It was time to set her wits to catching a would-be killer because her tortured musings about bringing Marco up to scratch would all be for naught if someone succeeded in ending his life.

* * *

MARCO ABHORRED that he was the worst of scoundrels as he slipped into his bed. Leaning over to put out his oil lamp, he thought about his admonishments regarding any potential courtship. What was it about Molly Carter which set him off balance? Or was it the knowledge that someone wished him ill for something that could not be helped? For circumstances beyond his control. He had not asked to be the baron's heir. His first reaction had been to refuse even a visit until his mother had persuaded him that it would do him good.

Was it the delectable Molly that was causing this tension, or being targeted for death by some unknown foe? Was he the victim of a cosmic jest, wherein forces beyond his awareness placed him in a Divine Comedy of his very own for their amusement? If he were to describe his current circumstances to a stranger, they would find the story fraught with melodrama.

Marco slowly drifted into sleep, only to find himself chased in his dreams by a nameless dread. Rousing from a particularly stressful encounter, his eyes flying open in the dark, he realized it was but a nightmare. Rolling over, he willed himself to fall asleep again until the veil of slumber carried him back into his ominous phantasies.

As he descended into the eighth circle of hell, Marco came upon a valley, deep and filled with fire. Shadows shifted on the outcroppings of blackened rock, and there was desolation in every direction. The flames moved like fireflies in the dark, and peering closely, he discovered that each flame held a tormented soul within its flickering form. The flames were not just fire, but an embodiment of suffering and punishment, and Marco could not help but wonder what he had done to deserve this terrible visit to such a desolate abyss.

His injured ribs throbbed, as if to protest his presence here, when one of the flames approached from the dark to reveal Molly dressed in the short tunic of Diana, her shapely legs exposed to his lustful gaze. But her expression was tortured as her hair streamed down like the flow of lava from the depths of the earth. He could smell cinnamon burning as he frantically sought water to cool her down, but there was none. The smell of singed hair filled his nostrils with its acrid stench, and helplessly he watched her lean close to him, her mouth a fraction of an inch from his, to whisper.

"You are burning."

He looked down, but there was no evidence of smoldering upon his person. Frowning, he brought his gaze back to hers. "I am not. I merely visit. I am not a resident of this shadow realm."

Her opalescent eyes glimmered in the red light, bright and glowing against the sooty smudges smeared across her lovely face. "Wake up, Marco. You are burning."

Marco sat up in his bed, his pulse racing and the echoes

of the dream yet so vivid that the stench of burning hair still plagued his senses. He tried to calm his breath, but the smoke of hell continued to plague him. The heat had followed him to the waking world, and the sound of crackling aggravated his ears. Had he woken from one dream into the next?

Flinging back the bedcovers, he sprang to his feet, only to be met by the sight of a blaze upon the rug. The logs of the banked fire he had fallen asleep to had somehow fallen from the hearth to set the room on fire!

Marco yelled out loud, hoping someone would hear him raise the alarm as he ran over to grab the water jug from the washstand. He threw it on the burning rug, then ran to grab his counterpane which he folded over to pound at the fire in an effort to smother it, but it was hopeless as the fire licked outward. Dashing out into his private drawing room, he threw open the door to yell again at the top of his lungs.

"Fire!"

Running back inside, he snatched up the tartan pillows from the chaise lounge to run back into the bedchamber and beat at the flames frantically as heat and black smoke bellowed up in clouds.

From the depths of the house, he heard an answering shout, echoing his alarm. "Fire! Wake up! Fire!"

He nearly wept in relief that someone had heard him, and within moments, Sebastian ran in and joined to stamp at the flames with his boots, while smoke swirled around them. Marco dropped a pillow, burying his face into an elbow to ease his coughing as he continued to thump at the flames.

A chorus of shouts sounded in the distance, signaling that more help was coming, but Marco continued to beat at the flames as if he were the only one to save this house. The thought of this elegant home burning to the ground was too horrible to conceive. Allowing beautiful Molly, or his ill uncle, or even the irritable Nicholas to come to any harm, was too awful to think about.

Soon more arrived with buckets of water, and Sebastian dragged him from the chamber, insistent despite Marco's resistance. "You need to catch your breath, my friend."

Out in the hall it was chaos, bodies rushing back and forth while shouts rang out in distress. Until, finally, Angelo called out from the interior of the room that the fire had been put out. Marco's legs went weak with relief, and he sank to his knees to hack violently as he tried to pull oxygen into his lungs.

Sebastian tugged at his arm. "Come with me. You need a drink."

Marco struggled to his feet, his eyes and throat burning from the smoke, but obeyed to follow the Norseman down the stairs.

"I am fortunate you were up so late," croaked Marco, gesturing to Sebastian's charred boots.

His friend glanced down, still fully attired in the early hours except for shedding his coat and cravat, his shirt hanging open at the neck and his waistcoat unbuttoned. "I am struggling to sleep. Being home is bringing back memories."

Marco nodded, understanding the sentiment as Sebastian led him into the library where he threw the terrace doors open and the clean, cool rush of air eased his discomfort. He slumped into an armchair.

It was his fourth day in England and his third brush with death.

Sebastian hunted about for a drink until Marco finally reminded him that they had been told that the house had been emptied of spirits after Nicholas had begun his dry spell. Cursing, the tall Englishman spun on his heel to depart the library without an explanation. A few minutes later he returned with Angelo who hurried to look Marco over, his own face covered in soot to make the whites of his eyes glow in contrast.

"How are you?"

"My throat aches, as do my lungs," Marco replied hoarsely.

Angelo nodded. "You will have the worst of the smoke inhalation. I shall prepare a herbal tea with honey from my supplies. That will calm the physiological effects for you and the rest who fought the fire."

His brother handed him a thick dressing robe, which was when Marco realized he was dressed in a thin linen nightshirt, which barely covered his knees. In fact, he was shivering in the breeze blowing through the open doors, his undercarriage tightening in retreat against the cold to signal that the robe was sorely needed.

The thoughtful gesture made him reach out to grasp Angelo's arm in gratitude, who nodded before hurrying off. Soon after, Molly appeared with her lapdog at her heels, and Marco was grateful he was properly robed for the encounter. He assured her that he was well, maintaining a proper reserve for the French companion, but wishing he could reach out and embrace her. The vision of her trapped in hell had been most disturbing to his peace of mind. More than that, he could not shake the whimsy that it had been the divine hand of fate, embodied by Molly's haunting presence, that had awoken him from his nightmares. He wanted to pack his trunks and leave England to end this train of death-defying incidents, but the urge to protect her and their family fought back with vehemence to leave him drained and reeling. Not to mention the searing pain of his throat, lungs, and eyes, added to the throb of his bruised ribs. Every aspect of this journey to England was turning into a veritable visit to Dante's *Inferno*.

CHAPTER 11

"It is the boldest fox who risks the hounds for a taste of freedom."

Impressions of England by an Unrepentant Foreigner

* * *

DECEMBER 3 1821

*M*olly tiptoed past the sleeping Miss Dubois, determined to seek out Marco for a private conversation. She had not slept a wink after finding him in the library. His expression had been haunted, exhausted, and she wished to verify for herself that he was all right, but Miss Dubois's presence had prevented any genuine conversation.

They had all got back to bed so late that her chaperon had not yet stirred, even past the normal hour of her waking, and Molly had finally concluded that this was an opportunity to not be missed.

Letting herself out into the hall, Molly hesitated when she heard her name being called out.

Blast! The poodle is up!

She tried to think what to do, casting about the hall before rushing toward the door that led to the servants' staircase. Not in the mood to wait out another opportunity, Molly elected to run for it instead. Behind her, she heard the door to Miss Dubois's bedchamber open, and the woman called out again.

Molly shut the door to the staircase, which connected every floor, including the attic and basement levels, determined to continue on. The interior was dim, lit only by the low light of wall sconces. Racing down the steep, narrow steps to the ground level, she threw open the door as she heard Miss Dubois enter the staircase above her, accompanied by a shimmer of light from the sunlit hall. Molly stopped, realizing she was being chased like a fox with hunting hounds on her tail.

If she took a direct route to look for Marco, her chaperon would soon catch up with her. Even now, the creaking of the wooden stairs announced she was descending.

Leaving the door ajar to suggest she had indeed taken this path, Molly turned back into the staircase. Quietly, she slipped down farther into the basement level, being careful to not turn an ankle on the well-worn stairs.

Miss Dubois would never look for her down in the servants' domain. Perhaps she could exit the house and search for Marco through the terrace windows. Even summon him outside to converse. If she were fortunate, perhaps she would even avoid the servants.

Reaching the lowest level, approximately midway up the length of the building, Molly stopped to orient herself so she could find the exit to the garden. To her left she could hear the sounds of the kitchen, which she had visited on occasion, and not wanting to encounter the staff, she turned right. She thought she was heading toward the servants' hall, with the doors to the butler's pantry and housekeeper's room on either side.

To her right, a door suddenly opened, causing her to shriek in surprise as her palm flew up to cover her hammering heart, and she came eye to eye with MacNaby, who had a ledger tucked under his arm.

The butler's brow furrowed. "Miss Carter?"

"I was … looking for the kitchen."

Through the door she could see a modest and exceptionally well-appointed butler's pantry. It was lined with stained beech cabinets, which were capped with workspace counters, and the upper sections were shelves enclosed by glass doors. Neatly labeled drawers ran up in a stack in one section of the cabinetry and fine pieces of silver and china could be seen through the immaculate windows, with a small desk just in view tucked against the opposite wall with account books neatly stacked next to quills and an inkstand.

The spine of one book was oddly out of place—

"It is this direction." MacNaby started to close the door behind him, apparently reluctant for her to view the room, and Molly quite forgot her manners as she tilted her head to view that spine for an extra second before the room disappeared, to—

"I wanted to learn about the tea that Mr. Scott made for the people affected by the fire," Molly murmured in explanation while her thoughts raced. If she had any standing in the household, she might demand he reopen the door. This notion made her painfully aware that she was currently alone in a dim hall with a man considerably stronger than herself and the best thing for it was to pursue her pretense and follow him to the kitchen. She smiled broadly as the butler pulled a key from his hip pocket and locked the door with a decisive click.

"Quite a rabbit warren down here," she commented nervously, as she swallowed her fear.

MacNaby nodded politely, but Molly could see something in the depths of his eyes that was cold and angry. At her intrusion belowstairs? Or something else?

Entering the kitchen, she made a show of asking the stunned cook and kitchen maids about the brew that Angelo had made for those who had inhaled smoke from the fire, while MacNaby made to leave, mentioning he had a tradesman in the servants' hall waiting for his return.

The kitchen staff could not answer any questions, the gentleman having prepared the tea in the kitchen but with his own stash.

"Oi can't say for certain, miss. Think there was licorice root, an' oi saw chamomile flowers, that oi did. Might be best to ask the gentleman 'imself, eh?" queried the astonished cook, wiping her hands dry on her apron. Molly hoped Cook found her invasion delightfully eccentric, rather than the lunacy of a woman gripped by terminal stupidity, well aware her ruse was as thin as paper.

Thanking them for their assistance, she headed back to the servants' staircase, her original mission thwarted by a far more pressing concern. Racing up two flights to the second floor, she exited to make her way to her bedchamber. She should find the others to inform them what she had seen, but her instincts told her it would take too long and she needed to return immediately—while Walter MacNaby was still speaking with the tradesman.

Entering her room, she quickly crossed to the *secrétaire à abattant* which held her papers, a drop-front desk which had been here when she had arrived in London. Pulling out the second drawer, she felt around the back of the drawer until her fingers found the small purse in a surge of triumph.

Pulling it out, she untied it and dropped the contents onto the desk. Two brass, hooked picks, gifted by Madeline the prior month.

Her friend had used them in her quest to help Simon uncover the true killer, and when Molly had heard about how Madeline had picked the lock on Lady Blackwood's desk, she had coaxed her friend to show her how to do so, too. It had been nothing but an idle lark to fill her otherwise boring days, but now it was going to perhaps solve the mystery of the devil at Marco's heels.

Hurrying back downstairs, she snuck down the basement corridor to listen at the servants' hall. She could hear MacNaby's subtle brogue complaining about overcharges on a grocery account, confirming her way was clear. Returning to the butler's pantry door, she dropped to one knee, inserted the picks, and pressed her ear to the door.

Each second was infinite as she listened for the clicks, knowing that MacNaby could appear at any moment. Or a footman. Or a maid. Her palms were damp with nerves as she tried to focus on the task at hand, nearly swooning with relief when she tried the handle and the door swung open.

Entering quickly, she shut it behind her and crossed to the desk, but the book that had brought her here was missing. She inhaled, thinking hard, and swung her head around to view the room. MacNaby must have stopped in here on the way back to the servants' hall, suspecting that Molly had caught sight of what he was concealing within this territory set aside for the most senior of servants. It was wily, a measure he had taken just in case, likely not sure that she had seen it. Which meant he would not have had time to do anything more than move the book to a temporary hiding place because he had been en route to finish his meeting.

Walking over to the cabinets, she began pulling them open as quickly as she could while maintaining her silence, leaning down to crane her neck and peer within the depths of their interiors. She found china platters and silver chargers. One cabinet had tureens, but no book. Moving on, she found more platters and sauceboats, and even vases for centerpieces, but no book. Not even behind the larger items. Moving over to the drawers, she drew them open, careful not to jostle the contents to avoid making a noise. There she found cutlery, ladles, and tea strainers, but there was no sign of the book.

Molly mumbled a curse, trying to think. She had been in here for at least several minutes, and her time was running out.

Suddenly a flash of inspiration hit, and she returned to the cabinet with the tureens. Dropping down onto her haunches, she took a second to study them before reaching for the silver lid of the largest tureen. Lifting it, she blinked, restraining a crow of victory. Within its sizable interior was a leather-bound journal, with ornate gold tooling and an embossed thistle on its front cover.

* * *

"You have become quite prone to accidents. Or someone is attempting to kill you, my friend. Two accidents in four days?" Lorenzo was tense, flinging his arms out in emphasis of his declaration.

"Three," interjected Angelo from his position at the window, where he was peering out to the garden with his arms folded to signal his worry.

"Three!" cried Lorenzo. "What is this?"

"It is nothing," Marco insisted, boneless in his exhaustion. He had been awake since the fire, and coupled with the physical exertion of fighting the flames, he was wholly wrung out.

"We must tell them the truth, brother. If that fire had spread, everyone could have been killed." Angelo's admonishment was unexpected. Marco turned to look at his brother, wordless, while his brother cocked his head in encouragement.

Marco sighed heavily. "Yes, someone is trying to kill me."

"Why?" Sebastian leaned forward in his chair, his expression uncharacteristically earnest. All of them looked rather haggard after spending half the night up in the aftermath of putting out the fire.

"I cannot explain all of it because it is a private family matter. But we suspect someone in the house is trying to clear the path for my uncle Simon to inherit."

Sebastian frowned. "Would that not mean Lord Campbell is involved?"

"No. Lord Campbell left London to protect his wife. Her bloodlines are not acceptable to whoever is behind this." Marco tried to think what to say without revealing the involvement of the late Lady Blackwood. "I cannot tell you all the details, but Lady Campbell is a target for this blackguard who is after me. Lord Campbell removed her to safety by taking her to his estates in Scotland, with servants from her own household. I am confident he is not involved."

"What of the third accident? What was that?" Lorenzo interjected.

Marco coughed hard, attempting to clear his throat of the ashes he had breathed in. "An urn fell from the roof the day after we arrived. I was able to leap out of the way."

Porca miseria!" Lorenzo cursed, resuming his pacing of the library at a frantic pace that could have powered a machine.

Sebastian fell back, whistling through his teeth. "Three

accidents in four days! It is true, then. You are a marked man."

"I understand if you wish to end your visit. Perhaps you and Lorenzo can move to your brother's home?"

The Norseman scowled. "Do not be absurd. We accompanied you as friends. We will remain to help defend you."

"I cannot ask that of you. I cannot even tell you the specifics of why this is happening."

Lorenzo stopped his pacing. "Sebastian is right. We understand enough. Someone in the house is trying to kill you, and we must all remain vigilant while you uncover who it is. Meanwhile, the more friends you have around you, the more difficult it is to make these attempts."

Angelo nodded, still staring out the window. His usual cheer was lacking—the stark possibility of fatality had muted his brother's spirits. "I agree. We must all remain watchful and, at night, we must lock our bedchambers so we cannot be harmed in our sleep."

"As if we are children afraid of ghouls and goblins lying in wait beneath the bed?" Marco's tone was sour, but his mood was worse.

"Exactly so," Angelo shot back in a rare show of fury. "You could have been burnt to a crisp if you had not woken in time."

"Maledizione!" Marco growled, wishing he could find a corner to curl up and fall asleep. Except that inevitably led to more of the awful dreams he had been suffering from since he had arrived.

"It is time to change our tactics, brother. Perhaps locking our doors is not enough. Perhaps we need to keep watch through the night. We cannot allow anything to happen to you."

As tempers rose between Marco and his brother, Sebastian rose to his feet to tower over them. "We have not had much sleep, so I understand the impulse to quarrel, but I believe we can plan out security measures to protect Marco from further ... accidents."

Marco inhaled deeply, digging deep within his soul to find a measure of composure, until he finally nodded in acceptance of Sebastian's proposal.

Suggestions were thrown back and forth, and over the next thirty minutes they hammered out a plan to protect himself, the baron, and Angelo before his friends left to eat their breakfast. Angelo waited at the door for him, as Marco rose to his feet, his entire body protesting with stiff rejection of movement.

As he stood, a familiar face appeared in the window across the room, pressing against the glass which fogged with her warm breath. Molly's eyes found his, and she gestured for him to join her, lifting her hand to reveal something he did not expect.

"Angelo, go ahead. I must see to something before I eat."

Shrugging, his brother strode off, eager to find repast after their long night. Marco closed the library door, then crossed to open the terrace doors and was somewhat dismayed at how happy he was to see her. "Molly?" he called in a low voice.

She ran over, holding her skirts up, and Marco took a moment to enjoy the sight of her exuberance as she held the journal up again in triumph. Her obvious excitement dispelled the horror of his nightmare, in which her hair had been burning and her face twisted in pain. The urge to pull her into an embrace was overwhelming, but he stepped back to let her in the room.

"I found it! It was in the butler's pantry! MacNaby attempted to hide it, but I did not let it stop me."

Marco grabbed her by the upper arms, alarmed at the unknown risk she had taken to obtain the journal, intermixed with pride for her enterprise. He had long since recognized she was unique, but he was still startled by the extent of his feelings. Dropping his forehead to hers, he sucked in the smell of fresh cinnamon—not the stench of burning from his terrible dreams—and just enjoyed holding her for a second before letting her go to step back. He should not toy with her by giving her false hopes when he still wished to return to Italy to tutor.

"You can tell me the rest later, but right now I should send for MacNaby so he can explain this."

She nodded and handed him the journal, her eyes shining in the morning light, and Marco was tempted to lean in for a kiss.

This provoked a mixture of reactions, nearly knocking him off his feet with their sheer force. Relief that she was well, dread at this ongoing campaign to kill him, perplexment that the butler might be behind it. Those did not even take into account his alarm at finding the fire blazing last evening, the horror of discovering Molly in the fiery other-world of his nightmares, or the fact he did not know what path to choose for his future. It all coalesced to revive his earlier temper to a sudden boiling point—

"Where is your *chaperon?*" he demanded.

Molly flinched as if he had slapped her across the face. "I … well … I wanted to speak with you in private to ensure you were … well. After the fire."

"You must stop running off from her! It is not safe—you could ruin yourself if you continue this way!"

Molly blinked rapidly in surprise, her face falling. "I … am sorry."

When she turned to walk away, Marco saw her distress, appalled at his outburst as he watched her depart. He wanted to call her back. To explain why he was being such a cad. That he had even argued with his own brother just a half an hour earlier, something that had never happened before.

Fantastic, you beast! Add shame to your list of stupido *reactions!*

Looking down at the recovered journal, he realized he would have to make it up to her later. First, he must find MacNaby and demand an explanation to secure this household. Rubbing his tired eyes, he strode out of the library to seek the butler because lives hung in the balance.

CHAPTER 12

"To chase the fox is bold; to halt mid-chase is wisdom."

Impressions of England by an Unrepentant Foreigner

* * *

*E*ntering the breakfast room, Marco dismissed the servants, requesting that the head footman, Duncan, locate MacNaby forthwith so he could meet with him. He quickly shut the door once they had left, and turned to find his brother and friends staring at him agog. Sebastian had a silver fork midway to his mouth, but laid it down carefully.

"What is it?" Angelo asked, after swallowing his eggs.

"Miss Carter has found the miss—" He cut off what he was going to say, realizing his friends did not know about the journal. "We need to locate the butler immediately. It appears he is connected to all this."

"Excellent. You have sent the footman to find him, so we can finish our breakfast," remarked Sebastian, lifting his fork up once more.

"I am uncertain the butler will cooperate with my summons. He may make a run for it, so I need you to help."

Sebastian dropped the fork with a loud clink, springing to his feet. "He could be the one who set the fire?"

"Sì."

Angelo and Lorenzo rose, too, speaking in unison. "What should we do?"

"I would ask you proceed to find MacNaby. Perhaps one of you can follow Duncan to check the butler's pantry, while the other two search the house for him? I will search the third floor and then I have something to take care of."

"I will follow Duncan and search the basement, if necessary," declared the Norseman, striding over to exit.

Lorenzo nodded. "This ground level, then. If I do not find him, I shall search the next floor, too."

Marco got the sensation he was a general commanding troops as his friend brushed past.

"Is that the missing journal?" Angelo had come over to join him, cocking his head to peer at the book tucked under Marco's arm. Marco pulled it out, displaying the thistle on the front cover.

"Molly located it. I did not have time to learn the details, but she said it was in MacNaby's possession."

"The butler? What would he have to do with this?"

Marco waved the book. "I hope this will reveal his motive if he will not tell us himself."

"I will search for him in the attic. Hopefully, we will find him quickly."

Marco followed Angelo out the door, then raced up the main staircase two steps at a time to the third floor where he marched down the east hall, knocking on doors before swinging them open to view the rooms. He found the bedchambers of Sebastian, Lorenzo, and Angelo, but was uncertain which was which with all their things stowed away.

Continuing on to the lower floor, he turned the corner and quickly found the baron in his small private sitting room, and he apprised him of the developments. John was still dressed in nightclothes, a colorful robe keeping him warm as he ate from a breakfast tray.

"MacNaby, you say. I would never have thought it, but his conversation with Molly at Elmstead did remind me that the man joined us at the time Lady Blackwood married my father. He served in her household in Edinburgh, originally working for her father—the late Lord Campbell."

"Perhaps that should have been mentioned."

John shook his head. "Lady Blackwood made a point of hiring staff from there, so no particular servant stood out more than the rest. You must have noticed the servants' livery is lined with green and blue tartan?"

Marco was impatient to deliver the journal to Nicholas, but did his best not to display any irritation as he had done with Molly earlier. Whom he had yet to do something about, after being so rude. "Yes, what of it?"

"Lady Blackwood was a member of the Highland Society of London. It has become fashionable in recent years to boast of one's Scottish title, and, as you have likely surmised, most of the footmen hail from Scotland. Most from the Campbell clan. There was no reason to suspect one servant more than another, and MacNaby's background was a drop of information in a sea of facts."

"I should have interviewed all the servants, I suppose."

The baron laughed at this. "Dear boy, until I heard about the fire, even I could not credit that we had yet another murderous fiend living under our roof. This is the stuff of gothic novels. Even Ann Radcliffe could not invent suspenseful stories such as what has unfolded here these past weeks. Simon did not tell you the half of it the other day."

"Nevertheless."

"I will have you know the servants were interviewed by both the Duke of Halmesbury and the Earl of Saunton, and neither were able to learn much from doing so."

"Was that before or after the truth came to light?"

The baron rubbed his chin, contemplating the events of the earlier month. "Before," he finally replied.

"Then I should have interviewed the servants with the knowledge of the facts His Grace and his lordship did not possess at the time."

The baron tilted his head to consider Marco carefully. "That is an astute observation. Perhaps you will be a competent lord in Simon's stead when it is your turn."

Marco rolled his shoulders at the comment. "I am uncertain I wish the role."

"Ah, but the role wishes to have you."

Marco politely left, but once out in the corridor, he took a moment to grit his teeth. He would not have England and this title thrust upon him without a say in it. His new family acted as if it were a *fait accompli*, but he was a free man who could exercise his own will. If he wished to live in Italy, and use a man of business to see to the baronial affairs, he could yet do so. It was his decision to make.

Continuing on to the next door, he knocked, hearing a gruff reply which he took as an invitation to enter.

It was a large bedroom without a sitting room, but large enough for a seating area by the fireplace. The cross-as-crabs Nicholas lay on a chaise lounge with his leg propped up with pillows. He had the stack of journals at his side and appeared to be reading them for the second time.

"What do you want?" Nicholas's tone was belligerent, but

after their recent confrontation, Marco surmised it might have something to do with the reading material he was engaged with and the violent pressures of living in the Scott household.

"We have found a journal. I think it is the missing one you spoke of."

Nicholas frowned, swinging around to lower his legs to the floor. "What? Does that mean you know who is behind this?"

"I do not know the specifics, but Molly found it in the butler's pantry."

"MacNaby!"

"We are looking for him now."

"I thought to go through these again after what happened last night, but I have yet to find anything new." Nicholas gestured at the stack in explanation.

"Now you have three new years to read about."

"Give it to me."

The other man reached out to take the journal, opening it to check the first entry. He turned the book and scoured the last few pages to find the final entry, then nodded. "This is the three years."

Marco winced at the spider's scrawl he had glimpsed. Then, too, was the awful subject matter. Perhaps his uncle Nicholas had more strength than he let on, to volunteer for such a formidable task. Marco would hate to read his own mother's journals, and Bianca Romano Scott Rossi was a woman of sound mind, not a demented murderess. "Good luck. I do not envy you your chore."

Nicholas pulled a face. "Perhaps, in the end, it will prove cathartic after all that has unfolded. Knowing the truth is uncomfortable but ... necessary, I suppose. When these dark days are behind us, perhaps these journals will answer enough questions to close those chapters and seek something better. One can only hope."

Marco smiled in commiseration, his own poor behavior with Molly this morning providing him with some insight into Nicholas's belligerence. Not to mention ... Marco glanced at the injured leg. It must be difficult.

Nicholas noticed the direction of his gaze and grimaced. "Lady Trafford has informed me she has found someone to assist me. Something to do with Chinese treatments and massage. She would have visited today, but I sent Lord Trafford a note the day Simon left for Scotland to inform him I could not attest to their safety. We shall have to make new arrangements once this muddle is resolved."

"I am sorry your treatment is delayed. Perhaps, in the meantime, you should speak with Angelo. He might have liniments to ease both stiffness and any pain. He is a gifted pharmacist." Marco rubbed at his bruised ribs. "It was most painful after the carriage overturned, but Angelo has made it tolerable."

His young uncle gave a noncommittal nod, and finishing with Nicholas, Marco continued on down the hall checking rooms, completing the west side before returning to the main staircase to check the front rooms facing the street. Completing the task, he ran down the stairs to return to the breakfast room, where he found Molly and Miss Dubois eating their breakfast.

"I beg your pardon, Miss Dubois." He bowed slightly. "I have news to impart to Molly. Would you mind if she joined me in the hall for a minute?"

The chaperon frowned, then quickly straightened her features as if she recalled herself, unable to refuse the heir to a baron. "*S'il vous plaît*, remain in sight of ze door, Meester Scott, so I may keep watch."

Molly rose and followed him into the hall and, in a low

voice, asked about the butler. Marco noted she did not make eye contact, and folded her arms as if protecting herself from his earlier unsolicited scolding.

"I sent everyone on a search to find him, as well as requested Duncan summon him, but I have not yet heard if he is still in the house."

"Oh. What of the journal?"

"Nicholas is reading it now. He confirms the missing years all appear to be present."

"That is good."

"Molly … I wish to apologize and explain about earlier. Is there any possibility of losing your companion to visit me in the study?"

She shook her head, loosening one of the silky curls that haunted his dreams. "Miss Dubois is quite angry about this morning. She is watching me like a hawk today. See?"

Marco looked back at the breakfast room to find a fierce French poodle observing them closely, her large brown eyes narrowed with unexpressed resentments. Perhaps she was irate to have her breakfast interrupted. The servant seemed quite taken with her meal times, if the drive to Elmstead was anything to go by.

"When can we speak?"

Molly's lashes swept down to fan her cheek, and he wondered if she was thinking of refusing him after his unwarranted rebuke earlier. The fact that he was asking her to break away from the paid companion, after admonishing her for it, had to be grating.

"This afternoon. She will leave me in my bedchamber to read while she sees to my—" Molly colored, and Marco realized she had been about to mention her delicates. Despite his tiredness, the thought sent heat rushing to his groin, and he almost groaned out loud at the thought of Molly undressed in just her underclothes. A thin shift. Stockings. Garters fixed to shapely thighs. "—laundry, so I can meet you in your drawing room."

"That was damaged in the fire," he replied in a hoarse voice, still imagining those garters.

She nibbled on her bottom lip in thought, and Marco beat back the urge to lean in to capture that plump flesh in a kiss. He beat it back as hard as he had beaten at the flaming rug hours earlier. Apparently, his exhaustion had loosened not just his temper, but all of his inhibitions.

"Meet me in the formal drawing room at the top of the stairs. I will be there in about two hours."

"*Grazie*, Molly. I promise to be on my best behavior."

She pulled a slight face at that statement, appearing to be mildly disappointed as she returned to her breakfast, but he did not have time to consider what it meant because the sound of Sebastian approaching from the direction of the servants' staircase had him turning on his heel to learn about MacNaby.

"Did you find him?"

His Nordic friend shook his head. "I am afraid not."

"*Accidenti*! I was worried he might bolt!"

"Duncan informs me he could have stepped out on an errand but was surprised to find the butler's pantry standing open, and there was some disarray. From the looks of it, I think MacNaby may have grabbed some of his things and made a run for it."

"That would make sense."

"I wonder how he knew we had learned of his involvement?" Sebastian was prodding for an explanation, but there was no simple answer to give him. Revealing the journal would lead to more questions.

"We shall need to speak with the baron about hiring someone to search him out, I suppose. I wonder how you go about that in England?"

"I could call on my brother and see if he has resources. He seems familiar with—" Sebastian stopped, clearly at a loss for words to describe the bizarre events he was not privy to. "—whatever is going on here."

"*Sì*! The duke's man who visited me in Florence mentioned runners. Call on His Grace. Perhaps he can help us hunt this MacNaby down, so we might learn what this is all about."

"And what of the servants? Do we tell them anything?"

Marco rubbed his temples, trying to think what was the right thing to do. "I think not. We hope that MacNaby returns because it is possible he is merely running an errand. If we involve too many people, one of the servants might scare him off before we know about it."

"Agreed. Perhaps the duke can provide some insight into what to do because this is beyond my experience, while he has dealt with unusual legal issues on behalf of his wife's brother, from what I understand."

* * *

MOLLY WAS EXPERIENCING a mix of reactions to the morning's events. On the one hand, they now had a suspect. On the other, much to her disappointment, the annoying Miss Dubois was not guilty of attempted murder. How fortuitous it would have been if she could finally have rid herself of the annoying shrew. Alas, the evidence implied Miss Dubois was innocent of heinous crimes.

"Ze servants, zey are slipping without Lady Blackwood to manage ze 'ouse."

While she could agree that the late Lady Blackwood had ruled the house with an iron fist and exacting standards, Molly had found living here more enjoyable since the baroness had removed herself from this mortal coil.

"She was a gracious baronezz, who knew well 'ow a grand 'ouse'old should be kept. If she were 'ere, never would we 'ave such a terrible fire!"

Molly quelled her response, but she could not help thinking what she wanted to say.

But Lady Blackwood, and her ominous plotting, is the reason we had a fire—you horrible, stupid woman!

"Zis shows great *incompétence* from ze servants, all because milady ees not 'ere to keep ze discipline."

In Claudette Dubois's version of events, which Molly could at least confirm was what the servant truly believed, the household had experienced an unexpected accident rather than a deliberate act of sabotage. But, if that was the case, Lady Blackwood had hired the hypothetical incompetent servants, so would not the baroness then be the source of the problem? The poodle's babbling claims were preposterous and illogical.

"What would she say of 'er bedchamber being ruined? All 'er beauteeful things!"

Molly assumed Isla Scott would likely have been quite angry with MacNaby, but mostly because he had failed to murder Marco in his sleep. Truly, if there was anything more telling of the late Isla Scott's character, it was that she had tolerated Miss Dubois's corrosive presence for as long as she had.

Molly checked her timepiece and noted it was close to the time when Miss Dubois was to remove her pesky self. It was best to hold her tongue so she did not delay the departure of her delightful chaperon, because she had a meeting with Marco to look forward to.

Initially, after he had scolded her, she had been quite hurt. But then she had realized how pale and drawn he had appeared. The gentleman was trying to make life-changing decisions about his future while dodging death at every turn.

It was worrisome enough to be living in a home stalked by such mayhem, but she could not conceive what it must be like to know one was the subject of such plots. Molly, fortunately for her, was just a bystander.

"Milady would be gravely disappointed to see what 'as 'appened in 'er absence."

Molly frowned at the intrusive prattling, her irritation rising. If the despicable *milady* was here, after all the evils committed, Molly would be greatly disappointed, too.

But back to her own problems. If she could not make a match with Marco, perhaps she could ask Simon again to join his household next door. It was an imposition, but she would wager that Madeline would agree to find her some sort of position at their stone manufactory.

She might give up her place in polite society, but what place did she lose? That of a gently bred virgin whose days were overshadowed by bitter paid companions? Would she be giving up all that much?

I would not need a chaperon if I were to marry Marco.

She squashed the errant thought. It would not do to get her hopes up. She planned to continue her quest to bring him up to scratch, but she must be willing to live with the fact that she might fail.

"Is it not time to see to my delicates?" It was sheer manipulation to hurry Miss Dubois out, and Molly did not care a whit. She had reached her limit. For now, at least.

Miss Dubois checked her own timepiece and grumbled anew that she had the duties of both paid companion and lady's maid. Molly ignored her because she knew Simon had committed to considerable wages to secure the servant's agreement. Perhaps she should have pressed to join the household next door, but when she had mentioned it, Simon had pointed out she would lose standing in society if she were to live with common tradeswomen. Despite the brilliant success of Madeline's family, Molly was still ranked higher than them, despite her lack of achievements. Or was it precisely because of her lack of achievements?

It was with great relief that she heard the click of the lock when Miss Dubois finally left with a basket of Molly's delicates. Springing to her feet, she ran over to check her appearance in the looking glass, fixing her hair before she hurried out to the hall. Checking about for servants, she raced to descend the stairs to the next floor, and crossed to enter the formal drawing room.

It was intended to impress. This floor had the highest ceilings, with sweeping windows and luxurious drapes dropping from on high. Above her head were painted fascinating frescos that could entertain a lover of art for hours with their magnificent details and historical symbolism. The extensive rug was rich in color and design, and the elegant settees and armchairs beckoned one to settle in and drink an aromatic cup of tea. Large and exquisite masterpieces adorned the walls, but Molly only had eyes for Marco who was looking out one of the windows.

Her heart skipped a beat at how handsome he was in profile. That distinctive Italian nose, that sweeping brow, those sculpted lips. How could she ever hope to attract a man such as him into something as permanent as marriage? Surely such a man could choose any woman he wished?

Fortitude, Molly! You have zero chance of success if you do not even attempt it!

"Marco?"

He turned and smiled. "Molly."

He walked over to join her at the door, reaching out to shut them in.

"I wish to apologize."

"Yes, you mentioned that earlier."

He raked a hand through his hair, and Molly realized he

was nervous. Was that a good or a bad sign? That she made him nervous? She wished she had more experience with courtship so she could decipher the meaning of their interactions. If only Madeline were here to converse with. Perhaps she should write to her friend as she had offered?

"I want to ensure you understand that my … *scormposi?*"

"Discomposure."

He bobbed his head in acknowledgment. "*Sì.* My discomposure is not aimed at you. I have big decisions to make, and I do not want to give you expectations I cannot meet."

"I understand."

"I suppose, given my lamentable behavior, I should at least confess that you are a factor in my process. If I were to choose to remain in England."

It was not clear what he meant—did he consider her one of the advantages of remaining here? That was something, at least!

"That is … encouraging."

"But I do not wish to encourage. It is not my habit to dabble with the feelings of young ladies."

Molly feared it was far too late to shield her from her feelings. They had taken root deeply, growing with alarming speed since the first moment she had caught sight of him. She could scarcely think of anything but him.

Reaching out a hand, she rested it on his lapel as she gazed up at him.

"I understand that you have much to consider about your future, and I will confess that I hope you choose to stay."

His black eyes found hers, and he smiled. "I cannot promise anything, but I can assure you if I were to do so, you would be a prize beyond comparison."

The words burnt a hole through her soul and, for a moment, she envisioned the true possibility of being his wife. What that might entail, what freedoms it would unlock, and the joy of spending time with him unfettered by etiquette.

"I would ask one thing while you make your decision."

"What is that?" His voice had grown husky, and she realized they were now staring deep into each other's eyes.

"I would take at least one more kiss, no matter the path you walk."

His sensual lips spread into a knowing smile. "Would you?"

She nodded, never breaking eye contact as her cheeks warmed, and she wondered if she glowed with radiance or had merely taken on the appearance of a beetroot. But this was not the time for such vain anxieties. She had been thinking of that first kiss and hungered for another.

"I confess I have … had improper thoughts … about you."

Her heart thundered against her ribs as she leaned forward and rose on her toes to press her mouth to his. To her mortification, Marco did not respond, remaining perfectly still. It was not at all like the last time when he had flung her to the ground to save her life!

She dropped back onto her heels in confusion, disappointment sweeping through her like a torrential downpour. "Did I do it wrong?"

He stared at her for several seconds as if he were sorting through his thoughts until, finally, she saw him reach a conclusion.

"*Sì*. Very, very wrong. As a tutor who has helped dozens of students these past years, it is my duty to—how do you say this—demonstrate the correct method?"

He pulled off his glove, using his naked hand to cup her face. Those soulful black eyes stared into hers. The heat reflected in their depths made her melt and throb as the pad of his thumb gently stroked over her cheekbone with maddening patience.

Marco appeared so calm while she felt so wild, fascinated by his presence, his touch, until nothing existed but him and the artistry of his unwavering gaze and the clamoring of her chaotic heart. His head descended and his lips brushed over hers.

All thought was lost as she panted with the intensity of her desires, but he drew back. Then he leaned down and brushed his mouth against hers once more with such aching deliberation, she wished to reach out and grab him. Thankfully, when he brushed against her a third time, he pressed forward to deepen their kiss until she thought she would melt into a quivering pool of liquid on the floor.

Their tongues tangled in aching intimacy while he ran the backs of his fingers down the length of her throat to send a riot of delicious shivers spiraling out … and down. Her heart beat like a wild bird attempting to escape captivity as his lips left hers to follow down her throat and nuzzle at the frantic pulse which revealed her excitement. The dark grain of his shaven whiskers was rough against her soft skin, signaling the contrast between their bodies and drawing a deep sigh from the recesses of her soul.

He slowly drew away, his gaze blazing with languid heat.

"I am afraid I cannot continue."

"Why?" she whispered.

"Because I shall not be able to stop, and all decisions about my future will be taken out of my hands."

She licked her lips, the pressure of his mouth still vivid even as he backed away. Molly pressed her fingers to her flushed cheeks as she tried to collect her wits. "I … should go. Before Miss Dubois returns."

He reached out to open the door, standing aside for her with an expression of regret, and Molly realized what he had said was true. He truly considered her one of the advantages of remaining in England!

As she walked away, she turned this revelation over in her mind to consider it from all angles. And decided she was comforted that, if nothing else, she would always have this moment to hold on to.

The man she was growing to love had been sorely tempted to accept her heart as his. It was better than the alternative—that she had been inconsequential.

CHAPTER 13

"*Some inherit a title, others a vendetta. Both can prove fatal if left unexamined.*"

Impressions of England by an Unrepentant Foreigner

* * *

*M*arco regretted unleashing his base impulses on Molly. All he had achieved was to make them each yearn for something he could not commit to. But she had been so damned tempting. And perhaps he had owed her a kiss without apologies after ruining her first the way he had.

He should be recognized for having the strength to stop at all. When she had told him she had improper thoughts— there were no more erotic words in the English language than to have a well-bred young lady such as Molly reveal such a thing. The only thing that could make it more erotic was if she had detailed the thoughts she had had.

Maledizione! I cannot think about that!

There was a man trying to kill him, whom they could not find. It was time to run this MacNaby to ground!

"I searched the attic level again, after Angelo, and found a maid or two up there for my troubles. No signs of this scoundrel," Lorenzo stated, his irritation palpable.

"And I searched the basement, and this floor," Angelo added.

"The grooms in the mews told me they had not seen him today at all," Marco reported in a gloomy voice.

He, his brother, and Lorenzo had returned from their second search of the house and grounds, but it appeared that MacNaby was not merely out on an errand. A missive from Sebastian had arrived to inform them that the duke had sent for runners, and they should expect them to arrive shortly and begin their own search for the missing butler whom no one had seen for three hours or more.

"Mr. Scott?" He looked up from the seat he had taken in the library to find Duncan. "His lordship has asked that you and your brother join him in the study."

Marco nodded, getting to his feet. He should report to his uncle that the runners would be arriving, so it was an excellent time to talk. Truthfully, after searching the house, there was nothing more to be done for now. Marco did not know England, so it would be useless to try searching the neighborhood. Best that task was undertaken far more efficiently by the runners who would arrive at any minute.

He headed to the study down the hall, Angelo joining him.

"Do you think there is news?"

Marco shrugged as they reached the baron's door and knocked.

A voice invited them in, and when they entered, Marco found Nicholas sprawled in an armchair with the ottoman propping up his leg. Molly was seated in the corner, and

Miss Dubois was installed outside the window in a bitter stance. At least on this occasion, he knew the cause of the servant's brooding. He had been hit with a sharp, chilly breeze when he searched the grounds. The late November weather was uncomfortable, but he could not help feeling the chaperon deserved it for how she annoyed Molly so.

"Please, Marco, close the door. Nicholas has news, and we shall have to keep our voices low. Miss Dubois is an infamous gossip, and we cannot allow her to overhear anything we say."

The reminder was appreciated, even if they had been making a habit of these meetings with the petite watchdog glaring at the window.

Angelo and he took their seats and looked to Nicholas expectantly.

Their young uncle sighed with disgust. "I can confirm that the butler is our man."

"You believe we do not need to search any further for more accomplices? The baroness could have hired more than one," Marco rejoined.

"MacNaby was not hired. My mother may have left him with some coin to complete her foul crusade, but his motive is not money."

The baron leaned back in his swivel chair. "More's the pity. Unfortunately, MacNaby is a true fanatic with personal reasons to seek Marco's death. And Angelo's. I think I have been spared his wrath because of my poor health."

"Wrath?" Angelo's brows had shot up to almost his hairline, his low voice flabbergasted. "What have we done to invoke his wrath?"

Nicholas scowled. "Perhaps wrath is not the correct word, John. I would say it is his … ambition."

The choice of words startled Marco, leaning forward to urge Nicholas along. "The journal from thirty years ago somehow reveals—" He stopped, cocking his head in confusion. "—ambition as a reason to pursue multiple murder attempts?"

"It is complicated, but let me begin with the short answer to illuminate the matter—MacNaby might be Simon's father."

Silence fell. Even Nicholas, who had proclaimed the news, seemed rather bemused to state it, as the repercussions of the statement trickled into their minds. In his peripheral vision, Marco saw Molly fold her arms as if defending against the news.

"That would explain his willingness to enact Lady Blackwood's revenge," she finally squeaked into the prolonged quiet.

Nicholas remained silent, as if to allow them all the time to absorb the revelation. After another minute or two, John encouraged him to continue.

"Walter MacNaby joined the household of Lord Campbell in Edinburgh when my mother was a girl. Shortly after, when the marriage contract had been signed for her to marry my father, Lord Campbell died suddenly. My mother inherited the title and the entailed properties when she was just seventeen. Which was when she took it into her head that if she had a son, that son would one day ascend to the rank of baron, but only if she could clear the way to make that happen because the late Lord Blackwood already had two heirs in place."

"No disrespect intended, but … she was cracked in the head even then?" Molly questioned.

Nicholas nodded. "And just as manipulative. She decided she would need someone belowstairs in her new London household to carry out her will, and she wished MacNaby to accompany her as part of the retinue of servants she would bring. He, however, wished to remain in Scotland, so she …"

He was pale, drumming his fingertips on the journal he had just read with a haggard expression. "Perhaps Molly should not be here."

She jumped to her feet, bristling with alarm. "No!" Then, casting a glance out the window at Miss Dubois, she lowered her voice and sat back down. "This affects me as well. I have a right to know the truth. Do not attempt to treat me as some mere shrinking violet just because something in that journal is improper!"

"I agree. Molly can hold her own. She proved her mettle when she took care of me after my collapse. I do not think it would be right to exclude her." The baron's show of support placated her, and Molly settled back into her chair with an expression of relief.

Nicholas soughed. "Even I cannot process what I had to read, but so be it. My mother went to lengthy measures to seduce MacNaby into joining her. They had a brief but torrid affair in the months before and after her wedding. Simon was born within the first nine months of her arrival in London."

Silence fell again, until at last, a soft, feminine "ick" broke the tension, prompting Marco to huff out a humorless half-chuckle.

"Ick, indeed," agreed Nicholas.

"What of you?" Angelo asked. "Are you … the son of Lord Blackwood or …"

"Reading these journals has revealed that my mother had a habit of singling out male servants whom she recognized she could manipulate. It is not impossible that I am a result of one of those manipulations. She was obsessed with her mission, and the excessive quantities of laudanum she partook in did not help clear her thoughts. Some of her entries are pure rambling."

"I am sorry," Angelo replied.

Listening with disgust, Marco felt he had re-entered the circles of hell. Before he could stop himself, the words left his lips. "Will these sordid English intrigues never end?"

Molly turned to him, her lips parted in surprise at his vehemence. "I assure you that these sordid English intrigues are isolated to Lady Blackwood alone. No one in this room played any role in this."

Marco shook his head, still seething. "And yet, for some obscene fling from three decades past, a man has tried to kill me not once, but three times! I should never have come! It feels as though the devil himself beckons me to my death over events that predate my very birth!"

Molly flinched ever so slightly, refraining from responding as her face settled into desolate lines. Marco realized he had wounded her with his words, yet his frustration continued to simmer. "I apologize, Molly. That was not directed at you. I am simply not accustomed to hearing of such despicable behavior."

She nodded, but her shoulders remained a little slumped. What had he said to produce that reaction? She had the glum appearance of someone who had received terrible news, when all he had done was allow some of his outrage to escape.

Angelo glanced at her, too, a question in his eyes, but he apparently decided to ease the tensions with a shift in subject. "Nicholas, I wish to acknowledge your fortitude in reading your mother's journals. It must have been difficult, and I am not sure I could have done so if I were placed in a similar position."

Nicholas shrugged, his lean face exhibiting his usual belligerence. "It was the right thing to do. Simon wished to keep the less relevant contents private out of respect."

"Nevertheless, it took fortitude. Thank you for shedding light on the past few days."

"I am yet curious," interjected the baron. "What exactly is MacNaby up to?"

Nicholas straightened, lowering his feet to the floor. "I believe he helped her all these years. She would have needed him to intercept the mail from your late father. From what I can tell, my mother sold MacNaby the same dream she once pursued for herself—convinced him that his legacy could be a son raised to the rank of baron. At least according to these entries, where she describes using a combination of guilt over their affair and pride in Simon, whom he believes to be his son, becoming someone of high standing."

John frowned, shifting in his chair as if to ease some discomfort. "Is it not enough that he is a viscount?"

Nicholas shook his head, leaning forward with his elbows on his knees. "She speaks of the truly great houses as English. She claims that until she married the baron, she was an inferior peeress from Scotland, but the wedding elevated her status. She was welcomed into important homes, even enjoying state dinners and important events with the King in attendance. Rank was her obsession, and I believe she convinced MacNaby that his son could one day rub shoulders with royalty."

"Do we believe he will continue the quest to kill Marco?"

"I cannot say. I suppose it depends on how committed he is."

* * *

MOLLY FELT the need for privacy after the meeting. Witnessing Marco's angry disgust over what Isla Scott had done, she had realized that convincing him to remain in England was a lost cause.

She was going to lose the man she thought she might very well love because of the dead Lady Blackwood, and it was not fair. How was she going to be enough to make up for his terrible experiences since his arrival? Three murder attempts? Dreadful family secrets about people he had never met which had made him a target of such plots? If she were in his position, she would choose to return to Italy, too.

Marco was repelled by what had happened here in this beautiful but terrible home. By what was happening even now.

He had said as much.

"I should never have come!"

As soon as she had heard the words, the ground had disappeared from beneath her feet.

Was their unprecedented connection to be another casualty of the venomous Lady Blackwood's schemes?

Meeting Miss Dubois out in the hall after leaving the gathering in the study, Molly found her spirits as low as they had ever been. As low as the day her mother died months earlier. When Mama had died, Molly had lost her entire life. All familiar people and places had been left behind to join the baron's household. Now she was losing the only hope of building her own future. Lady Blackwood might be dead, but her legacy of destruction lived on.

What would it have been like if she had met Marco without the specter of danger and discreditable secrets to ruin their introduction? How was she to tempt him into staying when there were such excellent reasons for him to return home?

"Lady Blackwood, she never made me sit out in the cold. It is ... 'ow you say ... freezing. I miss her so much, I do."

Molly ignored Miss Dubois, requesting her coat and bonnet from Duncan, who was on duty in the front hall.

"What would she say about so many unwed men in residence? *C'est impropre!* It is scandalous, no?"

She had heard quite enough about the paragon of vice,

Lady Blackwood. She needed some time alone to collect herself.

Duncan assisted her into her coat, then she put on her bonnet and tied the ribbons.

"Where are we going? *Mon Dieu*, it ees so very cold! Surely, you do not truly wish to go outside?"

Molly did not reply, making her way toward the back door and wishing that Madeline was still here to talk to. She had not realized how much she had begun to rely on her friend's presence, but she was feeling her absence now. Perhaps she should write to Madeline and ask about joining her household. Perhaps she could move in before Madeline and Simon even returned from Scotland. Then she would have a distraction while she tried to pick up the pieces of her broken heart when Marco eventually announced his departure.

Reaching the exit, she turned with a gasp of dismay. She hoped the ploy might work one more time, because she needed the poodle to leave her to her thoughts.

Miss Dubois frowned, before relaxing her face to prevent wrinkles, as Lady Blackwood had advised. The French pest truly had idolized the late baroness. "What ees it, zen?"

"My gloves! I quite forgot them!" She was not sure it would work a second time, but she did not think Miss Dubois was clever, so it was worth a try.

"You must wait 'ere, yes?"

"Of course! It is far too cold to leave the house without them."

Molly watched the servant hurry away. As soon as Miss Dubois turned the corner, Molly swung the door open and strode away. There was only one place to find peace, and Miss Dubois was not the companion to take with her. She lengthened her stride, so she may extend her time alone as long as she could.

Entering the walled garden where she and Madeline had shared tea and conversation, Molly dropped onto the bench under the magnificent urn, closed her eyes, and leaned back to think, tucking her chilly fingers beneath her thighs to protect them from the cold. It was not like her to be pessimistic, but something about Marco's tone had told her he was reaching his decision and it was not the one she had hoped for.

While she attempted to regain her equilibrium, a crunch of gravel had her sighing in despair. She had thought she would have at least a few minutes before Miss Dubois caught up with her.

She slowly opened her eyes and yelped in surprise.

MacNaby stood facing her with a flintlock pistol pointed to her chest.

And there was madness glinting in the blue depths of his eyes.

"Miss Carter, I believe I have you to thank for my worsened circumstances," he fumed, his Scottish brogue more pronounced than usual.

"I … that is …"

"You searched through my things and removed a personal item. A gift that was not yours to take."

Molly frowned, a little confused that he called it a gift. Had Nicholas not said it revealed the details of Lady Blackwood's seduction and manipulation of MacNaby? "Did you read it?"

"That is none of your business."

She thought that probably meant no. Several questions flashed through her mind, but she deemed it poor timing to raise them as she tried to think of what to do about the angry would-be killer threatening her.

"What … are you doing here?"

MacNaby raised his free hand to swipe at his forehead

with a handkerchief, evidence of his nerves. "I am here to finish my ... work."

"Oh."

"But now that you are here, I am thinking it would be better to lure Mr. Scott out than to enter the house."

"What do you mean?"

"Stand up, Miss Carter. We have a journey to take."

Molly complied, and MacNaby gestured her along. She tried walking slowly in the hopes Miss Dubois might arrive, but he grabbed her by the arm and hurried her through the back garden gateway. Leading her to a narrow corridor that ran alongside the mews, he used his free hand to remove a key from his pocket and unlock a recessed door to the alley.

Molly realized she was being removed from the property, but she was not sure what to do about it and, for the very first time, she longed to hear the poodle approaching—but she had thwarted her own safety by tricking Miss Dubois to go away.

Once in the alley, he tugged her along and Molly peered about, looking for an opportunity to escape, but they were surrounded by high walls and no one was in sight. Not to mention, he still had the pistol trained on her with his finger resting near the trigger. If she tried to run, he might panic and shoot her.

They entered a street where she saw a small cart tethered with a single horse, and finally noticed he was dressed as a workman in a large overcoat with his hat pulled low. He must have rented the wagon with the coin that Nicholas had mentioned had been given to him by Lady Blackwood to fulfill her quest.

Molly was in trouble, fear eroding her composure. MacNaby was going to make her vanish without a trace. She could only hope that Miss Dubois would sound the alarm, but that might take some time, because her chaperon would believe she had merely run off to escape her company.

Molly hesitated, but felt the stock of the pistol jammed against her ribs.

"Do not think about causing any trouble."

"No trouble, Mr. MacNaby. Would you like me to drive the wagon for you?"

The butler's brows arched, taken aback by her offer. But Molly had decided her wits were her one defense against the man. Offering to take the reins might help coax him out of his agitated state. If she could calm him while reminding him that she was a real person with hopes and dreams, perhaps she might be able to reason with him.

Would Lady Blackwood's vile corruption of his mind relent in the face of persuasive logic?

"So you can hold your pistol steady. We do not want it to accidentally fire, do we?"

CHAPTER 14

"In every heart lies a reckoning—whether born of love, fear, or vengeance. Only the brave dare meet it head-on."

Impressions of England by an Unrepentant Foreigner

* * *

*S*itting this close to the butler, Molly had discovered that he smelled of silver polish, cedar wood, and starch. Not wholly unexpected, given his profession. She could also smell the sweat of fear seeping from his pores, and now that he had her away from the townhouse, he appeared to be dithering about what to do as she drove the wagon down a street for a couple of blocks. He swung his gaze back and forth as if he were trying to determine a direction. Likely, he did not know where to take her now that he had her.

It would work against her if he grew nervous. If he grew fearful or unsure of himself, he might decide to tie her up. She glanced down at the pistol in his grasp.

Or worse.

Molly tried to think what to do—the man was susceptible to manipulation, according to the secrets they had unraveled. She should continue to cultivate *camaraderie* with him, she concluded.

"Where are we going, Mr. MacNaby? To the Elmstead manor because it is locked up for the winter?"

He stiffened at her suggestion, but she saw him pause to contemplate it. "Yes … We are heading to Elmstead."

His demeanor improved as he directed her to turn in to the next street. Molly blew a subtle sigh of relief. They were headed to familiar ground, rather than disappearing her into the boroughs of London where MacNaby might not be the worst peril she faced. Trying to run off from him in a seedy neighborhood could result in a worsening of her current circumstances, but at Elmstead, she would have a single person holding her captive. The drive, with the wagon and just the one horse to pull them, would take a minimum of three hours. Three hours that she was out in the open, with a destination she knew how to navigate. MacNaby might have been easy to convince because he knew the lay of the manor, but so did she. Maybe not as well as him, but Elmstead boasted displays of old swords and rifles in the halls. Or she might find an opportunity to lock herself in a room or closet to await a rescue.

They left the structures of London behind, the rhythmic clopping of shod hooves on packed earth marking their passage between tall hedgerows. MacNaby, ever the resourceful senior servant, had secured a Shire—a large, powerful draught horse well suited to pulling substantial weights over long distances. By her estimation, the horse stood a full eighteen hands high—a bay with a striking white feathering of silky hair around its fetlocks that added to its handsome appearance.

The gentle giant pulled them along placidly, and Molly found the steady drive a balm to the initial panic that had coursed through her. It gave her time to think. To plot.

"Are you doing … this … to ensure Simon inherits the title?" Her question broke their long silence, and MacNaby started from his introverted bemusements.

"It is none of your business, Miss Carter." His growl was guttural with menace, the pistol pointed straight at her heart.

Molly's thoughts raced as she tried to think what she might talk about to establish a rapport. Surely, if they were friendly, it would be more difficult for him to do anything dastardly?

Finally, she nodded. "I agree. However, you have taken me hostage and you have a pistol pointed at me in a most threatening manner. I would propose that it may have become my business?"

MacNaby frowned, peering down at the pistol as if he were surprised to see it. "The pistol is the reason you should hold your tongue!"

Despite his barking, Molly was not entirely convinced he was committed to his task. She had interacted with MacNaby daily since joining the Scott household, and he did not strike her as an evil man. Lady Blackwood had been an enigma, and as it turned out, her veneer of perfection had hidden a corrupted soul. But MacNaby? She was sure she could reason with the butler.

She nodded again, her eyes on the road ahead of them. "I can do that but … It is just … Simon seems so happy since his nuptials. He has married his childhood love, visited his estates in Scotland. He even bought shares in the stone manufactory. It is the happiest I have seen him since I joined the household."

MacNaby straightened, scowling at her fiercely. "Shut it!"

Molly's heart skipped a beat as he swung the pistol in her

direction with deliberation, and she swallowed hard as she tried to calculate whether it was worth the risk to continue talking.

They fell back into a silence, broken by the creak of the wagon and the metallic clank of the wheels, which mingled with the rustling of cold wind through the hedgerow leaves. Molly tried to warm her bare hands with a quick rub, all the while keeping the reins steady.

The winter chill crept from her fingers to her wrists, numbing her limbs, and her coat proved woefully inadequate against the prolonged exposure. Yet it was the thought of dying without ever having truly lived that sent the deepest chill through her veins.

* * *

MARCO HAD JUST FINISHED MEETING with the duke's runner, Briggs, who had written notes in a small notebook. Marco and Nicholas had discussed what they could and could not reveal to the man, and he felt considerably better that Briggs had assured him that several runners would begin the search for MacNaby. He might be missing from their household, but it did not mean the butler would not sneak back in and attempt to kill him in his sleep again.

Several hours had passed since the family meeting, and there had been no word of MacNaby's whereabouts yet. Rising from the baron's desk, and without anything to occupy his time, Marco decided that perhaps he should find Molly to learn what he had said to upset her so. Striding across to the door, he swung it open and bumped into a soft body, which emitted a low shriek in a French accent. He dropped his gaze to find the tiny chaperon, shivering and clasping herself in protection as if Marco was attempting to whip her.

"Miss Dubois? My apologies! Are you well?"

The servant glowered at him, but then her sharp little chin quivered fiercely, and she unexpectedly burst into tears. Marco blinked in alarm, not sure what to do.

"I am so sorry, Miss Dubois! I did not mean to hurt you. Should I summon a doctor?"

"*Non* … it ees not zat, *Monsieur* Scott … I must tell you … somezing."

Marco exhaled in a puff, relieved to hear that he had not inadvertently injured the companion.

"Please, come in and have a seat. I shall request some tea to calm your nerves."

Miss Dubois nodded, brushing past him to sink into an armchair at the window where she covered her face and sobbed quietly. His brow furrowed in consternation. Perhaps Miss Dubois and Molly's tense relationship had descended even further. Was she here to tender her resignation?

Marco walked over to ring the bell, then pulling out a handkerchief, he crossed to the sobbing servant to thrust it in her hand. She took it, wiping at her face, but her misery did not diminish. He looked about, trying to think what to do and feeling torn. He did not care for the shrewish companion, sympathizing with Molly for the position she was in because of his and his companions' presence in the household, but a crying woman must be dealt with gently.

"Miss Dubois, please, I will assist you. What is it?"

"I do not know 'oo to speak to … I thought perhaps you should know … Duncan said you 'ad met with a runner, so I thought …" Her words were garbled as she cried into his pristine linen square.

"Runner?" Marco echoed in perplexment.

"It ees Miss Carter. I cannot find 'er anywhere."

Marco suppressed a smile. Her mistress had managed to escape again. Her weeping seemed a bit of an overreaction, but the Frenchwoman had not impressed him with her composure before, so it did not seem all that surprising.

"Come, Miss Dubois, there is no reason to cry. I shall help you look for her, then."

The chaperon shook her head. "*Non*, I 'ave searched for 'er. For hours! She ees simply not 'ere. I think you must call the runner back, no?"

He frowned, walking over to take a seat. "How long has she been missing?"

"Since your meeting zis morning, yes?"

Marco tensed. Confusion and fear were just two of the emotions that surged through his body.

"That was some hours ago."

"*Oui.*" Her voice was muffled and lashes flickered up as if to assess how irate he might be. Anger started to prickle as comprehension trickled in, and Marco realized what the tears had been about. Miss Dubois was not crying out of concern for Molly, but rather she was afraid of how it affected her position. It would appear the diminutive chaperon might harbor some anxieties about finding a new position in the wake of Lady Blackwood's death, and had delayed informing him of Molly's disappearance in the hopes she would reappear without the necessity of taking responsibility. He had been right—she was a dreadful companion!

"*Maledizione!*" He sprang to his feet. What if the butler had somehow got hold of her? Molly could be lying dead somewhere. Had MacNaby concluded Molly had taken Lady Blackwood's journal? Would he attempt to get it back from her or harm her out of vengeful wrath? Marco should have taken steps to protect her, but they had believed that it was he, Angelo, and the baron who were at risk. "Where did you last see her?"

Miss Dubois flinched at his curse, but he did not have the patience to deal with her.

"I went to fetch 'er gloves, so she might visit ze garden."

Without an acknowledgment, he ran from the study. They needed to mount a search immediately. Duncan approached down the hall, en route to answer his earlier summons with the bell, and Marco quickly dispatched the head footman to gather the other servants to search for Molly.

Then, striding into the library, Marco found Angelo reading a book and sipping a cup of coffee, the aroma rich in the cold air. To Marco's nose, Angelo must have brought some coffee with him from Florence.

"Molly is missing."

Angelo snapped his book shut, getting to his feet. "What is this?"

"Miss Dubois lost track of her after our meeting this morning, and has not seen her since."

"Then we must search for her."

"I have sent Duncan to gather the servants. They will search the house, but Miss Dubois informs me that Molly was on her way to the garden when she last saw her."

"Do you think MacNaby might have returned?"

"Molly only disappears from Miss Dubois for short periods."

Angelo arched an eyebrow, his curiosity evident about how Marco was aware of Molly's habits, but he did not comment as they headed out through the terrace doors into the cold without their overcoats. Marco was not quite ready to discuss his numerous clandestine encounters with the young lady, which would reveal too much. Angelo would know this was unusual behavior for his older brother.

They searched through the gardens but found no sign of Molly until Marco entered the walled garden and saw that a small square of lacy linen had been dropped beneath the stone bench. Hurrying over, he knelt down to get it. It was embroidered with M and C, and his blood ran cold as he realized Molly might have left it here as a signal.

Running from the walled enclosure, he entered the mews to question the grooms, where he learned that MacNaby had keys to a recessed entrance where he sometimes let merchants in who were delivering through the alleyway.

He rushed out into the alley and looked about, but there was no sign of anyone. Running down to the end, he checked the street to no avail, then backtracked to check the street on the other end of the block. His intuition told him they were gone. He would need to summon the runner back.

Hurrying back into the gardens, he hollered for his brother until he appeared around the side of the house.

"Any sign of her?"

Angelo shook his head.

"I think MacNaby took her." Marco held up the lacy handkerchief to display the initials, and Angelo rubbed his face in distress.

Guilt racked Marco as he blurted out, "We should have informed the servants!"

"It would not have helped if he took her from here. It does not appear he entered the house."

"This is my fault."

"That is a leap, brother. MacNaby is trying to kill you, not her. There was no reason to suspect he would take Molly."

His brother's assurance did not help. All he could think about was his vision of Molly in hell, with her face covered in soot and her hair burning with molten lava. How disturbing it had been to witness her suffering in the world of dreams, only to wake to this living nightmare where she could be killed by a madman in search of revenge.

If she was harmed, it would break him in two, and he realized that despite his best efforts, Molly Carter had found her way into the very heart of him. Her forthright nature, her sensual form, her courage living in a household beset by such devious curses! It was more than he could bear, to think of something happening to her.

They returned inside, and Angelo sent a footman with a note to find the runner because Marco's hands were shaking, unable to hold the quill steady to write the note himself.

"How has he grown so bold? To kidnap a woman?"

"Bold, indeed. Also rather stupid, I think."

"What do I do? She must be terrified!"

Angelo bobbed his head back and forth with skepticism to this statement. "Fearful, perhaps, but Molly has fortitude. Perhaps I should find Lorenzo and Sebastian? We need to formulate a plan to rescue her."

A knock on the library door drew their gazes sharply toward Duncan, who stood holding a letter with an apologetic expression on his broad face. "Sir, an express rider from Edgware delivered this," he announced. "It is from Mr. MacNaby."

"Edgware?"

"It is a small village in Middlesex, sir, a few miles from here. It lies on the route to Elmstead. You would have passed it on your visit, if I may say so."

Marco grabbed the letter. Confirming that MacNaby had sent it, he dismissed Duncan and closed the door. Quickly unfolding it to read the contents, his heart skipped a beat. It was true. The butler had taken Molly hostage.

"What does it say?"

"He has taken Molly to Elmstead. By now, they must have reached the manor. He wants me to meet him there without accompaniment."

"That is rather melodramatic. Does he plan to kill you, then come and murder the baron and I one at a time? How can he know you will arrive on your own?"

"It says if he sees anyone else, he will put a musket ball through her head."

Angelo threw his hands up in the air. "This is a half-hearted plan at best. He does not seem as committed as he should be, but I shall find Sebastian and Lorenzo, so we can leave for Elmstead. You summon the carriage and a spare horse to approach the manor *without companions* once we reach there." The last was said with heavy sarcasm.

"Damn it, Angelo! We must take this seriously! Molly's life is in danger."

"I know, brother, but the four of us will execute a rescue."

Marco hesitated, then relented. He was more certain of recovering Molly with help, despite the dire warnings in the letter. "Call the others."

While awaiting Angelo's return, Marco went upstairs to briefly inform the baron about what was happening. He could only hope his uncle's resulting distress would not harm his vulnerable health. Marco then went to the entry hall and lifted one of the ceremonial daggers from the display on the wall. Testing the edge for sharpness, he gathered up several more and returned to the study. He hunted through the shelves until he located a walnut box. Inside lay a single dueling pistol with a flintlock, along with a few musket balls. The second pistol was missing from its indented space, and a chill ran through him as he realized MacNaby would have had access to the missing weapon.

This was how the butler must have coerced Molly into leaving with him. How long had the servant had the pistol in his possession? Had he tired of making his attempts to murder look like accidents and decided to go a more direct route? MacNaby would have had to have taken it even before Molly had uncovered his corruption.

Soon the four of them waited out in the entry hall for the carriage to be brought around, Marco bouncing on his toes with impatience while Lorenzo distributed the daggers Marco had gathered up.

"I think we should take the rifles, too."

"I could not find any gunpowder. They are useless," replied Marco.

"Yet a Brown Bessie can be used as an effective club," commented Sebastian.

"Then take one."

Lorenzo and the Norseman nodded, grins spreading across their faces as they each took up a rifle from the display—a circle of firearms radiating outward from a central point on the wall.

Marco pondered their difference in moods. They seemed almost excited to hunt MacNaby to the ground, while he could not stop thinking about what would happen if he failed her. A world without Molly Carter was … inconceivable.

"You hold her in more esteem than I realized." Angelo spoke from behind his shoulder, Marco watching the street to see the second the carriage approached.

"I do not desire it—to hold someone in such high regard, knowing the frailty of life. It is … dangerous to one's state of mind."

"Molly is not frail."

"We are all frail."

"That is rather … *pessimista?*"

"I think … Pessimistic. And it is my experience."

"You mean because of what happened with …" Angelo paused, as if searching the depths of his memories. "Miss Dashwood?"

"*Sì.* And our father."

"Marco, I am disappointed by your cowardice."

Marco frowned, spinning on his heel to glare at his brother. "Cowardice?"

"Chi non intraprese mai nulla non realizzò mai nulla."

"He who never undertook anything, never achieved anything?"

"Sì. You cannot compare Miss Dashwood to Molly. Molly is strong. Unafraid."

Sebastian chimed in. "Miss Carter? That young lady has gumption. She will be alive and well when we get there—I am sure of it."

The sound of the carriage approaching had Marco turning back to the window, ripping the door open to hurry outside as fear for Molly's safety continued to make his heart pound against his bruised ribs with an unrelenting vengeance. His woman needed him.

"I hope so. MacNaby is a lunatic."

CHAPTER 15

"It is a bitter fate when a man discovers too late that love is his strongest armor—and his deepest wound."

Impressions of England by an Unrepentant Foreigner

* * *

*C*reeping dread was making her hands and feet both numb and tingly as the wagon passed through the gates of Elmstead. Her earlier fears had been realized. Just outside of Edgware, MacNaby had directed her to bring their vehicle to a stop within a copse of trees, and ordered her to remove her stockings.

That in itself had caused a surge of panic, but it had turned out he had merely wanted them to tie her wrists and ankles so he could send a message back to London. She had lain in the bed the empty wagon, a tarp beneath her shivering body, and stared up at the sky without seeing a thing. Lost in her thoughts, she had begun to contemplate the worst outcomes.

She could be killed!

Her breast heaved as if she had lost her breath, thinking what it would feel like to have a musket ball pierce her chest or head. Would she die immediately or slowly in abject pain?

After about five minutes of panic, she had realized there was an alternative outcome. What if she survived unscathed, but Marco was killed in her stead?

Despite her will to remain composed, tears had eked out the corners of her eyes to run down her cheeks, the icy weather affixing them painfully to her skin rubbed raw by the incessant and brisk breeze.

How would she live with herself if she were the cause of his death?

Why had she sent Claudette Dubois away?

Did she wish for Marco to arrive to rescue her, or would she rather he remained safely in London to leave her to her fate?

Sheer relief had made her head giddy when MacNaby had returned to untie her and instructed her to drive them to Elmstead. At least she had some measure of control back with the freedom of her limbs restored.

As they drove between the archway of elms, Molly licked her lips and regretted it when the cold wind gusted against the moistness. Teeth chattering, her legs bared against the elements that swept up under the skirts of her gown, she tried to think what to do.

Considering the possibility of Marco's arrival to rescue her made her fairly lose her mind at the thought of him lying dead on the floor while she sobbed and lamented her role in his demise. The thought of his handsome face wreathed in the pallor of the eternal mists, innocent of any wrongdoing other than a happenstance of birth, was nauseating.

She supposed, as a member of the weaker sex, she should accept her role in this terrible comedy of a tragedy. But she could not bring herself to act the damsel in distress. She would have to risk the ire of her captor because failing to act, failing to prevent Marco from being harmed because of the deluded phantasies of a dead woman, was too awful to consider.

She would have to risk debating with the butler. If the words of great orators could echo through the millennia, surely she could convince one misguided man to abandon his murderous quest—especially when the originator of that quest was no longer in this world to urge him on.

If she failed, if he hurt or killed her, she would enter through the gates of midnight with her honor yet intact.

Molly brought the wagon to a halt in front of the manor, which loomed eerily in the silence, framed by the iron gray of twilight. It had seemed so inviting on their last visit, but now, under these grim circumstances, it leered with a menacing air in the half light, its darkened windows like the gap-toothed smile of a cackling hag.

There was a caretaker when the manor was closed up, but it was an old man who could not help her, even if he was somewhere inside. Molly could count on no one other than herself.

Fortifying her courage, she inhaled deeply to steel her nerves. "You have hurt no one yet, Mr. MacNaby. It is not too late to repudiate Lady Blackwood's request."

The butler growled in outrage, turning an angry face to glare at her with madness lurking in his eyes. "You know nothing of what you speak! If you do not shut it, Miss Carter, I shall tie you up and gag you to force some quiet!"

* * *

WAS THERE a special place reserved in hell for him? He who had allowed the vibrant Molly to be left defenseless? Would his departed father be disappointed in him to learn of his failure if he were to visit from the afterlife?

A lurch of the carriage brought Marco back to the moment as he stared out at the gathering darkness, and he slipped his fingers into his pocket to caress the gold watch. His thoughts returned to how his father had been disowned by his grandfather because of his father's desire to wed his mother. How Peter Scott had left everything he knew—everyone he knew—to return to Italy with *Mamma*. How he had married her, given up his life in England, to do right by her. In comparison, Marco had weakly vacillated between returning to Florence and committing to the Blackwood title. His final conversation with Molly in the formal drawing room had been to inform her that she should not get her hopes up.

Now she was a hostage at Elmstead. She might die at the hands of a madman, a madman who had taken her as bait for Marco, and she would believe she died in place of a man who had not held her in sufficient esteem to make her his wife.

The very concept made his gut coil and writhe in protest, but what did his regrets matter when it was Molly whose life was in the balance? He would pass forever into Dante's City of Woe if he were to fail her now.

Was she terrified? Did she know he would come for her? Did she blame him for putting her in harm's way? These were all questions that plagued because he had too much time to think, and they could do nothing effective until they reached the manor.

"*Molly ha grande coraggio.*" Angelo's voice interrupted his spiraling thoughts.

Marco scowled, barking back before he could stop himself, "She should not require great courage. She plays no part in this."

"*Starà bene quando la raggiungeremo.*"

"Dear Lord, I hope so! If she is harmed because of me—" Marco stopped, too overcome by rage and fear to complete the sentence.

Sebastian stirred from his bench, moving his gaze from the window to regard Marco with sympathetic gray eyes. "It is not your fault, my friend." Then he frowned. "At least—I do not think it is your fault? I confess I have a thin understanding of what is happening here."

Lorenzo snorted, muttering a curse beneath his breath. "I have no understanding what is happening here." He glanced at Marco. "But if you need us to fend off a maniacal butler, we are here for you."

Marco nodded in appreciation. He might yet be a stranger to England, but it had been a wise choice to travel with family and friends at his side. Even if he succeeded in distracting MacNaby, he might not be able to save Molly in the aftermath. It was going to take working together to secure her safety.

They lapsed back into silence, the night arriving so that all he could see were the hedgerows racing by in the glow of the carriage lamps, and he could not help but feel he was Dante entering hell itself. He half expected to pass through its gates, to read the inscription, "Abandon all hope, ye who enter here."

The sound of the carriage wheels rumbling through the night was loud in his ears, or else he was certain he would have heard the laments and wails of fellow tortured souls who had neglected their duty. He had allowed a woman as compassionate as Molly, a woman full of life, to be caught by a criminal. Even if they succeeded, what if MacNaby had hurt her? Or— His stomach lurched, and he closed his thoughts off from considering her innocence removed without the presence of love. He had already entered hell. There was no reason to descend further into its fiery pits.

Fortunately, the carriage drew to a halt, and Duncan appeared at the window to open the door and lower the steps.

"We are close, sir. The lane to the manor is beyond this copse of trees."

Marco nodded, descending to walk down the road and peer in the direction they were traveling to. It took a few seconds for his eyes to accustom to the full dark of night, but eventually he could make out the outline of the archway of elms on the horizon against the star-studded firmament with only the moon to mark the difference between the earth and the heavens with its silvery light.

The rustling of the wind through the trees, and the hoot of an owl hunting, were the only sounds in the great, empty darkness.

Angelo came to stand by his side.

"The dark will hide our approach."

Sebastian arrived, gazing in the same direction. "It is a good night to catch a scoundrel."

Lorenzo joined them last. "A thorough thrashing is in order."

Marco again reminded himself of his good fortune that he had comrades with him, even if he were a stranger to this island realm. "England is turning out to be rather unpleasant," he finally commented.

Angelo cocked his head. "I would propose we are on a fine adventure with a beautiful woman awaiting rescue and fine friends at our side. It might not be the day you wished for, but it is the day the fates have bestowed on you, and a life of no risk is a life not worth living, perhaps?"

Lorenzo nodded in agreement. "No truer word has been said. I do not know this Miss Carter well, but I think a magnificent prize awaits you at the end of your quest."

"If I survive the quest," muttered Marco. "Angelo, I need

you to promise me if I am … unable … to assist Molly myself that you shall see to her well-being?"

Angelo paused, and Marco turned to find his brother in deep thought. "I shall go in your stead! If I wear an overcoat and hat, I can approach the house as you. MacNaby will not be able to tell the difference."

"No. This is my responsibility."

"But you are the heir. And Molly and you deserve to walk the future together."

"And if I lose both you and her tonight? How shall I live with myself? No, this is my task to undertake."

"But … what if he simply shoots you the moment you arrive? How will I live with myself if I allowed that to happen?"

Marco reached out to pat his younger brother on the back. "Then you take my place as the baron's heir, and you see to Molly's future knowing that I gladly entered to save her."

It took some discussion, but Angelo finally relented on his offer. They calculated that Angelo, Lorenzo, and Sebastian would approach the manor from the back, while Marco would ride up to the front. They considered including Duncan, but decided against asking the servant to risk life and limb.

"Sir, I don't presume to know what's going on, but if Miss Carter's in danger, I'd like to help." Duncan had approached soundlessly, making Marco flinch in surprise. He supposed servants were accustomed to discretion, careful not to impose their presence on their employers.

"I cannot ask that of you."

"You haven't, sir. I'm offering freely. I'm a good man to have by your side in a fight."

Marco considered him through the gloom. The Scotsman was tall, broad of shoulder, and muscular—the perfect footman favored by the upper classes to display their wealth. "If you are certain? I am afraid I cannot explain much of our purpose. Only that Mr. MacNaby has taken Miss Carter hostage, and we must retrieve her at all costs."

Duncan nodded, his square face calm and steady. "Miss Carter's a fine young lady. I don't know what MacNaby's playing at, but I wish to help, sir."

"As footman, Duncan knows the manor better than us." Sebastian tilted his head in question, waiting for Marco to decide.

He nodded, and his Nordic friend pulled out a dagger from his overcoat to pass it to Duncan. "Here you go, friend. Does MacNaby have access to gunpowder or firearms in the manor?"

"He does."

"Do you know where we might access some for ourselves? Mr. Scott has only a dueling pistol and a single shot to fire, while we have only blades."

The footman pointed into the distance. "The gamekeeper has a cottage nearby."

Lorenzo laughed at this, shaking his head in disbelief. "Visiting the gamekeeper is a much better plan than daggers and clubs. Why did we not involve Duncan before this?"

"Because it is the first time I am managing a rescue, and I did not think of it," replied Marco. "I suppose we should leave the carriage here with the coachman."

Sebastian nodded his head to the gelding tied at the back of the carriage. "Bring your mount and we shall set off by foot."

Within thirty minutes they had obtained rifles, the game-keeper had elected to join them, and they set off toward the manor. Marco left his friends behind, relieved that Molly would have their protection if he failed to survive the night, and rode off to serve as a distraction. Reaching the front garden of Elmstead, he dismounted to watch the house while he waited for them to get into position. The gelding snickered into the quiet, perhaps Marco's state of tension communicating to the beast as he watched the house with a pounding heart.

Inside was a killer and his fair Molly. Visions of his nightmare, when he found Molly smudged and burning in hell, plagued him every time he blinked. He wished he could run up to the house right now, and thump the door with all his pent-up anger, but instead he had to wait. Pulling out his timepiece, he squinted in the dark, angling it to catch the light of the moon and check the time to discover he still had ten minutes to wait.

He turned back to the house, noting that one of the windows was lit. That must be where MacNaby was holding her captive. Perhaps he had the caretaker held there, too, whose presence Duncan had informed them of.

Impatience raced through him, but he quelled the desire to pace. It would not do to make unnecessary commotion until he was timed to approach.

He attempted to distract himself by thinking of his journey to England, the revelations of the past few days, and the responsibilities which had been thrust upon him. And he realized he would gladly accept these upheavals of his life if it secured Molly's life. Marco checked his timepiece again, his jaw tight. The minutes dragged, each one laced with visions of Molly in danger. He drew a slow breath, willing himself to remain calm, though his thoughts refused to quiet until, finally, it was time to act.

Taking the pistol from the pocket of his coat and the gunpowder in a twist of paper, he carefully loaded the lead shot. His friends were circling the house, and Sebastian had declared he would find the room where Molly was being held so he could break through the window if MacNaby left her to answer the door. It was not much of a plan. Mostly, Marco hoped the butler would let him in and provide an opportunity for him to fire the pistol into the reprobate's chest.

Marco grabbed the horse by the reins and began to lead it through the garden. The gelding was to help suggest that Marco had arrived alone, so that MacNaby would not be alerted to his friends' presence.

His heart raced ever faster as he approached the manor. Reaching the front drive, he tied the horse within view of the front door and inhaled to fortify his mind. This might be the final act of his life, and he needed to make it count. Hiding the pistol in the folds of his overcoat, he rested his finger on the trigger guard. His feet crunched on gravel as he approached, and he assured himself that his giant friend was even now peering through the candlelit window, ready to use his bulk to rescue Molly.

Reaching the front door, Marco paused, his thoughts fixed on Molly's safety. He took hold of the brass knocking ring, lifted it, and brought it down hard to announce his arrival, just as instructed.

CHAPTER 16

"A woman's strength lies not in the sword she bears, but in the truth she speaks when all others fall silent."

Impressions of England by an Unrepentant Foreigner

* * *

Marco could hear his knock echoing through the bowels of the manor; from the sparseness of the entry hall and the deliberation of his thunk, it sounded like a crack of overhead thunder. MacNaby would certainly know that he had arrived.

Putting his ear to the door to listen for the butler's approach, his finger hovering over the trigger and ready to fire, Marco sought to keep his calm as the desire to break the door down made his heart pound in his ears.

He heard nothing for a couple of interminable minutes, but just as he stepped forward to bring down the knocker a second time, the creak of a metal key in the lock informed him his foe had arrived.

Marco tensed, aiming the pistol to where the door would open, but reminding himself that the butler could be using Molly as a shield. The door swung open to reveal a shadowy form.

He blinked, hastily pointing the pistol down at the ground lest he accidentally pull the trigger.

"Molly?"

She was framed by flickering light from the dim wall sconces, and she was … alone?

"What took you so long?" she asked, her tone almost annoyed, but then her lip quivered and she burst into tears. Despite it being the second weeping woman to disrupt his day, Marco found that, unlike Miss Dubois's tears which had merely made him uncomfortable, Molly's tears were devastating. It was as if he had re-entered the eighth circle of hell from his recent nightmares.

Peering into the hall behind her, he saw a few small furnishings, covered by dust cloths and leering like tiny specters in the low light, but he could see no evidence of a lurking blackguard. Marco tucked the pistol away and quickly entered the manor, shutting the cold winds out behind him. Then he wrapped his arms about her in a tight embrace, tucking her head under his chin so that she wept into his overcoat.

It took a few moments to compose herself, and when the last of her sobs had subsided, he leaned back to gaze into her face. "Molly, where is MacNaby?"

Her eyelids were puffy and red, and he wanted to place kisses to soothe them, but he needed to address the danger first.

"I convinced him to leave."

Marco shook his head, hoping that would clear his befuddled thoughts, yet he remained just as confused. "What?"

"I tried it a few times, but eventually when we reached

Elmstead, I pointed out that he had not hurt anyone. That Simon was happy in his new role. That Madeline might even now be bearing his grandchild. He threatened me repeatedly, but I did not let up. I reasoned that MacNaby is not a bad man. He had not hurt anyone yet. I even pointed out that if he had truly intended to kill you, would he not have succeeded? That perhaps his failure to do so was a sign he did not wish to walk that path."

He blinked rapidly, but he still had difficulty gathering his wits. "And that worked?"

"Not at first, but I persisted. I think the notion of a grand-child was what swayed him. Lady Blackwood had used his desire for legacy to trap him into this grim pact, so I used the same to break her thrall over him."

Pride in her courage and ingenuity swelled in his chest. He should have guessed, as his brother and friends had suggested, that Molly would find a way to take care of herself. The intrepid young woman must have persisted with her arguments for hours if the butler had got her all the way to Elmstead before finally relinquishing his mission. Marco supposed he was well aware that she was a tenacious nego-tiator, finding himself wholly entangled these past few days by her compelling nature.

"Where is he now?"

"I advised him to take the coin Lady Blackwood had given him to complete her mission and perhaps find the closest port. I expect he will sail from English soil by the end of the night because he left some hours ago. I confess, as part of our negotiation, I encouraged him to raid the silver so he would have sufficient funds to make his escape. I thought the baron would not mind."

He shook his head in disbelief. Part of him wanted to holler out for his fellow rescuers so they might chase MacNaby to ground. The butler would likely head for the

London Docks as the closest departure point, but he had several hours' head start and seen the error of his ways. "Uncle John will be overjoyed to recover you at such a low ransom to the Blackwood coffers."

Suddenly the dread of the past few hours coalesced, and Marco grabbed her firmly by her upper arms to stare deep into her eyes.

"You are the most—" Marco's English failed him as a tidal wave of relief, anger, and fear for Molly swept through him. "*—esasperante?*"

"Infuriating," she responded, staring back at him with those opalescent eyes.

"*Provocatoria?*" he continued.

"Provocative," Molly replied.

"*Allettante?*"

"Enticing."

"*Deliziosa?*"

"Delectable?" She said the last with a bit of a squeak, as if overpowered by his words.

"—woman I have ever met!" he finished, and his mouth found hers, tasting her salty tears and cinnamon essence with profound relief.

Time stood still as he unleashed his passion, kissing her with deep and pressing need until the flames of the eighth circle licked in his gut, and heat rushed through his veins. Molly moaned, her lips parting, and he claimed her mouth, exploring her with his tongue and cupping her head to lock her in place.

Why had he prevaricated about choosing this life? Molly was indeed the grand prize, but there was much potential to pursuing this course and he had been an imbecile to resist it. He hungered for her, pressing closer as he caressed and kneaded down her back until he found the luscious, rounded cheeks that sashayed so sensually beneath her skirts in his dreams and cupped them to pull her against him. She kissed him back with an ardor that provoked a stirring in his loins, clamoring with awareness of her femininity as he ground his hips against hers—

The sound of heavy footsteps had them pulling apart in alarm, and they turned to find Sebastian and Angelo had entered from the back of the manor. His brother had already dropped his gaze to examine his boots, while the Norseman folded his arms to grin like a pleased fool. "Miss Carter is well, I see."

Marco released her and Molly quickly scampered behind him in embarrassment, raising hands to heated cheeks before straightening her gown and checking her hair surreptitiously.

Angelo coughed into his fist, clearly uncomfortable at finding his brother in the throes of passion, and Marco thanked the heavens he was wearing a thick overcoat to hide the evidence of his lust. "Where is MacNaby?"

"Miss Carter convinced him of the error of his ways. He is likely at the docks negotiating his passage to—" Marco shrugged. "—the Continent? Constantinople? The Americas? It is far too late to catch up with him."

Sebastian arched his blond brows, clearly impressed. "Well played, Miss Carter."

Molly had apparently recovered her equilibrium, dropping a quick curtsy. "Thank you, Lord Sebastian."

Marco roused himself, his passion finally receded, to check on the caretaker, whom they found uninjured. After a while, Angelo rode his mount to summon their carriage. When it drew up, the four men and Molly stood staring at it in consternation.

"Did we not plan how to return Molly home once we rescued her?" Lorenzo asked, his irritation obvious.

"It would appear not," replied Marco.

"Lorenzo can ride your mount back to London," Sebastian suggested.

"Why must I ride the horse?" Lorenzo grumbled.

"Because I am decidedly heavier than you," laughed the Norseman. "The fresh air will do you good, my friend." He slapped the lean frame of the Italian on the back, perhaps with more force than he realized when Lorenzo appeared slightly unbalanced.

Duncan held out his hand to Molly. "May I assist you, miss?"

Molly hurried forward, accepting his help to clamber into the dark interior, which was when Marco caught a flash of bared ankles to rekindle his earlier passions. Where had her stockings gone? Then he groaned inaudibly at the thought of those long limbs locked around him. Did she still wear her garters?

Following her into the carriage, he took his place on the bench beside her—eager to maintain their proximity and to feel the warmth of her unharmed body as confirmation that this nightmare had finally ended.

Angelo and Sebastian took their places, and the carriage rolled forward.

"Do you think we have to worry about MacNaby returning?" His brother had addressed his question to Molly.

"I do not think so. His heart was not committed to doing evil."

"How do you know that?" Marco queried, genuinely curious why she seemed so confident.

"I just think that his attempts were halfhearted. He could have done something more decisive, such as poisoning you. Instead, he chose methods that were prone to failing. Sabotaging the carriage? You were traveling within London, so the vehicle was never going to reach lethal speeds. The urn on the roof? The noise of it attracted your attention, and you had time to fling us from its path." Molly stopped, looking at the others with mild embarrassment. Marco realized she had just revealed her presence during the second murder attempt. She licked her lips before continuing. "And the fire could have been orchestrated to take hold far more quickly than it did, yet you had time to awaken and sound the alarm. When he took me hostage, I sensed him dithering and uncertain of what he wished to do with me. His discomfort when he tied me up in Edgware was palpable. Lady Blackwood is no longer here to encourage him, and deep down I believe he could see Simon did not need any more strife. I think it was just difficult for him to change his mind about the course he was on, and he needed a reason to release himself from his promise to Isla Scott. I might be naïve, but to me, he appeared unburdened when he made his choice to leave."

Marco nodded and went quiet, lost in his thoughts about the day's events.

It was intimidating to realize that Molly was pure strength. A formidable woman who knew how to take care of herself. But Marco wanted to be a man she could lean on, someone who added to her strength. How was he to demonstrate that he was such a man when the confounding female had rescued herself without his help? How was he to prove his worth under such circumstances?

While he was eternally grateful she was safe, it did offer a puzzle to reflect on how to display his esteem in a meaningful manner when his rescue effort had proved ... how to say it ... *ridondante* ... redundant?

He could imagine his mother tearing up with mirth at his ridiculous circumstances. His English girl who made him both proud and humbled had now relegated him to basking in his irrelevance as an ineffectual *mollaccione*—how did the English call this? Milksop!

One thing was for certain: Angelo was right. Molly was

incomparable. No one like her had come before, and none would come after. She was a priceless jewel who had cut his pride off at the knees like a ruthless enemy in the heat of battle. It smarted. It smarted as if he stood within Dante's gates of hell. If he could not balance their character traits and place them on equal footing, despite his desires, she would remain out of bounds.

Marco recalled how he, his brother, and his friends had secured the manor with Duncan, including ensuring that the old caretaker, quite shaken by the evening's events, was well. Sipping on a brandy that Sebastian had poured for him, the servant told them how he had been convinced that the mad butler was going to off them with the pistol he had been brandishing with a wild look in his eyes. From the caretaker's account, Marco was able to confirm that Molly had been relentless in the face of repeated threats of violence from MacNaby, wearing down his resolve until, to the caretaker's astonishment, the reprobate had abruptly decided to leave without further word.

"I were afeared for 'er, I were. But Miss Carter, she just yammered on 'bout babies 'til Mr. MacNaby give up! I ain't never 'eard the like!"

Marco had listened to the account with a knot of fear in his stomach—what a risk that Molly had taken. It was still difficult to credit that it had worked.

* * *

MOLLY HAD DOZED OFF, her head coming to rest on Marco's shoulder. When she awakened, she pretended to sleep a little longer so she might draw in the scent of his shaving soap and recall the feel of his hard body pressed against hers. After such an awful day, his arrival and passionate kiss had improved her general outlook.

She still considered herself a complete ninny for bursting into tears, but she supposed the stresses had finally caught up with her in that moment when she had finally seen him and realized they were both safe from harm.

Eventually, she straightened up and opened her eyes to find they had reached the outskirts of London.

Licking her lips, she asked into the dark carriage, "What will happen now?"

Marco glanced at her before returning his gaze to the window. "What do you mean?"

"Are you returning to Florence?"

He hesitated, and her heart sank. Somehow, during her escapade, Molly had convinced herself that when they were reunited … they would remain reunited. She had been so desperate to see him, and his embrace at Elmstead and the heady words he had voiced—they had increased her hopes that there was reason to believe that being taken hostage should tip the scales. It might have been wishful thinking on her part.

Her eyes prickled as tears threatened a second time. Molly fought them back, unwilling to release them with such a large audience. Although Lord Sebastian was making a point of inspecting his gloves, and Angelo had taken a sudden interest in the hedgerows, as if they were attempting to grant them privacy within the cramped interior.

Marco released a sigh. "Are all English girls so forward?"

She winced at the forthright question, but she supposed she had brought it on herself. Waiting to speak in private would have been more discreet than questioning him about his future in front of others.

"No, just me."

Marco reached up to thump the roof of the carriage, which slowly rumbled to a stop. Creaking announced Duncan's descent, and he appeared shortly in the window.

"We are taking a brief break to stretch our legs," called Marco. Duncan nodded, opening the door and setting the steps in place. Angelo and Sebastian quickly exited, apparently understanding that Marco sought to speak with Molly.

When they were out of earshot, Marco turned back. "I am considering … everything. Finding you unharmed—it was sheer, sweet heaven to find you unharmed. But my thoughts are—how do you say—scrambled, and I need time to sort them out."

"I understand." She did, but her impatience knew no bounds. What she wished for was that he would take her back in his arms and finish their kiss. She wanted to join him in his bedchamber so he might make her his forevermore. After facing the possibility of death, she yearned to savor life. But it was understandable that he felt drained while she felt energized to grab life with both hands and take what she wanted in case she never had another opportunity to do so.

Waiting for his arrival, she had had time to consider the frailty of humanity. How one could not take it for granted that there would be another morning, and that regret was a bitter mistress. To be fair, she had had time to digest what had happened, while Marco had arrived at Elmstead unaware that she had secured her safety—believing she might be hurt or dead.

But he had come to the door as MacNaby had demanded. Surely it meant something that he had believed he was risking his life by knocking on the door?

Marco leaned over to buss her on the cheek and caress her fingers as if to assure her. It raised a lump in her throat that made it almost impossible to swallow.

"Perhaps we can discuss this in the morning? It has been a long and difficult day, no?"

"In the morning," she agreed, mollified by his gentle words as she hovered between disappointment and hope.

What were they to discuss? It was impossible to read his mood and assess whether he considered that their conversation would be good or bad news.

Marco turned back to the open door and called out. His brother and Lord Sebastian returned, entering, and she saw Angelo glance at his brother with a questioning look, but Marco refused to react. He was keeping his thoughts to himself, it would seem.

CHAPTER 17

"He who stands at the threshold of love must first shed the garments of fear."

Impressions of England by an Unrepentant Foreigner

* * *

DECEMBER 4 1821

*M*arco faced a towering white marble wall carved with images. He stared at his reflection in the polished finish, and his reflection moved with a life of its own, gesturing to him as if to question his past choices and consider the future. And as he stood there, attempting to make sense of his gesticulating self, Marco became aware of a heavy weight upon his back.

Realizing he was carrying the stones of his indecision, he peered about to find an exit from this in-between place. He did not belong here because he had every intention of reaching a decision and *earning his place at Molly's side. With great relief, he noted that there was a narrow pathway leading toward a cliff, and he hurried in that direction, eager to leave and find the gates to paradise—*

Marco awoke with a start, disoriented at first until he realized he was in his new bedchamber. Smaller than the one that had been damaged in the fire, but pleasantly appointed. He rolled over to find that morning had arrived and groaned. He supposed he should be comforted that the landscape of his dreams had shifted from hell to purgatory, apparently a sign that his worries had evolved from when danger had lurked in the shadows, but it was disturbing, nevertheless. Thankfully, there were several guards posted downstairs at the baron's insistence.

The marble wall had confirmed that he had not yet earned his place as Molly's husband, and he knew he should arise and find a path to earn his own esteem after he had disappointed her too many times with his indecision.

A knock on the door signaled that the baron's valet had arrived to assist him in preparing for his day, so Marco got out of bed to wash and dress.

An hour later, after having breakfasted with the baron who had been in fine spirits regarding the resolution of the MacNaby situation, Marco had gone to the baron's study to sit at the desk and peruse Simon's notebooks about the estates once more.

It would not be such a terrible thing to pursue a new life here. Notes about the tenants and their lives had turned out to be thought-provoking, as their day in Elmstead had proved. It was a difficult thing to let go of the life one had had, the goals one had envisioned, but Florence was a long sea journey away and he must consider his place here in England.

Perhaps before he tried to solve the problem of his worthiness to offer for Molly, he might take a small step regarding the barony to carve out his role here in London. Something to take ownership as the baron's representative.

Staring at the notebooks, he tried to think about what he could possibly do to take charge. No tenants were due to sign their leases until the following year, so there was nothing there to negotiate, and rent would be collected by the stewards, so no action was required from him. The same with the servants and their wages—

A knock on the door interrupted his reverie, and he called out with permission to enter.

Duncan came in, slight smudges under his eyes after their late night returning, but it was comforting to see him.

"The coffee you requested, sir."

The head footman was neatly dressed despite his fatigue, apparently undisturbed by their nocturnal rescue attempt, with his livery in perfect condition. It was dark blue, with blue and green tartan just visible within the lining of his coat. He was carrying a large silver tray with a tall, tapered coffeepot and cups, crossing the room to set them down. Marco vaguely recalled he had requested a tray in the breakfast room. Rubbing his weary eyes, he savored the heavy aroma of rich coffee with great pleasure, his mouth watering in anticipation. Rising to pour himself a cup, he watched as Duncan made to depart and was suddenly hit with a flash of inspiration.

He could grab the reins of this new role with a relatively small, but important, decision. Perhaps he should clear it with his uncle John, but perhaps not. Perhaps he must make this decision on his own and address any concerns with the baron after the fact. Would it not raise his confidence about his place here in England if he acted like his own man?

"Duncan, I would like to discuss something with you."

The footman stopped. "Sir?"

"Close the door, please."

Duncan complied, then returned to the desk where Marco gestured for him to take a seat before returning to his own. The servant was nonplussed, unsure of himself, as he perched on the edge of an armchair.

"I was impressed with your mettle last night, Duncan."

"Thank you, sir. Miss Carter is well-liked belowstairs, and it did not seem right what Mr. MacNaby did ... Not that I am entirely clear on what he did, but, in regard to Miss Carter."

Marco nodded, appreciating that the servant was in an awkward position. But it had not been expected when he offered his assistance the night before, or led them to the gamekeeper's cottage so they might arm themselves. Duncan was an honorable man who had proved he could be relied on.

"How long have you been in the baron's household?"

The footman cleared his throat. "More than ten years, sir."

"And how would you feel about a promotion to the role of butler?"

Duncan's eyes widened in surprise. "I ... Are you certain I am qualified, sir?"

"I would say you have experience managing the footmen, and have likely assisted MacNaby with the silver and china. You must know our merchants. And I could speak with our man of business to obtain any training you feel you might be lacking. The Duke of Halmesbury would likely be willing for you to spend a few weeks with his own butler, if you feel it necessary."

The footman hesitated, likely to think about accepting the prestigious position, but Marco noticed a glint of excitement in his blue eyes. The promotion would be a significant increase in status, responsibilities, and wages, and Marco patiently allowed the servant to consider the ramifications of accepting the post.

"Yes. I would greatly appreciate the opportunity, Mr. Scott."

Marco nodded. "The role is yours. I shall prepare a note to summon our man of business to finalize the details."

Duncan rose to his feet. "Thank you, Mr. Scott. You will not regret this." He dropped a bow and left the room, but despite his stoicism, Marco caught the flicker of a smile playing on his lips as he exited into the hall.

Sipping on his coffee, Marco located a page and quill in the drawer of the walnut desk and jotted a note to summon the agent who dealt with their business affairs that Simon had detailed in the notebooks. It was high time he meet him, and he requested a meeting for the following morning before folding it up and ringing for a footman to deliver the letter.

That action behind him, Marco experienced the swell of confidence. Of a man who had finally accepted the role thrust upon him and begun to make it his own. He would fill the boots of his uncle Simon, and his next step would be to correct an oversight. Simon had made a mistake that Marco was aware of, and he was going to address it to provide relief to the wronged individual. With decisiveness in his step, he headed to the second floor to fix his uncle's egregious error in judgment.

Approaching the door to Molly's chambers, he paused at the berating of a plaintive French voice. Pressing his ear to the door, he eavesdropped without shame because he suspected he was about to uncover the perfect cue to enter.

"You could 'ave got me in great trouble, disappearing like zat! It could affect my chances to get a position in ze future."

As Marco had suspected, Miss Dubois's tears from the day before had not been about her worries for Molly's safety, but rather for her own prospects. His skin crawled with irritation. The chaperon was an obnoxious shrew.

"I assure you, I was not trying to inconvenience you."

Molly's tone was dry, responding with her polite English manners, which made him smile. He was sure she wished to put the servant in her place, but the constraints of her situation, along with her gracious character, forced her to keep the peace. How awkward would it be if she were to quarrel with her shadow? Molly might have defeated a pistol-waving madman with a convincing argument, but she had yet a dragon to slay. And it would be he who slayed this particular dragon on behalf of the woman he … shutting his lids for a moment, Marco finally confessed the truth to himself … the woman he loved. The admission was unexpectedly freeing.

"Very selfish of you, truly! So *inconsidérate!*"

Reaching the limits of his patience, Marco chose that moment to knock on the door. Silence fell inside the room. After a few seconds, the handle turned and Miss Dubois's pretty but sharp face appeared through the crack.

"Meester Scott? May I be of azzistance to you?"

His lips spread into a polite smile. "I wish to speak with you and Miss Carter. Will you join me in the hall?"

The chaperon was perplexed, but swung the door open to reveal Molly, who was dressed but her hair hung free. Her face lit up with hope and, for the first time, he accepted her admiration without reservation.

They had not completed preparing Molly for her day, but Marco gestured for them to exit the servant's temporary bedchamber, and threw a quick wink to the beautiful woman who haunted his dreams.

They stepped out into the corridor, Marco's gaze running appreciatively over the silky curtain of hair falling down Molly's back. Soon her locks would be spread out over his pillow as he—he quickly cleared his thoughts before they ran away with him.

"Miss Dubois, I am delighted to inform you that your services as a paid companion are no longer required. Miss

Carter has graciously accepted the role of the future Lady Blackwood, so her need for chaperoning has diminished. You shall return to your duties as lady's maid, and you can speak with Mr. Campbell about moving your things back into your old room."

Molly and Miss Dubois both dropped their jaws at the same time.

"Mees Carter ees to marry ze baron? An' please forgive me—who ees zis Meester Campbell?"

Marco smiled, offering his arm to Molly, who took hold of it with a grin spread from cheek to cheek, her eyes incandescent with joy. "That is incorrect. Miss Carter is to marry me. I think she will do the Blackwood title proud in the years to come."

Miss Dubois blinked in surprise, her dismay clear as she likely considered the ramifications of the tirades she had directed at her mistress when she had believed Molly to be inconsequential. He noted from the corner of his eye that Molly was biting her lower lip as if to contain her elation.

"And Duncan Campbell, the head footman, has been promoted to the position of butler this morning. He now manages all servants in this household, hence his new address as Mr. Campbell."

"Yes, sir." The chaperon dropped a curtsy.

"Miss Carter, will you join me in the formal drawing room?"

Molly nodded, and he led her down the hall before noting the sound of pattering feet—Miss Dubois was following them. Coming to a stop, he glanced back. "It is a private meeting."

Miss Dubois's face fell. "You conduct ze meeting alone, sir?"

"I believe when two people are betrothed, the proprieties are relaxed. Is this not the way of British society?"

"I ... eh ... it depends on ze family, sir."

"Then I absolve you of your duties, and his lordship will confirm my wishes. We may call on you for the sake of modesty if there is a public event to attend, but I think that unlikely."

The servant's face creased into lines of worry—evidently worrying about her own reputation if she was in proximity to such circumstances. "But, sir ... it could take weeks to marry, *non?*"

He thought about this for a moment, making up his mind. "I do not believe so. I believe Miss Carter and I shall take our vows immediately. Why would any gentleman wait when such a magnificent beauty hastens the ... *velocità?*" He glanced at Molly for a translation.

"Velocity."

"When such a magnificent beauty hastens the velocity of one's pulse?"

Miss Dubois frowned in what appeared to be genuine confusion. He supposed Molly was not what the upper-crust would consider a diamond of the first water, not being an English rose or a proper miss. But she was lively and attractive with a deep-seated courage that would put even hardened warriors to shame.

"Be sure to move your things, Miss Dubois. Miss Carter should have her drawing room back, so she might prepare for a wedding."

He felt Molly bouncing on her toes, her arm hooked through his, and he suppressed a smile at her obvious excitement and led her away. Turning the corner, he glanced back to ensure that the servant had returned to her chamber and then hurried Molly to the door of his temporary bedchamber. Once they were inside, he quickly locked the door so they would not be disturbed.

* * *

"That was ... splendid!" Molly exclaimed in a low voice, aware she could not alert any servants to her being in Marco's bedchamber, and brimming with joy. "Did you mean it?"

He swung around to face her as she released his arm, the heat in his black eyes causing her to shiver as if she had contracted a fever. He reached up to cradle her chin with his hand, angling her face up so he might steal a kiss.

"Every word," he whispered.

"You were magnificent! I have never seen Miss Dubois speechless before. She forgot herself to such a degree, she even frowned despite Lady Blackwood's edict against emotions!"

Marco's brow furrowed in incomprehension. But Molly did not wish to describe the late Lady Blackwood's reign of endless stoicism. Not when there was a wedding to discuss! How strange to think she would one day fill the shoes of the dead baroness, something she had not considered in her clumsy pursuit of the fine gentleman who had captured every iota of her esteem.

"I think your companion might have just discovered that treating someone as inferior can have lasting consequences if they unexpectedly elevate their position. It pays to treat everyone with respect."

"What made you reach a decision?" Her voice was breathless, but she was feeling overcome by the past few minutes. Listening to Marco put Claudette Dubois in her place had been pure bliss. She supposed the time of stepping on eggshells had finally passed, and she had regained her free will. Once she wed, she would never need to answer to others again. And what a husband she was gaining!

Marco stared down at her, the pad of his thumb softly

caressing the line of her jaw back and forth, as if enthralled—by her!

"You. I confess that reading Simon's notebooks helped, and I found myself intrigued by the work he had done to improve the estates. The potential that exists grew my interest. But the primary motive for considering it—was you."

"Me?"

"You are brave and strong and clever, Molly Carter. I would have no other, *mia bella*. With you at my side"—he paused, running a fingertip over the curve of her cheek—"*troverò l'ingresso al paradiso?*"

She licked her lips, which had gone dry at such beautiful words. "You shall find the entrance to paradise."

"*Sì.*"

Molly's heart thumped, beating against her ribs as if to escape the confines of her earthly form as they locked gazes, and he slowly lowered his head. Their mouths fastened together, his velvet tongue delving to find hers with a growl of approval and Molly let him. Floods of sensation surged like a tidal wave to sweep down into her lower belly, where desire blossomed to make her intimate core pulse and swell with anticipation. Marco pillaged her mouth like a marauding pirate, and she wanted it. All of it. His passion unleashed.

Her arms wrapped around his neck, clinging to him as if she were drowning and he was her one hope of surviving the lurching waves of desire coursing through her quivering form. He flexed in response to her touch until he yanked away to reveal his cheeks were flushed with ardor—ardor for her!

"I cannot yet claim you as my bride but … how do you say this … *Dipingerò il tuo corpo con la mia lingua.*"

Molly nearly swooned, not quite sure what it meant but fully prepared to learn. "I wish to paint you with my tongue?"

"*Sì.*"

His husky whisper made her giddy at the promise of great pleasure to be had. The growing heat between her legs swelled, bursting into flames to roar through her veins.

"When?" she squeaked in amazement.

His sculpted lips curled into a wicked smile that reached deep into the organ pounding in her chest with sweet, sweet emotions.

"*Ora.*"

With her brain liquefying in her befuddled head, it took a second for Molly to translate the word for … now?

"Zooks! When I awoke this morning, I did not know what mood I would find you in. Now you are suggesting—" Molly glanced to his bed that dominated the room, and fairly lost her breath at the thought of what he was proposing. After her terrifying experience the day before, she wished to begin living. To exit the cage of expectations and take hold of life with both hands.

She turned back and nodded in muted supplication.

It was all the invitation he needed as his mouth descended to possess hers again. This time, she kissed back, tangling her tongue with his as his fingers worked over her back. She vaguely realized he was unfastening her bodice, but she was far too fascinated by the smell of his shaving soap, the olive-toned smoothness of his shaven cheek, and the feel of his hard body to do more than moan and press against him in imploring turmoil. He continued to kiss her as he wordlessly stripped her of her gown, her stays, her shift while continuing to kiss and nuzzle and nip until she was a mindless puddle of raging heat.

Suddenly he pulled away, and Molly became cognizant that she was entirely naked, her clothing pooled at her feet as Marco unwound his cravat, unbuttoned his waistcoat, and shrugged out of his coat. She should have been mortified, but her attention was riveted to the masculine form being revealed. Next, he kicked off his boots to stand in his stockings. When he finally tugged his shirt from his buckskins and lifted it over his head, she gasped in awe at the flat abdomen and muscular form revealed.

She had tried to imagine what he might look like without his clothes, but because of her inexperience, it had been a hazy imagining at best. She barely had time to process such masculine perfection when he pulled her back into his embrace. Their skin came into contact as she rubbed her cheek against the crisp curls matting the expanse of his chest, her mewling escaping in throaty approval as his hands ran down her back in sweeping caresses. Molly raised her head in anticipation of a kiss, but his lips instead trailed down the slope of her breast until she felt the nerve-tingling sensation of his tongue swirling the hardened bud at the tip. She keened softly, arching back in sensuous delight. It was all the invitation he needed to stroke the delicate flesh with a flickering tongue until all thoughts had been washed away in a vortex of passion.

Reaching down, he lifted her into his powerful arms and strode over to the bed, where he lowered her onto the counterpane and joined her, coming to rest between her knees. His mouth found hers briefly before returning to lap at the turgid nipple, hard and pleading as she arched up in a mindless ecstasy. Then he moved to the other breast which he cupped and plumped with a hot palm and fingers, lifting it to swirl his tongue again and again until the pleasure racked through her in uncontrollable waves.

Molly thought this was what he meant by painting her with his tongue, squeaking in alarm when his smoldering mouth began to descend, causing her belly to ripple in reaction until he finally arrived at the curls that shielded her womanhood.

Her eyes shot open as she suddenly realized what he had truly meant, his hot breath tickling at her crease until she was gyrating in an attempt to relieve the tingling thrill building between her legs when a large palm ran down her midriff to where his face now rested.

A blunt fingertip ran over the seam of her womanhood, causing her to jump and gasp in elated reaction. It passed again, before he slipped it between the folds and she was sure she would pass out in heady delight.

That tip discovered the very center of her pleasure, spreading her nectar as he explored with an enthralled expression. Waves of pleasure built at the sweep of his circling finger, and she found herself rising to a hitherto unknown realm when she felt his mouth descend so he could lap at her with fervent interest. The sensitive nub he had been caressing burst into flames, and she threw up her hand to bite at her fist, emitting a muffled shriek as she reached for the heavens themselves. A white flash of heat exploded throughout her entire body as she entered the paradise Marco had spoken of.

Marco groaned, rolling off her and onto his back to pant with a smug air as Molly attempted to catch her own breath. She was feeling rather smug herself, eyeing the straining falls of his buckskins—tangible evidence of his lustful passion for her.

"We need to say our vows," he eventually declared in whispered frustration.

Molly bit her lip in aroused trepidation. If this was a prelude to their wedding night, heaven help her!

CHAPTER 18

"It is one thing to desire paradise. Quite another to walk through its gates with open eyes."

Impressions of England by an Unrepentant Foreigner

* * *

DECEMBER 7 1821

"What about a special license? How long would it take to procure?"

The baron cocked his head thoughtfully. "Given my rank, I believe we could secure it within a day or two. Simon arranged for Vicar Stone to conduct his ceremony in the garden, so we might call upon him to perform the service. However, it would require that you convert formally to the Church of England."

"I am already baptized in the church," Marco replied. "My mother converted before marrying my father during their time in England, and we attended Anglican services in Florence."

The baron's brows lifted, clearly pleased by this revelation. "That is excellent."

"But … I should like Madeline and Simon to attend," Molly interjected, to Marco's quiet dismay.

He could not stop thinking about how she had felt, her silky-smooth skin, or … her taste. He was determined to leave her virtue intact until their wedding night, but sending word for Simon and his bride to return could take up weeks at this time of the year.

Molly must have noticed his frustration, her fingers reaching out to touch his. He glanced down to find she had made sure the folds of her skirt disguised the motion.

"I cannot wait that long, *mia bella*."

Molly colored, and her lashes dropped to fan her cheeks. Her blush brought to mind her glow of satiation in the aftermath of their lovemaking, and Marco suppressed the urge to roar with the satisfaction of a feral jungle beast. Molly was astute and knew what his haste was in aid of. His groin tightened at the recollection of what they had done in his bedchamber. In his bed. His heart picked up a beat at the memory of her writhing naked in his sheets.

"Oh." She sounded rather pleased.

"We should send word for them that it is safe to come home, I suppose," mused John. "It seems the danger has finally passed."

Marco nodded. "I sent a letter this morning."

"Then summon our man of business; I shall have him procure the special license. A letter from me should be sufficient to persuade the archbishop. I will explain that it is a matter of urgency to secure your position in England because of my health. We must present a unified family front, and your marriage to an Englishwoman will be advantageous to establishing your place within high society and strengthening your claim to the title."

Molly leaned forward, her lovely face creased with concern. "I thought your health was improving."

The baron grinned with a mischievous glint. "I am, but he does not know that, does he?"

Marco rose from his place to ring for a servant, impatient to get their nuptials under way now that he knew what he wanted.

Molly. I want Molly.

He rubbed his cheek, a little mortified to discover how obsessed he had become with bedding Molly since seeing her naked in his bedchamber. This wedding could not happen fast enough!

* * *

MOLLY AND MISS DUBOIS were getting along much better since Marco's intervention. The servant's skills were far more suited to lady's maid, and she did excellent work as such. In fact, Molly was on the verge of tears as she examined the gown she had picked for her wedding vows which the servant had taken from storage and refreshed for this evening's ceremony. It was the gown she had purchased with her mother when they had planned to finally bring her out in society, and she had never worn it because shortly after ordering it, Molly had entered the mourning period for her beloved parent.

Blazes!

She pressed a lacy square to dab at the tears, which no longer threatened, but had arrived. How she wished her mother could have lived to see this day. Then Molly realized, if her mother had not been called to glory, she would not have arrived to live in the baron's household. And without the macabre events of recent weeks, she would not have met Marco. Everything that had transpired had led to this moment where she could weep like a ninny over a pretty garment.

From the ashes of the past, they would build anew.

"Ah, you will be beauteeful in zis!" The exuberant declaration from Claudette Dubois was unexpected but appreciated. For once she agreed with her French poodle, who had become quite tolerable within the past day.

"We shall see."

Miss Dubois assisted her, buttoning up the bodice and tweaking the folds and sleeves, until she bobbed her head to the mirror in satisfaction.

Molly shut her eyes, hoping that the gown would not disappoint now that she was in it—a key component of the final presentation. Turning toward the mirror, she glanced up and gasped with awed delight.

A rich, deep shade of amethyst perfectly complemented her warm brown hair and hazel eyes, bringing out the green and golden flecks in her gaze.

The gown was of the finest silk, catching the light with a soft, elegant sheen. The bodice was delicately gathered to enhance her figure, with a square *décolleté* edged in intricate lace to draw attention to her collarbone and shoulders. Subtle puffed sleeves sat just off her shoulders, adorned with tiny seed pearls to add an air of tailored charm.

A high waistline was cinched with a matching silk sash that accentuated her taller silhouette and flowed into a graceful skirt that flared slightly as it reached the floor, embellished with a hint of pearl-beading along the hem. Enough to catch the eye, but not distract from the gown's simplicity.

Turning, she viewed the back where a column of small,

cloth-covered buttons ran down the bodice, allowing the gown to hug her figure in an elegantly understated way.

Miss Dubois sighed in happiness, stepping back to admire her handiwork.

"*Oui*, it is *très élégant*, fit for a future baronezz!"

Molly nodded in agreement, reflecting that the change in her lady's maid's behavior was rather remarkable. She might even relent to addressing her as Claudette, since she was no longer gritting her teeth every moment they spent together. Which were significantly fewer moments since Miss Dubois —Claudette—had her old quarters back. Perhaps she had been just as aggravated with their enforced proximity as Molly had been. Their disparate temperaments were easier to manage with the increased distance between them.

Miss Dubois brought out a delicate pearl necklace from Molly's jewelry box and strung it around Molly's neck, balancing on her tiptoes to reach.

"Ah, pearls—just right for a bride. Zey show purity ... to tell Meester Scott he has found ze one he love, forever."

Molly smiled in acknowledgment, too overcome to respond. Claudette was an artiste, having styled Molly's hair in a soft chignon at the nape of her neck, allowing a few delicate curls to frame her face and highlight her hazel eyes. This simple yet refined style supplemented the squared bodice and intricate lace detailing, while creating an air of sophistication befitting a future baroness. Along with a pair of white gloves and a soft, gossamer shawl in sheer silk, this dinner gown was a wondrous choice for a quiet, romantic wedding.

Sighing with joy at her reflection in the mirror, Molly prepared to leave. As she reached the door, she turned back.

"Would you like to attend the ceremony ... Claudette?"

Claudette's mouth fell slack, her expression stunned.

"Ah, truly—you mean zat, Mees Molly?"

Molly pursed her lips and thought about it. She was not

one to hold a grudge, and considering their new circumstances, it seemed appropriate. Given the other woman's occupational aptitude, attending a noble family's nuptials would be of great interest to someone so fashion-minded, and Molly supposed she did not mind if it resulted in detailed recounting belowstairs from the gossiping servant.

"I do."

"Zen, *oui*! I would be honored to bear witness!"

She beckoned for the servant to follow her in her progression to the formal drawing room where she found the baron waiting for her out in the hall. Smiling with sheer happiness, Molly hurried over to take the arm he offered her. John had asked to give her away, which had touched her deeply.

"Molly, you are … utterly ravishing, dear!"

With a nod to Campbell, the doors to the formal drawing room swung open, revealing tall windows glittering in the candlelight from flickering beeswax tapers set into silver candelabras—candelabras Molly remembered last seeing stored in the butler's pantry. Elegant vases filled with hothouse flowers: soft pink roses, lavender, and white lilies, symbolizing passionate love, loyalty and grace, purity and new beginnings, enriched the restrained opulence of the room.

A fire crackled in the grand fireplace to fight back the chill, and their guests were seated on plump armchairs that had been collected from around the house. Molly felt the prickle of threatening tears to see so many gathered to celebrate this special occasion, as the guests rose in acknowledgment of her entrance.

His Grace and his duchess stood in the front row of the impromptu seating, the duke towering over Lord and Lady Saunton. Molly did not know Her Grace or Lady Saunton well, having met them only once in the past few weeks, but she appreciated their attendance because she and Marco would need help to enter British society. From the next row, Lord Trafford and his wife smiled broadly in greeting despite the proprieties of such an occasion, but the couple was unconventional and had been instrumental in saving their household just weeks earlier, so Molly beamed back.

Lord Sebastian was tugging at his cravat with the nettled air of someone who had grown unfamiliar with the starched rigidity of British attire, while Mr. di Bianchi leaned against the back of his seat with the flippant posture of an artist unimpressed with such goings-on. Nicholas gave a curt bow of his head, his recent foul moods not in evidence as he glanced at her up and down before tilting his head in approval.

But Molly paid little mind to their guests because her eyes were riveted to Marco, who was smiling with great appreciation at her entrance. He wore black trousers and a matching cutaway coat that revealed crisp, white linen and a luxurious silver silk waistcoat which perfectly accentuated his olive skin. His high-standing collar was pristine, while his cravat was intricately tied in a style she was unfamiliar with but assumed to be Florentine. Silver and black onyx pinned its folds, the perfect complement to his soulful eyes, and Molly grew lightheaded with disbelief. This man, with his slightly tousled black waves and refined Latin features, was to be her husband, and she was sure she was marrying the handsomest man in England!

John patted her arm and began their walk up the aisle, which provided Molly the opportunity to note the vicar who had wed Simon and Madeline last month. Dressed in simple ecclesiastical robes, he held his Book of Common Prayer while watching her approach with a welcoming smile on his rounded face.

Finally, they arrived and John deposited her by Marco's

side, whose expression was that of a man well-pleased. The vicar cleared his throat and spoke in a soft but resonant tone while Molly did her best to quell the elation threatening to overwhelm her.

"Dearly beloved, we are gathered here in the sight of God, and in the face of this company, to join together this man and this woman in holy matrimony ..."

* * *

MARCO'S IMPATIENCE TO get Molly alone had been growing over the past hours. Since the moment she had walked into the drawing room, he could scarcely think. His head swam with repressed passions as it had all through dinner. Now he was finally headed up the stairs with Molly's hand clasped in his. The smell of cinnamon toyed with his senses, while the feel of her delicate fingers wrapped around his made him think of her soft touch on his aching body.

With undignified haste, he dragged her down the hall, but he noted Molly raced along with him eagerly.

They finally reached her chambers, and he flung the door open. A shriek sounded from inside, and he found the French lady's maid holding a fall of satin with eyes widened in shock.

"Miss Dubois."

"Meester Scott." She dropped a curtsy, but Marco's gaze was riveted to what appeared to be one of those French *négligés*, relishing the thought of Molly poured into such a garment. He had planned to undress her himself, but now he was tempted to allow the lady's maid to do her duty as he considered the ivory silk and lace confection pouring through Miss Dubois's fingers.

"I shall be in the hall," he announced, releasing Molly to exit and shut the door behind him—the tightening in his groin urging him to return to his own room so he might strip down. He did not bother ringing for the baron's valet when he reached his bedchamber, removing his clothing to place it carefully over an armchair before pulling on loose linen trousers that he tied off at the waist. Rifling through his closet, he found his banyan, embroidered in black and red with the heraldic symbols of Florence, and drew it on before returning to wait outside Molly's door.

In the morning, he would speak with the baron about getting his old rooms repaired—they were far larger to accommodate him and Molly. He knew these Englishmen of the upper classes preferred to live in separate rooms, but now that Molly was finally his, he was not about to release her.

Eventually, the handle turned, and Miss Dubois exited with a smug expression.

"Ah, Madame Scott ees very beauteeful tonight, *non?* Truly, fit for a baronezz!"

Marco arched a brow, astonished at the maid's change in temperament—she seemed almost happy? Had the role of chaperon been as difficult for her as it had been for Molly? Her improvement in mood would suggest so, which he could accept, but he would not forget the many hours she had waited to inform him of Molly's disappearance. However, as lady's maid, her personality flaws were not as relevant as they had once been.

He smiled politely, then waited for her to disappear around the corner before he entered Molly's chambers.

She was not in the small drawing room that had been Miss Dubois's, so he crossed over to the next room to lean against the doorframe and smile at his bride. He was afraid his expression might be akin to that of a ravenous wolf as he took in his lithe beauty in the glow of the oil lamp and the flickering light from the fire in the hearth.

Molly was gorgeous, ravishing with her hourglass figure draped in her ivory nightgown, waiting for him with her delicate bared feet peeking out from beneath the silk folds. Miss Dubois had proved her merit as he took in the flowing fabric with discreet panels of lace that framed her *décolletage*, her olive skin a striking contrast in the shadowed room. Rich brown hair cascaded over one shoulder to coyly hide one of her rounded breasts while the other ... *maledizione*! The outline of a tawny nipple was visible through the thin fabric, causing his mouth to water as he recollected the taste of cinnamon, woman, and creamy skin.

Then he realized a facet of tonight he had not considered —Molly was an innocent maiden. How precisely would he remove her of her maidenhood? It was not like he had any experience doing such a thing.

He folded his arms and considered his bride, calculating what was the best method to ease her into married life.

"I shall describe what I plan to do," he announced, striding over to wrap an arm around her waist and pull her into a tight embrace. Molly's head fell back, and her opalescent eyes focused on his mouth. He had noticed her inclination to do so before, his lips curling into a smile of triumph— Molly's intense desire for him was matched only by his own for her. Tonight would be the culmination of heated glances and magnetic intensities of the past days.

"I shall worship your ... *contorni*?" He knew the word he wished to say, but the sound of Molly's husky voice translating his salacious musings was too enticing to resist.

"Contours," she breathed, a blush of color settling on her cheeks.

"Until you are ... *cantando le mie lodi*?"

"Singing my praises." Her lashes fluttered, and she swallowed hard, appearing dazed by his proposal.

He gave up all pretense at the Anglican tongue, leaning

down to whisper into her ear, *"... con quei gemiti gutturali che tormentano il mio sonno ..."*

She began to pant as he nuzzled against her cheek. "With those guttural moans that haunt your sleep ..."

"... e poi ti reclamerò con il mio acciaio ..."

She gasped, blinking in confusion as he himself was almost unmanned by the very image of what he described and the thought of hearing it in her melodic voice. "... and then you shall claim me with your steel ..."

"Fino a quando i cieli stessi tremeranno al suono della tua passione."

"Until the heavens themselves quake with the sound of my passion," she finished weakly, both fearful and excited.

"Sì."

He cupped her face, large palms wrapped around her delicate structure, lowering his head with a loud growl. Marco captured her mouth with his, merciless as he demanded entrance to the soft cavern. She moaned, as he had predicted, and he took advantage of that slight parting of the lips to tangle his tongue with hers, his frustrated craving from when he had brought her to her peak finally unleashed as he cradled her head with his palm and walked her back. A bump informed him that her knees had found the bed, which was all the encouragement he needed to lower his free hand over her luscious curves to reach down as far as he could.

Molly mewled, kissing him back with a fervor that lit his passions, and he could feel himself growing and lengthening with pulsing desire as he slowly took her silk nightgown between his fingers and began to work the fabric upward with agonizing patience.

He may have adopted this foreign land, but his Latin nature howled in his breast to tear the garment in two and toss it aside like a marauding god laying waste to a mortal woman. But he banked those fires of lust to continue his painstaking raising of her skirt until finally it was bunched in his hand.

Releasing her skull, his mouth moved to stroke her delicate jaw while he reached down to caress a velvet thigh that had been bared by his careful work, fondling the smooth skin until he found the damp curls between her thighs. Throwing his head back, he howled softly at the feel of slick petals against his fingertips, returning his mouth to find the frantic pulse in her throat as he continued to explore her as the most fascinating of treasures.

Molly was mindless, moaning loudly, and Marco was thankful that the room was recessed from the hall by her small drawing room because he had no desire to silence such glorious cries. Lowering his head farther, he took a diamond-hard nipple in his mouth through the silk and lace to swirl and lap until her hips were gyrating against his with the instincts of a female who knew what she wanted. And what she wanted was him. The evidence was there in her blushing skin, the slick nectar between her legs, and the rhythmic grind of her hips against his erection as she sought their joining.

Marco straightened up to pull the counterpane and sheets back, coaxing her to lie down. Her *néglige* was up around her hips, her shapely legs bared and her silk garment transparent, where he had soaked it with his hungry mouth to reveal the very shape of her pleading nipple. He untied his robe to toss it aside, then undid the tapes of his cotton pants, which dropped without the benefit of their restriction, baring his manhood to her with the full strength of his desires on display.

Her eyes moved down over his exposed chest, down over his flat abdomen, and widened when they came to rest on the erection that spoke of his unfulfilled passion. An audible inhalation could be heard as she stared, enthralled, before finally lifting molten eyes to his and licking her lips as if they had gone dry.

Holding her gaze, he approached. Settling onto the bed, his hard body pressed her soft curves down into the mattress as her legs fell open in mute invitation. His flesh was throbbing and heavy, urging him to claim her as it came into contact with her slick crease. With great difficulty, he restrained himself to find her mouth with his, and he reached down to explore the lush petals that had released the subtle scent of womanhood until he was drunk with lust and realized he must bring her to her peak before he lost control!

He circled the nub that controlled her pleasure, stroking with deliberation while Molly grew more agitated beneath him, continuing without mercy until she finally yelped and stiffened; waves of gratification racked her slender form as he smiled against her mouth in masculine victory.

When she finally relaxed, he renewed his exploration, his finger nudging at her entrance to coax her acceptance of his invasion. She was tight—so very, very tight—which in turn made him harder than he had ever been, his cock demanding immediate satisfaction as he worked a forefinger into her pulsing channel, then another, to massage her into acceptance.

When he was satisfied that she was ready, he lined her up with the hard ridge of his arousal, nudging at her intimate entrance with suggestive thrusts that made her rub and pant in pulsing unison with him until he finally penetrated her with a long thrust, deciding decisiveness was the best strategy. She stiffened, grunting in surprise at what must be a rather painful sensation as he held himself still inside her.

The clasp of her slick sheath was agony as he waited, every nuance of motion acting as a seismic deluge of teasing sensation, but he gritted his teeth and buried his face into her shoulder, determined to wait for her signal. Eventually she relaxed, her touch trailing down his taut back to dig into his buttocks, and gyrated against him to encourage his resumption. He began to move and thrust with tightly controlled passion, settling into a delightful rhythm that made her sheath ripple around his staff. He continued on, a man with a mission, reaching down to slip his fingers through her slick petals again, until her moans resumed. And on he continued, finding just the right angle to work the secret pearl hidden in those folds as he thrusted, until she emitted a loud shriek and peaked with deep spasms gripping at his swollen flesh.

Marco finally released all self-control, thrusting frantically into her wet heat until he groaned loudly and the waves of climax took him to the heights of paradise where he spent his seed deep into her waiting womb—aroused to hitherto unknown heights by the thought of Molly rounded with his babe in her belly.

He rolled to the side, bringing her with him in a tight embrace as he buried his face in her hair and sniffed the spice of cinnamon as a man obsessed with the woman who repeatedly visited his dreams—an emissary of the great Dante Alighieri, tasked with escorting him to paradise itself.

EPILOGUE

"Even a broken compass points north when the storm has passed."

Impressions of England by an Unrepentant Foreigner

* * *

DECEMBER 8 1821

*M*arco entered the breakfast room with the air of a victorious Roman general returning from a glorious campaign. His head was held high, his chest almost puffed out in smug triumph, and he beamed as a man who had acquired new aspirations and was heading down a promising path.

He was well aware that anyone who encountered him would know that he had been properly bedded—had properly bedded? He waved the distinction away—he was wed and well satisfied from a long night of bed sport with his incomparable Molly. They had completed the act just the one time, Marco mindful of her inexperience and the soreness she was sure to feel this morning, but there had been other delightful activities to engage them well into the dawn of a new day. His bride had not stirred even a little since she had eventually fallen into an exhausted slumber.

Gathering up a plate from the sideboard, while a footman deposited a silver coffeepot on the table for him, Marco heard muffled voices quarreling in Italian. It would seem that Sebastian and Lorenzo were at it again, in the family drawing room adjacent to the breakfast room. He paused—angling his ear to shamelessly eavesdrop through the thin connecting doors and ignoring the footman's presence. His friends' continuing standoff had been piquing his interest since Florence, and he wondered if he might learn something about their disagreement.

"We have been here an eternity! Our friend has met a maiden and married, while you continue to delay!"

Lorenzo sounded agitated, and Marco grimaced in sympathy. His impatient friend was growing ever more frustrated, it would seem.

"The time is not right."

Sebastian's low growl was hard to hear. Marco pursed his lips, staring down into his coffee cup while contemplating Sebastian's continuing reluctance and wondering what he should do to help.

"The time is never right! What is it about this ... this ... this bit of muslin that has you hiding under the stairs like a schoolboy?"
    "Watch how you act!"

"No! Not this time, Sebastian! You keep delaying, and it is unlike you to behave so cowardly. We need that painting if I—"

Lorenzo broke off, apparently defeated. At least, for this instant.

Marco sighed heavily. He was afraid whatever their strange quest was, if Sebastian did not act soon, he might rend their lucrative partnership in two. Which would be a pity because the two men had been close friends for a long time, and Marco wanted them to continue their success. Who on earth was the woman who caused a man such as Sebastian to balk so?

There was a long pause, until, finally—

"You are right. My apologies, Lorenzo."

The scraping of a chair announced that the Italian—the lighter of the two men—had left, perhaps storming out, loud footsteps sounding out in the hall. Marco picked up his cup and sipped while he thought about what he could do.

Sebastian appeared seconds later in the doorway, stalking over to the sideboard and rifling around until he turned to take a seat at the table with a laden plate.

Marco refrained from commenting, watching the Norseman with a sympathetic gaze.

Sebastian stared at his plate but did not pick up his fork, or commence eating.

"You overheard our argument."

It was not a question, so Marco said nothing.

The giant Englishman raised two large arms to comb through his mane of hair, his elbows bracketing his head as he exhaled deeply.

"I know you were not the same after that English girl died of consumption. It makes me wonder how you have found the courage—" He stopped, evidently overcome by a tempest of emotions, and Marco wished he knew what comfort to provide as Sebastian rubbed his jaw to peer out at the garden with unseeing eyes. "How do you find the courage after your heart has been so utterly crushed beyond repair?"

Marco understood his friend's pain even if he did not understand the circumstances of his heartbreak. He weighed his words carefully because Sebastian needed a hopeful answer. Despite his good nature, it would appear his Nordic friend had been burdened these many years, which he had hidden well until the day Marco had announced he was leaving for England.

"What choice do we have, my friend? We cannot give up on the future when it has so much more to offer than the past."

"You believe I should stop delaying?"

"I think you have an opportunity to close the door on an old chapter. As painful as it might be, it must be done if you are to … resuscitate."

His friend's face was blank over the next few minutes, but Marco waited with patience as he allowed Sebastian to think. Something Lorenzo was ill-equipped to do due to his restive character, which had likely prolonged the arrival of this moment.

Sebastian nodded, exhaling a puff of air as he finally reached a decision and announced, "Then the time has arrived to pay a call on Lady Slight."

* * *

Lady Harriet Slight wants to begin again. Sebastian wants to set things right. When goals collide, can a renewed courtship lead to a second chance at love? Find out in *The Courtship Trap*, Book 1 of Inconvenient Ventures!

DOWNLOAD TWO FREE BOOKS

Enjoyed the story? The adventure isn't over yet …

Subscribe to Nina's newsletter at ninajarrett.com and receive two novellas—absolutely free!

Interview With the Duke – What happens when an ambitious writer corners society's most elusive duke? Sparks fly in this witty prequel full of secrets, scandal, and charm.

The Captain's Wife – A runaway bride. A brooding army captain. And a reunion that could change everything.

Join thousands of Regency romance readers who love exclusive content, behind-the-scenes peeks, giveaways, and early access to new releases. Your next favorite story is just one click away.

AFTERWORD

Impressions of England by an Unrepentant Foreigner is a fictitious work, loosely inspired by the travel memoirs of Giuseppe Baretti. Styled as a satirical and romantic companion to the events of this novel, its excerpts are the imagined reflections of an outsider navigating the contradictions of English society with both admiration and irreverence.

While writing *Lord of Intrigue*, I discovered Molly is rather a capable young woman for her time. It soon became obvious she could not be content sitting on her hands, hoping Marco might express an interest. Recognizing what she wanted, she would work to make it happen. It was a natural progression that as the living, breathing character that she was, she would manipulate circumstances to help achieve her desired outcome. A trait which Marco recognizes and finds endearing, but intimidating, until he ceases to dither and commits to his new path.

Researching the relationship between Italy and England was deeply rewarding, and I hope you have enjoyed a taste of Regency-era Florence. Expect more to follow because Italy has been the top destination for tourism for centuries, inspiring the art and culture of the Regency itself, and making it the ideal counterfoil for romances steeped in English history.

If you enjoyed this story, I would be incredibly grateful if you'd consider leaving an honest review. Your words help others discover the book and support future stories.

Now that Sebastian has returned to British soil—and pays a call on the woman we love to hate—is it a Lady Harriet Slight we will recognize from earlier books? Or has Lily's blessing—which from a different vantage might be considered a curse—cracked the frozen heart of the ice queen?

She has had months to consider those venomous wishes from the annoying chit who stole her lover. What lessons might she have learned, or has she grown ever more embittered after losing a second paramour to an Inconvenient Bride?

And will Sebastian's visit tug her onto a strange path of symbolic art, hidden clues, and treasure-hunting—or will she betray his quest when he seeks to restore Lorenzo's long-lost family honor?

Find out in Book 1 of Inconvenient Ventures, *The Courtship Trap*, wherein Lady Slight extorts Sebastian into a fake courtship that will wreak havoc within the world of the Inconvenient Brides.

ABOUT THE AUTHOR

Nina began writing stories in elementary school but took a long detour through real life before returning to fiction. After finishing her studies, she worked in non-profit outreach with recovering drug addicts—serving communities from privileged suburbs to the shanty towns of rural and urban South Africa.

Then she met a real-life romantic hero. A fellow bibliophile, he swept her off her feet, and she promptly married him and moved to the United States. There, she built a successful career as a sales coaching executive at an Inc. 500 company. Today, Nina lives with her husband on the sunny Gulf Coast of Florida.

Nina believes deeply in kindness, resilience, and the power of transformation. Inspired by the extraordinary people she's met across the world, she writes mischievous tales of bold choices, unexpected love, and the courage it takes to change. She tells these stories while sipping excellent coffee—and heroically avoiding cookies.

Join Nina's Newsletter at NinaJarrett.com for two free books, fun Regency content, announcements, and exclusive discounts.

Follow Nina Jarrett on your favorite platform.

ALSO BY NINA JARRETT

INCONVENIENT BRIDES

Five daring heroines. Five unexpected heroes. One scandalous series of love, redemption, and happily ever afters.

In this sweeping Regency redemption arc, five flawed men seek forgiveness and love—with the help of five extraordinary women. Each story stands alone, but together they form a powerful tale of legacy, loyalty, and the courage to change.

Book 1: The Duke Wins a Bride

Book 2: To Redeem an Earl

Book 3: My Fair Bluestocking

Book 4: Sleepless in Saunton

Book 5: Caroline Saves the Blacksmith

INCONVENIENT SCANDALS

A tangled murder mystery to unravel one romance at a time.

In the elegant world of *Inconvenient Brides*, five couples find love in the most unlikely places—while uncovering a mystery that could ruin them all. Each book delivers a satisfying, standalone Regency romance, but together they unravel a shocking murder that shakes the nobility. Only by the final page will the full truth come to light.

Book 1: Long Live the Baron

Book 2: Moonlight Encounter

Book 3: Lord Trafford's Folly

Book 4: The Trouble With Titles

Book 5: Lord of Intrigue

INCONVENIENT VENTURES

Five unlikely couples unlock a legendary secret.

In the glittering world of *Inconvenient Brides*, five unexpected couples are swept into a thrilling race to unravel a centuries-old secret. From coded paintings to Arthurian relics, each courtship reveals another piece of a legendary puzzle—one with the power to shake the British Empire ... or crown new heroes.

Book 1: The Courtship Trap

Book 2: The Hidden Lord

Book 3: TBA

Book 4: TBA

Book 5: TBA

Printed in Dunstable, United Kingdom